AZRAEL

A Jessie McIntyre Novel

JOSEPH CASTAGNO

This is a work of fiction. Names, characters, places, and incidents are either the product of the author's imagination or are used fictitiously. Any resemblance to actual persons, living or dead, or to events, or locales is entirely coincidental. This story is purely for entertainment and is in no way intended to offend or cast any ethnic, religious group or country in a negative light.

There are a number of real places in this story the author's descriptions and use of them may or may not be accurate, you can visit them and develop your own opinions if you so choose; any particular descriptions are the opinions and observations of the author and may not represent historical facts or even current conditions.

TABLE OF CONTENTS

Prologue

Jessie McIntyre had left the Army, the Rangers to be specific, two and a half years ago — it seemed longer than that though. Things had been a bit boring working for Thompson Security protecting celebrities, mostly from each other, but the money was good and at least you traveled first class.

Boring that was until Tom Brady had entered her life and the Sokolov human trafficking cartel had made her target number one shortly after. A significant body count and what seemed a few short weeks later she had found herself in Odessa partnered with her dad's old CIA partner Jack Hardy face to face with Sokolov. She hadn't hesitated, two well placed 9MM rounds had ended that threat and cemented her future in the CIA.

Of course, things aren't always as simple as they seem, she had spent that summer training at The Farm preparing to become a bona fide CIA operative — she hadn't really thought too far ahead figuring things couldn't be nearly as insane as her first dip into the deep end. That was more than six months ago, and she had been wrong, so very wrong...

St. Eustatius

The howl of the gusting hundred and thirty mile-an-hour winds brings Jessie back to the moment, she had a real fear the ramshackle block building she had been forced to hunker down in wasn't going to make it. She glances over at the man lying in the corner among the empty air tanks, the steady thump of the compressor had stopped when the electric had flickered for the last time hours ago, but none of that had mattered to Ismael, he had bled out rapidly, before the wind even picked up and without giving her the information she wanted - needed - had come here for in the first place, another dead end.

Jessie McIntyre had joined the Agency almost a year earlier, and at thirty-three years old it was much later in life than most operatives, but then again Jessie wasn't like most operatives, her Army Ranger background was a significant advantage. It didn't hurt that her first assignment had ended with the elimination of the international human trafficker Alexi Sokolov – the details were hazy, but the leaked pics out of Odessa showing two neatly placed 9MM holes had pretty much cemented her "bad-ass" status and had insured her a special assignment to Deputy Director, Vance Simpson.

Being an operative had seemed like a good idea last October while sitting in a comfy Georgetown townhouse eating pancakes and joking with her dad, Big Lou, and her mentor Jack Hardy a thirty-year veteran of the agency, but that was before the Director had tossed the file simply labeled "AZRAEL" in her lap.

There wasn't anything positive about being holed up on a small Caribbean island in the middle of a hurricane with a dead Israeli informant – in fact there hadn't been many positives before this latest fiasco and she was beginning to wonder if she had made the right decision all those months ago.

There had been a running debate within the Agency if Azrael was even real, a singular human being seemingly able to dispatch death at will appearing and disappearing without so much as a whisper and that alone had earned the moniker "AZRAEL". It didn't help that Azrael didn't appear to be motivated by anything more than his own psychosis – no known group had claimed the kills and there didn't appear to be any ideological or political motivation in the target choices – just a general disdain for the world's most powerful governments. No one had developed anything more than a sketchy profile, certainly no pictures, prints, or even a megabyte of electronic surveillance. But for all that the legend grew, some said rogue Mossad operative dissatisfied with the two-state solution that had been hammered out with the Palestinians three years earlier, others claimed he had come out of ISIS an agnostic killer not even they could embrace, a fanatic unwilling to concede defeat when the last cells caved in.

The kill list was impressive and growing, a U.S. ambassador in Egypt, the entire French trade envoy to Singapore - in public at a celebratory dinner no less, the highest ranking British officer in Afghanistan – in his bed at what was supposed to be the most secure NATO base in the world. Even non-traditional targets like the Russian Federation and the Chinese had lost ambassadors and diplomats. Never-mind the Japanese Prime Minister and his underage mistress in a scene that transcended disturbing on multiple levels, Azrael seemed able to reach out and effortlessly deliver death with impunity - a true angel of death. Then he had disappeared without a trace two years earlier about the same time the Syrian government had completely erased the "redline" employing a biological so potent it had to have come from one of the three superpowers – fifty plus thousand dead and a humanitarian disaster unprecedented since the plagues of the middle-ages. There were a number of assassinations he had been linked to during that time, but most agreed they seemed almost too mundane for the "Angel of Death".

The United States had erased Syria after that, what else could they do? The Russian Alliance had stood by quietly – there was clear enough evidence of whose weapon it had been. As usual the Chinese kicked up some noise but there was no way to diplomatically whitewash it, so the United States had eradicated anything that remotely resembled the Syrian government, or anyone even loosely associated with it.

The area was still under United Nations control, it had taken months to solve the public health issues, now there were only humanitarian peacekeepers allowed in and out, the Iraqi border locked down by the United States, the Turks were precariously guarding their side still at odds with the Kurds living there, the Jordanians had stepped up big though and were working hand and hand with U.S. Central Command to patrol the Southern end of the country. It was holding as well as it could, but the Western border and the Mediterranean coast were leaking like a sieve - there was only so much the Israelis could do at this point.

Then last fall word had come out there might have been mistakes made during the clean-up, at least one vial missing, and maybe the biological known only as VX17 had ended up in the hands of the one person no one could put their finger on – Azrael. The idea of an invisible killer with no known ideology possessing a weapon like VX17 went beyond frightening.

Jessie leans her back against the block wall. She can feel the wind vibrating the building and somewhere in the dark a piece of the metal roof is flapping and threatening to tear loose. Director Simpson had been clear enough, "roll-up whatever and whoever you need to, but find out who this bastard is..."

She had no idea how she was supposed to make that happen, but a new operative wasn't in a position to question The Deputy Director, so she had found an empty cube on the seventh floor and spent two plus weeks reviewing everything the Agency, Israelis, Brits, Russians and anyone else had developed – it was thin at best.

She had called Jack, he had been around for more years than most and had connections in and out of the Agency, he had agreed to put the word out, but he wasn't hopeful. They had even talked about trying to contact Mikhail Kirilov it was possible he might know something about VX17. He had come out of the Russian Spetnaz and GRU – and he was running the largest black-market arms empire in Eastern Europe, not ideal but you couldn't always choose your allies. Kirilov didn't really owe them, but they had kept him out of the Sokolov reports – you never knew when you might need a favor from the other side of the line and he hadn't been on the Agency's list – well not yet anyway – but neither of them really had any idea how to make that happen.

Her next call had gone out to her Dad at Paradigm Tech, the work they were doing on predictive analytics using AI and big data – a program they had affectionately named NEO - was yielding some impressive results, it couldn't hurt to run Azrael and VX17 through the system and see what dropped out the bottom, it hadn't been much.

Now it was early June and she had been chasing phantoms until three days ago when a cryptic message had shown up on her SAT phone: *Ismael – St Eustatius - Golden Rock Dive – Azrael* - the number had led nowhere originating somewhere inside the Russian Alliance, not even the crypto techs at Langley had been able to narrow it any further. Better than even odds it was a trap, but what choice was there? She didn't have anything else, except a nagging feeling that time was running out.

She had landed at the little airport in the center of the island on a prop charter from San Juan thirty-six hours earlier, before Hurricane Beatrice had decided not to take the sharp right turn North every meteorologist in the world had forecasted and Ismael had taken a bullet she felt certain had been meant for her. Clearly her cover as an ad executive out of New York down for some hardcore scuba diving had been blown before she even hit the island. That had ramifications she didn't want to think about, like was the Agency penetrated to the point that someone had known she was coming or worse had she been set up?

Now she was stuck here hoping the roof didn't blow off and turn her career into its own natural disaster. On the bright side, maybe she was finally making progress – someone wanted her dead and that had to mean something.

She replays the shooting looking for anything that might give her a clue, she had been surprised that Ismael had actually existed, but he had been genuinely shocked or relieved she couldn't really decide which when she had called his name out. He had looked wildly around, grabbed her by both arms and turned her toward the water, the round had penetrated his lower back and exited right above the left side of his pelvis. She had used him as shield dragging him the ten feet into the building, he had taken another round almost immediately, but it wouldn't have mattered. She had locked the door and squirreled herself into the far corner, pistol at the ready, waiting for something to happen – it didn't.

The more she thought about it – assuming she survived the storm – the hurricane was going to be her best bet for getting out of here in one piece, at least that was what she was telling herself as the wind howled and the rain beat ceaselessly against the metal roof. She figured she might have as many as thirty to forty minutes during the eye to make a move, she wasn't going to get far, but better to be on the move than caught like a rat in a one room maze. *Then again, if whoever had taken a shot at her had managed to stay put, it won't matter anyway*, she thinks.

She checks her backpack, four extra clips, her tactical knife, SAT phone, a change of clothes, bikini, passport and ten thousand in cash. There seems to be a slight decrease in the wind and she can see a sliver of grey light under the door, *well, nothing to else to do but get to it* she figures, pushing the door open halfway, waiting for something to happen. It only takes a second for the wind to smash it closed again though. She pushes it open and dives straight out rolling to a crouch pistol drawn. Nothing, no shots, nothing – slowly standing up she takes a look around, the dive boat is straddling the road on its side, trees are strewn around like match sticks and the angry waves are breaking over the sea wall swamping the parking lot to her right. It looks like a couple of giant petulant children decide to wreck their playroom leaving everything strewn all over.

She gathers herself and starts off at jog toward the Inn a half mile down what's left of the shore road, she needs to be where other people are, she needs to find a way off this island. It didn't occur to her that she may be the first survivor of Azrael's attention.

Odessa

It had taken Kirilov a little more than six months to absorb the Sokolov arms business, absorb was probably too benign an adjective - he had taken over - any loyalty issues dispatched with rapid prejudice. The two American operatives had come for Sokolov accelerating his timeline, but it had all worked out. He still smiled when thinking about that dark night in Odessa – Jack Hardy the man was a legend even in GRU circles. Of course, it was the girl, Jessie McIntyre, he had learned her name later; that had gotten the drop on him – he was going to have to keep tabs on her.

Kirilov's Spetnaz and GRU - the Russian Military Intelligence Agency - training brought a precision and discipline to the operation that had been lacking in the days of Sokolov, he also had the connections needed to secure the sophisticated weaponry today's clients were demanding, it was big business and business was very good. The resurrection of the Russian Alliance, a thinly veiled attempt at reconstruction of the old Soviet Union had actually made it easier for profiteers to access the aging stores of Soviet era weapons and erased most of the border issues that had been natural trip points for intercepting illegal arms.

He knew very little about VX17, but he knew where it came from - the Soviet germ factory known only as – Compound 19 – the place was legendary, and he had a greater understanding of it than most, of course nobody expected someone to be insane enough to actually let anything out of there. When VX was used in Syria, he had made discreet inquiries - he needed to know if he was working for someone blind enough to deal in WMDs, but nobody he knew, was talking. Which of course meant it had to have been sanctioned at the highest levels, some political idiot trying to send a message to the West about how powerful the Alliance still was. It had just given the Americans an excuse to show how powerful they really were.

Then last year VX pops up again, this time rumors pointing to the lunatic Azrael. Kirilov was a business man, he had no desire to deal with a madman like that, they were generally bad for business and brokering anything considered a weapon of mass destruction was a sure way to end up on every intelligence agency's list – something he wasn't the least bit interested in. He had consolidated the Sokolov empire, focusing on supplying high grade weapons to people intent on killing each other – the way it had always been; let someone else supply the fanatics.

The arms business made for strange bedfellows, you had to have an open mind about these things. He was cultivating some early business using government back channels with Israel and the Americans. It wouldn't do for the Israelis to openly arm moderate Arab groups or for the Americans to be selling M16s to Venezuelan separatists – he provided a blanket of deniability and they paid oh so well!

It was one of these early deals that had introduced him to Ismael, Mossad was secretly arming a moderate Iranian group – no one believed they had any chance at success, but any internal discord within Iran was a win regardless of the outcome. The deal had been mostly small arms, RPGs, and plastic explosives. It had been at one of their first meetings Ismael had mentioned Azrael in passing, Kirilov had assumed it was a test question, but the man had seemed fixated on the assassin, mentioning him multiple times in their subsequent meetings. Kirilov for his part had pleaded ignorance, not wanting any part of Azrael. He didn't need some invisible, unstoppable assassin dropping in on him; he had even told Ismael as much at their last meeting.

He thought that had been the end of it, but three months later Ismael had called him pleading for help, he should have just hung up, but the man had been so distraught he had relented. The Mossad agent had said he was running from Azrael, which seemed unlikely to Kirilov, but he had played along asking what he could do to help. The request had taken him by surprise, contact the CIA and tell them I need protection... he had tried to explain he didn't have any contacts, but Ismael had been adamant – "I know you worked with Jack Hardy and Jessie McIntyre on the Sokolov hit, I know you did..."

He had almost hung up then, there was no way Mossad could have known that, not unless his organization or the CIA had been compromised at the highest levels. "Okay, fine Ismael, I don't want to know how you found that out, but two questions: why me and how do I reach them?"

The Israeli had explained that his own people were now hunting him, and he couldn't take the chance of reaching out directly and it was unlikely anyone would connect him with Kirilov and Kirilov with the Americans. He didn't like it but that made sense in a roundabout way; Ismael had provided a phone number, he claimed belonged to the McIntyre girl.

Kirilov had grudgingly agreed, "ok, ok, I'll try to reach her, but what am I supposed to say?"

"Tell them I'm on Saint Eustatius, Golden Rock Dive Center, and hurry, I need to get out of here," he had said before abruptly hanging up.

Kirilov had waited the better part of a day debating what to do, the scrap of paper with the phone number and scribbled location sat on his desk, a beacon he couldn't ignore. He had finally located the tiny Caribbean Island on Google Earth, shaking his head he brought up the text messaging app and dials the number in. He wasn't worried about it being traced back to him, his security was better than the Russian military's – but still, the thought of getting involved in anything even remotely related to Azrael bothered him.

That had been seventy-two hours earlier, he had no way of knowing whether they message had gone through or if the Americans had even paid any attention. He needed to let it go, he couldn't put his finger on it, but something about the whole episode had him anxious.

He picks the phone up and dials a number he knows by memory, "Uncle Yuri, it's Mikhail, how are you?"

"Mikhail, you shouldn't be calling me here... it's good to hear your voice though," the older man answers. Yuri Semonovich was the senior officer, a Major General, with the permanently assigned regiment to Compound Nineteen - he had taken over the unit after the Syrian debacle and was probably the only person Kirilov could trust enough to ask a few questions.

"Uncle what can you tell me about VX17 and this maniac Azrael?"

He is met with a long silence, "Mikhail these are not questions you should be asking..."

The old man pauses before continuing, "I don't know much, they say Azrael is Mossad, was I should say, his wife and daughter killed by a Hezbollah rocket attack on Nahariya years ago, but it was the peace accord that broke him our people say. Couldn't be controlled and well, when his own people came for him he started picking his own targets, but who knows for sure."

"Fuck me," Mikhail whispers in Russian, "what about the VX," he asks.

18

"Mikhail, you know I can't speak about that, but if this Azrael has it then the world is not so safe for anyone, nephew."

"Thank you, uncle, I understand, be well…"

"Mikhail, remember, the more you know, the less you should talk!"

Kirilov loved his uncle's old sayings, they reminded him of his childhood when his father and uncles would let him stay up late while they drank vodka and told war stories from the brutal days in Afghanistan. He hangs the phone up thinking about what his uncle had said. If the information on Azrael was true, why hadn't it been shared with the Americans and even more disturbingly, why hadn't the Israelis cleaned up this mess already? They admittedly had one of, if not the best, intelligence agencies in the world. All questions he knew he shouldn't be worrying about, but he was still an intelligence agent at heart…

Tel Aviv

A warm breeze carries a hint of salt off the Mediterranean mixing with the murmur of the Jaffa Flea Market and the cries of hungry gulls circling the docks - David Eisen sits in the cracked leather recliner watching the slow roll of condensation soaking the napkin his mineral water sits on, the ice cubes having mostly melted while he is lost in his memories.

He had been "out of country" that night in late October it seemed like yesterday but had been almost nine years now – the rockets had rained down for hours killing thirty-seven civilians including his precious Raisa and little Tania, innocents in a war that had been raging for centuries. He had buried their broken bodies and thrown himself back into work fueled with a righteous anger, but even by Mossad standards he was pushing too hard. He was already a member of the elite Kidon unit, known for their espionage and assassination skills. They had tried to pull him back, counseling, down-time; none of it mattered, he would train on his own honing his skills, his physical conditioning, his fervent desire to kill. He was the perfect assassin, at five feet ten with dark hair and sharp features he could pass as an Arab, Italian, Turk and Pakistani – his superiors finally gave up giving him the impossible missions, the most difficult kills, he thrived on it.

Then three years ago everything had come crashing down, his country, the land where his girls were buried, where his daughter's laughter had filled his days; had finally capitulated to the Western powers and embraced a Palestinian state. He had been forced to serve a country no longer recognizable, a country that was embracing the murderers of his family, a country that was in his eyes defeated, his sacrifice had been betrayed. He had been in Singapore when the news had come through, he hadn't hesitated to go off grid immediately – he figured they would come for him sooner or later but hadn't anticipated the kill order they had issued almost immediately.

In retrospect, it probably made sense, he was already operating independently for the most part and his superiors had to know how was going to react. He had never returned to the small house on the outskirts of Nahariya, the palm lined boulevards, the fishing pier where his precious Tania had laughed chasing the sea birds, he missed the grottos just north of the city where the Mediterranean had over thousands of years created intricate sculptures out of the soft sandstone – he had made a final trip to their graves vowing to never return but visited often in his dreams and he knew the day was coming when he would rejoin his precious girls.

That first year had been the toughest, he was already immune to the killing, but executing those first jobs had been an outlet for his rage, but they were also means to an end - the mythical status of Azrael had to be established and what better way than a series of high profile kills that couldn't be traced to anyone or any ideology. The money had come after that, assassination for hire grated on his moral outrage and professionalism, but the money had been more important than his feelings.

The apartment was a sublet of a sublet, not unusual in these older neighborhoods, paid in cash six months at a time so no one asked any questions. He opted to stay in Israel, in spite of everything it was home and a short train ride to the end of the northern line where his girls were waiting. There were a half-million people living in Tel Aviv more than enough to disappear in. Years ago, he had participated in a joint CIA – Mossad training in the United States – he had been taught to "hide in plain sight" – a lesson he was taking to heart. The insanity of trying to integrate the Palestinian population into the Israeli government systems, including identification, passport, and surveillance had made disappearing almost too easy; further proof of the enormity of the mistake as far as he was concerned.

The scent of grilling meats and clatter of plates from St. George's below refocuses his attention to the task at hand. His MacBook Pro is using a pirated signal off the restaurant's Wi-Fi. He isn't worried about sending up any red flags, the search history is what you would expect from a normal user, another piece of the camouflage. He uses a separate laptop to read the encrypted thumb drives containing sensitive data exchanged with clients and sources.

The schematics race across the screen as he swipes right to left on the wireless pad — the piping and filtration system delivering water from the Zamzam Well in the center of Mecca was a convoluted collection of pipes and pumps under continuous renovation by the Saudis. A number of upgrades to the systems had been installed over the years and although security was impressive it wasn't impenetrable. New pumps and filters had been installed by a British firm after the last Hajj, *need to check into that*, he thinks making a note to look up their website. The plans had cost him a small fortune, but they had been cheap compared to the vial. He had played on the natural animosity between the Shia and Sunni sects that had erupted on a whole new level after the Syrian debacle to procure what he needed.

A year earlier he had helped a high-level Syrian extract his family from the "humanitarian" camps the UN had set up, the man had fled to Iran, a coward, leaving his family behind when the United States had initiated its purge. The safe passage of the man's two sons and wife had bought him access to a vial of VX17 and the man's nephew — a deeply planted mole in the Saudi police force. He hadn't had a plan at the time, but access to a high-grade biological and a well-placed mole were assets that couldn't be passed up, it's also where he had run into Ismael.

It had been one of those right place wrong time situations, turn right not left and everything changes another lesson from the CIA training. He had been in Tehran sitting in the last car on metro line four from downtown to the airport when Ismael had boarded. The man had spotted him instantly – they had spent enough years together so there was no chance of mistaking each other. David had just nodded when Ismael had taken the seat next to him, neither could afford to draw any attention, being Israelis in Iran was an inherently dangerous situation. Ismael had only asked one question, "why David, why...?"

David had looked at the man with tears in his eyes all he could choke out was, "they betrayed my girls..."

Ismael had nodded and said, "peace be with you my old friend," and had gotten off at the next station.

It pained David to think about it, but he knew that Ismael was now a danger to him – the last thing he wanted was to start eliminating his countrymen, he had broken bread with this man, they had trained together – but he was on a different path now and there were consequences he didn't want to think about but couldn't avoid either. Maybe he could have let it go, but Ismael hadn't let it be, the man had come looking for him, making inquiries, asking questions – he had finally confronted Ismael one dark evening in Odessa, a final warning to leave it alone. This wasn't a crusade, he wasn't looking for followers – he didn't need or want company on this journey.

It had been too late; Ismael's superiors were on to him and it wouldn't be long before they started rolling up the string in search of David. Ismael had run of course, everyone always does, and he had tracked him to the Caribbean and a meeting with the CIA. Maybe the man had gotten lucky, maybe David had been careless – either way he had saved the girl's life giving his in exchange, although David had planned to take them both. He hadn't waited to see how it turned out as he was experienced enough to know – when it didn't go as planned you didn't stick around to figure out why, that's what "next time" was for.

That was three days ago, it had taken two just to get back to Israel, a string of six flights and three passports, making it difficult if not impossible to track him, now it was time to get back to work. The Angel of Death had a date with the two million pilgrims making their way to Mecca in less than two months for the Hajj – Jessie had been right time was running short.

Paradigm

The Styrofoam containers were stuffed haphazardly in the trash can next to the oversized executive desk, Lou was studying the three large hi-definition monitors on his desk, one was linked to his laptop and the other two accessed the mainframe downstairs. Paradigm might not have the computing power the government had, but it boasted significantly more than most of the bigger hi-tech firms that had made Silicon Valley famous a few decades earlier and he had the best minds in the business period.

"What you lookin' at?" Jack asks from the couch, still slurping on his sweet tea and feeling like a nap after downing the Pig Pile Elvis style – a huge pulled pork sandwich piled high with coleslaw and a side of baked beans from KT's downtown.

"I'm lookin' at an old man that's going to get fat if he keeps eating like that," Lou laughs.

Jack pushes himself up from the couch with a groan and comes around the desk, pulling a chair from the small conference table with him, "seriously what are you looking at?"

"Well we were able to access some details on VX17 and I had the team combine that with what we learned out of Syria to build a profile on this bit of nastiness," he turns to Jack, "this is a very, very, ugly bug, let me tell you. If the Syrians had been even a little more capable the number of dead would have been in the hundreds of thousands..."

"Not for nothing Lou, but you know they usually lock hackers up for this kind of shit..." Jack smiles, "but I like your initiative, have we shared this with anyone yet?"

"No, we haven't, I'm going to send it to Jess but not sure who else, if anyone, my guess is the bastards already know anyway!" Lou might be taking hundreds of millions in government contracts for his work, but that didn't keep him from having a very healthy skepticism as well – fact is, he didn't trust the Agency, the FBI, or anyone else when it came to his daughter. Jack knew it didn't help reminding him they had done right by her during the Sokolov mess, in Lou's mind that didn't excuse their opportunistic use of her as bait, and he was probably right. Jessie was inside the Agency now though, an operative reporting to the Deputy Director himself, which hadn't made her dad feel any better about it.

Jack backed off, "so do you think this maniac Azrael really has some of it?"

Lou looks up from the screens leaning back in his chair, arms behind his head, he takes a deep breath, "I do Jack, I really do." He rubs his face with both hands, "There's too much chatter at the Agency about it, and the Russians are being way too cooperative, no he's got some – only question is, what's he going to do with it..."

"Listening by doors you shouldn't be at, again Lou?" Jack asks with a smile.

"Well, we have to test the encryption algorithms, might as well do it in a live environment, don't you think?" he answers with a sheepish smile.

Jack smiles back, "those boys at the FBI were right, thank God you're on our side!"

The two men had been friends for more than thirty years, having met in the CIA as young men. Jack had stayed in, a career officer; Lou had gotten out though, married the girl he loved, tragically lost her way too young, but gained a baby girl, and built one of the most powerful tech companies in the world - they had remained best of friends through it all.

Jack had left the field work behind a few years earlier, just happy to have made it through. He had retired, spending his time consulting or doing training for the Agency, the money was good and for the most part he got to sleep in his own bed. Then a year ago Lou had knocked on his door needing his help, Jessie had been the target of the Ukrainian mob and the bodies had started piling up pretty quickly - he had found himself reinstated and back in the field showing her the ropes. He had stayed on this time as a paid consultant, but his only real responsibility was to continue Jessie's training.

Jack retreats to the couch, "so, what's worst case scenario if this guy has... what did you call it?"

"A vial is how they are describing it, apparently it's a mutated protein; uhh," he pulls the screen back up, "named Ubiquilin, anyway it hyper escalates neurodegeneration at the cellular and subcellular level. It's very similar to ALS only it takes about thirty-six hours, not three to five years, the bastards grafted it to a live virus so it's not only stable but contagious for maybe as long as a couple days once distributed." Lou moves over to the love seat caddie-corner to the couch, "anyway, the Syrians released it as an aerosol, screwed the concentrations up and everybody got lucky, well if you call fifty thousand dead lucky." He takes a deep sigh, "my guess is this son-of-a-bitch won't make that mistake, so worst-case scenario is probably water or food supply in a mobile society - that will accelerate the contagion effect, the damn thing will simply overwhelm whatever healthcare system is trying to deal with it."

Jack lets out a low whistle, "I don't get the cell stuff but that's a pretty bleak picture – likely targets?" he asks.

Lou purses his lips, "well if his early kills are any indication we are probably looking at the US, Russians, Chinese or one of our allies, but," Lou hesitates, "...something about this whole thing just doesn't make sense to me, but I can't put my finger on it," he says, leaning forward.

"Go with it Lou, what are you thinking?" Jack prompts him sitting up again.

"Well if you think about the two theories on this guy, neither one really supports the initial targets."

"Explain what you mean," Jack says.

Lou gets a far-away look in his eyes, "well, let's take the first theory... rogue Mossad agent, okay the skill set makes sense, the precision, everything but the targets, right?"

Jack nods, "I guess so, no Middle East or Arab targets, I can see what you are saying and no reason to go after us or the Brits, and that thing with the Japanese Prime Minister, Jesus!"

"Right, so let's look at option two, super killer out of ISIS, I'm just not buying it, they've been decimated for almost ten years and why wouldn't we have heard of him before, we had excellent intel on those guys, and once again the targets don't fit, in fact this whole fucking thing doesn't make any sense," Lou says exasperatedly getting up and starting to pace around the office, he stops at the floor to ceiling windows looking out at the Flatirons, "unless..."

"Unless what?" Jack asks coming over to stand next to him.

"Unless those fuckers already know who he is and are standing down for some reason."

Jack sucks in his breath, "Uh, that's seriously fucked up if you're right Lou, and what does that mean for Jessie?"

Lou turns to look at his old friend, "I don't know, but you can be damn sure I'm going to find out!" the anger evident in his voice.

"Slow down, this isn't like marching into some mid-level FBI guy's office, we need to be sure before we go turning any rocks over on this, think about it anyone willing to put that many people at risk isn't going to worry about disappearing you and me."

Lou pats him on the shoulder, "you're right old friend, don't let me get us killed ok?"

"Haven't yet, but it's getting more difficult!" Jack answers with a grin.

Shelter

The wind is already picking back up as Jessie rounds the curve coming up on The Old Gin House, a small hotel and bar she had been planning to stay at before things had gone awry. The place is solid, constructed of old brick, but the doors and windows are boarded up and there doesn't seem to be any way in. Jessie skirts the pool area, avoiding the mangled palms and tattered awnings while circling around the back to the rear kitchen entrance, hoping she can find an open door before the rain returns. The wind is already whistling through the few trees that are still standing. She finds the rear door blocked with palm debris that has been blown into that corner of the building. Pushing aside the limbs and palm fronds she tugs at the handle — locked — in frustration she bangs with her fist. There isn't time to retreat to the dive shop, she looks around hoping there is somewhere else she can seek shelter.

"Child, get in here," the soft accented voice calls.

The kitchen door has been opened just enough for her to slip through, "thank you, thank you," she whispers trying to contain her emotions.

"Honey, let's get you dried off," the old woman, her mahogany skin making her almost invisible in the soft glow of the candle light says as she begins to pat her dry with a clean towel, humming and cooing over her.

Jessie leans against her the stress of the past twelve hours starting to bleed off, she looks around there are a dozen or so others sitting or leaning against the old brick walls, clearly staff still in their uniforms or aprons. "Is it only us?" she asks.

The old woman smiles at her, "oh, yes dear, they move all guests to the Fort, safer there," she pats her on the arm, "but no worries, plenty of food and drink here, plenty safe."

Jessie smiles and thanks her again, one of the young men hands her a bottle of water which she downs in two long swallows, she sits cross legged on a stack of twenty-five-kilogram burlap rice sacks, the rough material is itchy against her bare legs, but she is so tired she hardly notices. The group is quiet, only a few murmurs between them as the winds begin to howl again and the rain beats in rhythm against the bricks.

The gentle rocking wakes Jessie, she is disoriented at first the smell of burlap, coffee, and bacon mix with the salt air. She hears the whine of a chainsaw and the syncopated beats of a hammer, she stretches working the stiffness out of her muscles and neck before hopping off the bags of rice.

The old woman smiles and hands her a cup of steaming coffee, "time to rise young lady," she says.

Jessie yawns, "is it over?"

The old woman nods, turning back to the giant stove and sizzling bacon, "now time for cleaning up!" and with a cheerful chuckle, "and breakfast!"

Jessie extracts the Kimber 9MM from her backpack and slips it into the sleeve sewn in the waist of her shorts, the pistol fits snugly in the small of her back and is easily covered by her t-shirt. She makes her way over to the stove, "thank you again for last night, my name's Jessie, can I help...?"

The old lady hands her a metal bowl and whisk, "everyone calls me Mimi," she points to several cartons of eggs, "you whisk them for me?"

"Sure, all of them?" Jessie asks.

"Yes dear, many mouths to feed," as she turns back to the oven, opening the door and checking on golden loaves of cornbread. They spend the next forty minutes fixing the eggs, bacon, cornbread and cutting up fresh fruit – Jessie thinks it might be the most delicious breakfast she has ever eaten.

It's late morning by the time they have cleaned up from the meal, Jessie heads for the courtyard to see if she can get a SAT signal on her phone and check in with Langley. Turning the phone on she sees three messages from her dad. She hesitates, but they are going to have to wait.

The Ops Support Group at Langley has the luxury of never seeing the field, creating an annoying habit of believing they are doing you a favor – Jessie ignores the attitude for the most part, she just needs off the island as quickly as possible. "I understand there was a hurricane," she explains for the third time, "I was right fucking here for it!" she says exasperatedly. "Ok, Ok, just tell me how to get out of here, and I need everything Collections can get me on a Mossad agent name Ismael, no I don't have anything more than that," she hangs up in frustration. The Collections group was responsible for analyzing all the intelligence data collected by any method possible, but even they would need a starting point.

The best Ops had been able to offer was a Navy supply flight out of San Juan nearly two hundred nautical miles away. How the hell she was supposed to get to Puerto Rico was the real question, and Langley hadn't been real helpful on that score either – the CIA may be one of the foremost intelligence agencies in the world but it's still a government agency.

Jessie re-reads the text messages from her Dad and decides it's just easier to call him, checking her watch she calculates the time in Boulder. *Let's see, four hours so should be nine there*, she thinks.

She listens as the encryption syncs and the phone begins to ring, her dad answers without preamble before the second ring, "you ok?"

"Yeah, I don't recommend vacationing in hurricanes though," she laughs.

"I'll bet, find out anything?"

Jessie hesitates not willing to lie to her father, "no, somebody took my source out before I could talk to him…" She leaves out that she was probably the target, her dad already worries way more than he should. "All I have is his name, not even sure who gave it to us or why, I've got Langley trying to track down anything we have, but I'm not real hopeful," she takes a deep breath, "my biggest problem is finding a way off this island."

"Is the airport intact?" her dad asks.

"Actually, I don't know, it's only a couple of miles, I can be over there in thirty or forty minutes, but I don't think anyone is flying in or out anytime soon."

"I'll send a plane, Paradigm just acquired a jet charter group, if we have one close and it's clear I can have someone there in a couple hours."

"Uhh ok, you own a bunch of jets now? That's cool, give me forty-five and I'll call you back."

"Well, after all that travel last year it seemed like a good investment. By the way, how many people at Langley are working on this Azrael thing?"

Jessie knows the warning signs, knows how her dad is and knows he probably already has the answer so no point in not responding, "well - not really sure dad, I've got the analysis and support groups at my disposal, but I think I'm the only operative unless there is someone I don't know about, why?"

"No reason, just curious."

Jessie smiles, "bullshit dad, what's up?"

"It's nothing Jess, let me see about getting you out of there..."

"Ok thanks, I'll call you back," Jessie lets it go, she knows her dad well enough and if he doesn't want to tell her no amount of pleading is going to change that. She shakes her head, fact is her dad's five years in the Agency and time as a government contractor has amped up his conspiracy theorist levels to the point where he doesn't really trust anyone, of course she had to admit he hadn't been wrong about much either.

She bids farewell to Mimi and heads off towards the airport at a brisk jog thinking, *Paradigm must be doing better than she realized if her dad could afford to buy a corporate jet service.*

The airport is a wreck, overturned prop planes, the metal roof of the hanger is in shreds, but the strip itself is clear. Jessie looks around for anyone that looks even remotely official, not always an easy thing to identify on these small islands, but the place seems abandoned. She dials up her dad again, "strip looks okay, everything else is a mess though," she says not waiting for him to ask.

"Ok, well as long as they can land I think it's okay," he answers.

"Uh, you might want to ask about fuel and if the strip is long enough, not sure there is any way to refuel here and I had to take a small prop in."

"Ahh, good catch, I'll check. Can you hang there for a bit while I make some calls?"

"Yeah, just send me a text though, I've got to save this battery, nowhere to recharge here… dad, thanks."

"No problem baby, love ya," he says hanging up.

Jessie smiles to herself, here she was a badass spy chasing the "Angel of Death", but underneath it all she was still a daddy's girl.

Collusion

Each of the six ALPHA team operatives had been recruited independently their identities intentionally hidden from each other – they were simply addressed as their assigned number. ALPHA One, Two and Three were Israelis, Four was American, Five Russian, and Six was a cheeky Brit, the leader of this operation was a senior Mossad agent only referred to as "Control". The group had been formed to combat Azrael the year he had first burst on the scene, but more sinister and pragmatic minds had taken the reigns two years ago and the mission parameters had been updated.

They used a secure and encrypted satellite network to communicate via both satellite phone and shared screen computer to computer communications.

"ALPHA One, where is the asset now?"

"Control, he returned to Tel Aviv yesterday and hasn't left the apartment," One responds.

"What about Ismael Cohen and the girl?"

There is a clicking of keys, "Ismael's biometrics went offline three... no four days ago, sir... last word on the girl is she caught a private charter off the island." The Israelis had started chipping all their agents after Azrael had gone rogue, it wasn't going to help track him, but they weren't making the same mistake twice.

"So, he is fallible..." the Brit says with a low whistle.

"Doesn't matter, she is isolated, what about the water plant schematics, were they delivered?" Control asks.

"Yes, sir the asset has them in hand and the source has been neutralized... car accident – nasty business," the Brit answers, he's always been prone to a bit of commentary and just can't seem to help himself.

"Stay on task Six," Control cautions, "are we sure it was clean, we don't need any red flags."

"As far I can tell, it was handled as a routine traffic accident."

"Ok, do we have a casualty estimate from our friends up North yet, Five?"

"Dah, models out of Nineteen estimate seventy-two-hour casualty count at four hundred thousand plus and ninety-six hours topping out around six hundred thousand, they say the secondary impacts over the following weeks could top a million dead..."

There is silence, even these hardened operatives are sobered by the immensity of what they are discussing. A million dead will put this on the short and disturbing list of humanity's worst atrocities.

"Any concern about spread outside the Kingdom?"

"No Control, standard protocol will be to lock down the borders and well, it's surrounded by desert so unlikely it will travel beyond the immediate area." He pauses for a moment, then almost to himself, "but it always gets out somewhere, somehow?"

"Ok ALPHA team, stay the course, we all knew what we were signing on for…" That wasn't technically true, the team's focus had taken a pretty dramatic turn, but they were too far down this path to deviate from it now. "Ok reconvene in three days 2200 GMT as usual, Four, we will need an update on the McIntyre girl, she's in your yard – I want to know what she knows."

"Yes sir, on it."

Each of the operatives signs off, now alone with their thoughts. ALPHA team had been chosen for their loyalty, and experience – the original mission had been to uncover Azrael's identity and neutralize him. They had solved that mystery pretty quickly when the Israelis had capitulated, almost immediately admitting he had been one of their top agents - the bigger challenge was figuring out where Azrael was and how to eliminate him.

Six months in they had gotten lucky, no other way to describe it, ALPHA Two had been vacationing in Northern Israel and had caught a glimpse of Azrael boarding the train South, it had been as simple as reviewing station surveillance footage from there. Why they hadn't moved immediately was still a mystery to the team, but it hadn't been their call and now they were on a ride to hell with the Angel of Death driving the train.

It was a simple fact that most atrocities could be tied back to four constructs: economics, colonial expansion, religion, and race. There were a multitude of variations, and the aggressor always seemed comfortable with their self-fulfilling altruisms; this case wasn't any different.

In many ways, the die had been cast a decade earlier, failure of the continuing nation building experiment in Iraq combined with the expanding power of the Iranian regime – which was now openly displaying their nuclear capability had forced the hand of the Sunni majorities in the other Arab states, particularly the Saudi Kingdom. A second purge following the first consolidation of power in 2017 had taken place earlier this year, hoping to stave off a resurgence of the conservative clerics that had been chafing for control since their last insurrection in the late seventies. Controlling them was key to maintaining the moderate power base that had been established but was also another affront to the more conservative Shia factions.

The brewing confrontation did not serve the interest of the traditional super powers or the European Union, at least what was left of it, whichever side came out victorious was going to have cemented their power base in a region that was already slipping beyond the rest of the civilized world's control and that wasn't acceptable to anyone.

After much haranguing and back channel discussions orders had been given – dismantle the Middle East by whatever means necessary. Nobody at the top wanted to know how or who – that would have meant acknowledging complicity in the matter, heads of state were intentionally isolated and kept out of the loop – the careers didn't need a crisis of conscience interfering.

In the aftermath and under the auspices of the United Nations the Western powers, with their "friends" in Russia and China, would step in and create a system of "Protectorates"; in very much the same way they had carved up the world after the Second World War.

That it was going to take a million dead Muslims and a humanitarian catastrophe the likes of which had never been seen to kick off this party didn't seem to bother anyone – plausible deniability ruled the day.

In a classic case of "Black Ops" running unchecked, where more oversight or at least more rational minds would have recoiled at the sheer horror of the proposal; opportunity had ruled the day. The combination of the Syrian massacre and Azrael's rumored background as an ISIS killer had created the template for this disaster – an internal war between the Islamic factions; with a million casualties as the starting point – there was no model to forecast the dead after the finger pointing started. The rest of the world would stand by and watch, not willing to become embroiled in what was clearly a religious war – but waiting to pick up the pieces when it was all done.

The fact that each government had people in authority willing to rationalize these actions was a clear indication that humanity wasn't evolving nearly as quickly as we had convinced ourselves and just that simply Azrael had been transitioned from imminent and uncontrolled threat to pawn in a game larger than he could have imagined.

The Israelis erased his identity crafting a new one to suit the narrative, their recent integration of Palestine working in their favor. A computer entry error and a Russian double agent had facilitated the vial of VX17 making its way to Azrael. The plans for the Saudi water pumping stations had been the simplest to obtain as the engineering had been completed by a British firm – the hardest part had been getting them into Iran for the hand-off. Ismael had been an unwitting drone; that he had actually run into Azrael was mere coincidence.

With all the pieces in place the only wild card left was Jessie McIntyre, nobody had any real data on her and no one involved had expected the Deputy Director of the CIA to assign an independent operative to the Azrael file. It was a complication, but one ALPHA team felt was manageable, worst case scenario someone would have to sideline her. ALPHA Four had already made it clear it would have to be one of the others, he drew the line with killing his fellow countrymen – Control hadn't argued the point, but even Four knew that if it came right down to it there wouldn't be any choice.

Extraction

Jessie had waited nearly three hours before the whine of the jet's engine had broken the peaceful silence of the island. It had barely come to a stop before the door had opened and the stair had unfolded.

The pilot sticks his head out the door, "you McIntyre?" he asks.

Jessie nods grabbing up the backpack and climbing in, "that's me, thanks for coming, cool jet," she says looking around.

"Thanks, it's a PC24 made in Switzerland perfect for small fields like this one, I can set this baby down on a dirt strip if I need to, name's Davenport, make yourself comfortable."

Jesse sets her backpack on one of the plush leather seats and takes the one next to it, she's a bit self-conscious in the luxury jet not having been able to change clothes or really wash up since arriving a couple days earlier. She had changed out of her bloody T-shirt that first evening replacing it with the only other one she had brought; this trip wasn't supposed to have lasted more than a day. A quick application of more deodorant and a scrub in the restaurant bathroom had been the best she could do.

Davenport secures the door, "takes about two plus hours to Miami, you can chill back here, or I have an extra seat up front, your call."

"Ok, gotta make a couple of calls can I move forward after we're in the air?"

"Sure, no problem, there's a cooler with soft drinks, beer and water in the back and probably some crackers and fruit up here in the galley if you want didn't really have time to stock up, heads right here by the front," he says pointing to the door.

"Thanks, appreciate it."

"Just strap in for the next five minutes or so until I get us off the ground, then she's all yours," he says with a smile.

Clearly, he was trying to be charming and it wasn't that she was immune to charming, he was kinda cute in a Miami Beach sort of way with his boyish grin, sandy blond hair, and good tan; but she was working, tired, and God she smelled a bit! On any other day, she might have entertained it. Not a relationship, that was pretty much out of the question, since the whole debacle with Tom last year, but a girl did get lonely and there were times when Jessie wanted what Jessie wanted.

"Will do," she says with a smile dismissing the other thoughts and tightening the seat belt. She dials up her dad's office and waits for him to answer.

"Hey kiddo, the plane get there?"

"Yeah, taking off now, headed to Miami, guess I'll try to catch a flight to DC from there, thanks Dad."

"No problem, but why don't you head out here, I reserved the plane and pilot for a few days, we can catch up, I know Jack would love to see you... what'd you say?"

"I don't know, I don't have any clothes with me and honestly, I need a shower and like twelve hours of sleep."

"Well listen, I'll book you a room at the DoubleTree in Miami, spend the night, do some shopping and you can decide in the morning, Mark will fly you wherever you decide."

"Mark?" she asks.

"Yeah Mark, you know the pilot," he answers perplexed, "didn't he introduce himself?"

"Well yeah, I guess, said his name was Davenport."

"Oh, Ok, well its Mark Davenport, he'll take you wherever, but I think you should come out for a few days."

"Alright, I'll think about it, call you when I get to Miami – thanks again Dad," she says clicking off.

She unbuckles and heads to the back rummaging through the cooler, she grabs a Diet Coke and a couple of bananas from the cabinet. She looks around, the plane is smaller than some she has seen but is functional and has a surprising amount of space. She sits in the last seat, munching on the banana and sipping the cold drink. Not a lot about the past few days makes sense, the tip had turned out to be real, but it had also been a trap or at least seemed like it, either way Ismael had paid with his life for the meeting.

Ismael was Israeli they had been able to ascertain that at Langley; did that make Azrael Israeli also – probably but way too easy to assume that at this point. But it did mean Azrael had excellent sources or had figured out how to penetrate their communications either way it was bad news, she was going to have to talk to her dad about the coms problem. She was no closer to uncovering Azrael than she had been before the trip to the island, and who the hell had sent her the text in the first place? Was that a source, someone that could help her? She had more questions than answers at this point.

With a sigh, she dials the direct number she has for Director Simpson, she was two days late checking in and she was sure he wasn't going to want to hear about any damn hurricane. She listens as the phone clicks and crackles the encryption syncing up before it starts to ring.

"Simpson," he says abruptly.

"Yes sir, its McIntyre, sorry I'm late checking in," she says tiredly.

"Heard you had a hurricane, I'm short on time so give me the highlights, Ok..."

"Yes sir, short version is Ismael was probably the real deal, but took two rounds through the back and bled out before he could give me anything, probably saved my life though, no indication who it was, but best guess is Azrael. Anyway, I'm headed back to the States, I've asked the guys down in Collections to see what they can dig up on Ismael and forward it to me... that's the short version sir."

"Glad you're okay, I'll make sure you get what you need from downstairs," he pauses, "listen, be careful, okay, call me next week and we can talk next steps until then don't take any flak from the support group."

"Yes sir, thank you," he has already hung up. Jessie leans back in the chair, she didn't know enough about CIA organizational politics and protocol to determine if she had just been marginalized by the Director, but it felt that way. She sits up and heads to the front, time to see how interesting Mark was or wasn't.

"Want some company?" she asks, poking her head into the cockpit.

"Sure, come on in," he says pointing to the seat on the right.

She wedges herself in, awkwardly aware that she definitely needs a cleanup, to his credit Mark doesn't act like he notices.

"So, do you work for Paradigm?"

"Nope, for the government, Paradigm is my father's company." She already regrets saying it, she hated the poor little rich girl persona.

"Cool, what kinda work do you do?"

"Sorry can't talk about it, classified. I could tell you but then I'd have to kill you?" she says deadpan. The cliché is old and worn but elicits a big grin from him anyway.

"Well, that would be a problem, who would land this beast?" he asks playing along.

"I guess I'll keep you alive a little longer," she laughs. "You like being a pilot?"

Mark smiles and his eyes sparkle, "Oh man, I love it, I was made to fly – this is as close to free as you get, besides I get to travel to some really cool places," he gushes.

Jessie smiles at him, it's nice to meet someone that just loves what they do, no complications, no crazy, just every day regular. "Listen, when we get to Miami I'm staying at the DoubleTree but I really need to do some shopping. Lost all my stuff in the storm, is there a mall or something close?"

"Oh sure, Mall of America is right down the street, I could give you a ride if you want..."

"It's not a bother?" she asks setting the hook.

"Happy to do it, seriously," he smiles, not realizing yet that the player is getting played. "I'm on call to fly you wherever you want, so I'm at your service milady," he says with a horribly faked British accent.

"Oh mercy!" she says laughing.

They trade stories for another hour, Mark had grown up in Miami getting his pilot's license while still in high school and had finally graduated to jets ten years later, he had been flying for this company for the past three years and loving it. Jessie wove a tale around boring government work and growing up in the Rockies, a combination of truth and fiction, Jack had taught her well. She had already decided that dinner was on the docket, and after that, well, she would see where things went, if he was still interesting great, if not she could use the rest.

"Need to be in Boulder tomorrow, flexible on the time, but would be great to get in around lunch if possible."

"Sure, no problem, I'll file a flight plan tonight, it's about four hours or so out there, with the time change we could leave at ten or so and make it for lunch, that work for you?" Mark asks.

"Perfect!" Jessie says with a smile.

Kirilov

Kirilov had left four messages for Ismael before burning the SAT phone and switching to a clean one. He had inherited much of the security network and all of the paranoia from Sokolov – you didn't stay alive in this business by being careless. A fact Jessie McIntyre had succinctly reminded his boss of, with two 9MM rounds to the head. Kirilov hadn't expected that, the Americans were a by the book outfit and were supposed to have taken Sokolov back to the States, apparently McIntyre had different plans for him, *she really was something else*, he thinks with a smile.

The silence from Ismael had him worried though, the man had been panicked when they last spoke and then nothing. It didn't help that the Israeli was his only contact for the small arms he had been shipping to the dissidents in Iran. It wasn't big business, but anytime a buyer was exposed or disappeared you had to worry what might come back up the line. It was one of the reasons he had burnt the phone, he wasn't really worried about the Israelis or the Iranians for that matter, but Azrael well that was another story all together. Only a foolish man thought he couldn't be touched, and Kirilov was anything but foolish.

He had to be honest though it wasn't just Ismael, the McIntyre girl had him intrigued and he wasn't bothered at all by her apparent comfort eliminating people. She had gotten the drop on him that night on the way back from meeting with Sampson, sure he had been careless, but she was good and ruthless. He knew a true warrior when he ran into one and people like Jessie McIntyre were very few and far between, and damn if she wasn't beautiful too. *Fuck me, I need to get this woman out of my head!* he thinks.

Kirilov had recruited a group of five lieutenants from his days in the GRU to help manage his business. These were men he had served with and could trust – four he had given a specific sales geography they were responsible for and the fifth managed procurement and shipping. It was corporately organized the five could have been polished vice-presidents in any modern boardroom. Gone was the brutality and human trafficking that ultimately had spelled doom for Sokolov. Black market arms weren't exactly legal, but it didn't carry the stigma or law enforcement attention human trafficking and drugs did. He had kept the Sokolov residence for himself but had moved the "corporation" into one of the shiny new buildings in the center of Kiev's business district. He made changes, quickly hiring Krushenko and Associates, the international law firm based in Kiev and Moscow, to clean up and consolidate the corporate holdings of Sokolov – it had cost him north of twenty million US dollars, but he considered it money well spent.

The first step in the cleanup had been the anonymous delivery of twenty-two Terabytes of data to Special Agent in Charge Timothy Harrington's office in Washington DC, it was going to take the Bureau years to sort through it all, but they were already tracking down and rescuing young woman all over the US and coordinating with Interpol to handle the overseas cases. It was an unexpected windfall after the near miss in cracking the Sokolov trafficking operation in New York the past year and although it bothered Special Agent in Charge Harrington that the data had to have come from someone inside, it had probably saved his career and he wasn't going to look a gift horse in the mouth.

Kiev made sense for Kirilov as most countries he was dealing with had embassies located there and it gave him easy access to Russia a major source of legal and illegal weapons. Besides, there were times he missed home and it was a little less than two hours to Moscow in one of the two Gulfstream 650s he kept hangered there.

But it was June and he liked to spend the summer months in Odessa enjoying the sea breezes. Sitting on the veranda he can hear the cry of gulls from a couple of blocks away and the faint crash of waves on the shore. Having lived in Russia most of his life a summer tan was a bit of a new thing for him, but it went well with his sandy blond hair, high cheek bones and blue grey eyes. He had a classic Russian chin that had never held a beard very well and he had never been able to get used to having a mustache. He wasn't a very tall man at slightly under six feet, but he had an understated power about him, but more than anything Kirilov relied on his intellect as it had never been about brawn for him.

He pushes himself up from the chair and heads inside. He can smell roasting meat for the dinner meal being prepared in the large kitchen downstairs. He had kept the old cook and housekeeper on, she simply had nowhere else to go and had begged to stay. He had cleaned house though releasing and replacing everyone else, thugs were generally unreliable, he had upgraded bringing in only ex-military for security. The hardest part had been the girls, Sokolov had kept half a dozen young women in the compound – young, beautiful, and compliant. Kirilov figured they would be anxious to leave, finally free from a life of forced sex and abuse. The opposite had been true though, most were Eastern European girls from small towns and cities across the region, there was no-one to return to. They were stained and would be shunned by their families, at least here they had the best of everything and were comfortable; the sex seemed like a small price to pay. In the end, he had insisted on providing each with enough money to start fresh wherever they might choose, he didn't want or need the complication, maybe he was just old fashioned that way.

Looking in the mirror he combs his hair and bends to wash his hands in the marble sink before heading downstairs for dinner, *strange thing this life*, he thinks. Those days training in the Army, the cold barracks, harsh marches, followed by the years as an intelligence officer had all led here; *but that had never been the plan had it?* He would have been a career man, but politics had changed all that, well, politics and his willingness to crossover to what his countrymen like to call capitalism, everyone else called it organized crime.

Kirilov wasn't kidding himself though, he was well aware of where he stood and the choices he had made, it didn't bother him. He didn't consider himself in the same group as the Sokolov's of the world, truly psychopathic criminals with no moral compass, he had a code of ethics, even if it was technically a bit out of sync with civilized society. The thought made him smile, there was nothing particularly civilized about society, never had been, he just happened to be on the other side of this particular iteration of the law.

He fluffs the linen napkin out setting it precisely on his lap as the aroma of lamb stew and fresh baked bread surround him. He hesitates a moment, reaching into his shirt pocket and extracting his phone, he looks at the blank screen as the facial recognition scan unlocks the device. He taps the messaging app, keys in four words hesitating an instant before adding his initials and hitting send before dropping the phone back in his pocket.

He bends to the stew savoring the deep rich chunks of lamb, mixed with onions, carrots, celery, and potatoes. He had acted on impulse, but now that it was done he wasn't going to second guess it. Tearing off a hunk of the dark brown bread he dips it in the broth wondering what, if any, response he'll receive.

Boulder

Jessie snuggles deeper under the down comforter not quite ready to face the early morning sun, the steady patter of the shower brings a smile. What Mark lacked in sophistication he made up for with enthusiasm and the captain's cap was cute. She reaches over to the night stand and dials room service, ordering a carafe of coffee, fruit plate, scrambled eggs and a bagel, then adds a large OJ – it was Florida after all.

It had been nice to click everything off for twelve hours or so. Mark had driven her around town in his jeep before stopping at the mall where she had picked up half dozen casual outfits, a couple of pairs of shoes, and a generic rolling bag to haul it all in. They had stopped at a little hole in the wall Vietnamese place by the mall for pho and fried rice, before checking into the DoubleTree. Mark hadn't been bashful, which she appreciated, she had been up front with him – "this is a one-time deal so don't be a 'Nancy' in the morning."

He had smiled and said, "no problem, pinky swear!"

Jessie had laughed, holding up her little finger, "going to hold you to it, captain..."

Jessie is still in the bed as Mark comes out of the bathroom already dressed, using a hand towel to dry his hair. "Finally, up sleepy head," he says with a smile, "I've got to run by my place and pick up a few things, thirty minutes or so work for you?"

"Umm, let's say forty-five, downstairs in the lobby say eight thirtyish?"

"Perfect," he answers, grabbing his keys and wallet off the dresser.

Room service shows up a few minutes later and Jessie sits with her legs crossed on the bed, food spread out around her. She slathers her bagel with cream cheese wishing she had asked for extra and thinking about her dad. He had been evasive on their call, but insistent she come to Boulder. With her dad, that could only mean one of two things: he either knew something he wasn't comfortable sharing over the phone or he and Jack had cooked up some plan. She smiles to herself the two of them together were an amazing combination of skills and experience, but they could get seriously sidetracked as well. Finishing up the eggs and draining the last of the OJ she heads for the shower she'd be there soon enough no point wasting energy trying to decipher what those two were up to.

Jessie camps out in the back of the jet for the flight to Boulder, it wasn't so much that she didn't want to talk to Mark — but she didn't want it to be awkward and it wouldn't hurt to have a little more sleep. Science had refuted the whole catching up on sleep concept, but Jessie knew from her time in the Rangers you slept when you could — things could change rapidly, and you might not have the opportunity later. It's a few minutes past eleven local time when the gentle bump of touchdown wakes her, she stretches, slings the backpack over her shoulder and heads toward the front of the jet.

Mark shuts the engines down as the ground crew chock the wheels, he thinks briefly about last night, trying to put the images out of his head. This wasn't his first rodeo, but Jessie wasn't like most of the pampered women that tried to take him home, no she was more akin to a barely tamed jungle cat - ferocious enough to scare him just a little, no way she was some government bureaucrat — he had already decided the less he knew about her the better.

Mark opens the door and drops the stairs handing Jessie's new roller bag to the ground crew waiting for them. He steps aside so Jessie can deplane.

She turns to him, "thanks for everything, I appreciate it," she says with a bit of an impish grin.

Mark nods unable to hide his own grin, "my pleasure ma'am," he says tipping his cap as he heads back to the cockpit to update his logs and keep from watching her walk across the tarmac.

Her dad's 1973 black Bronco is parked in the circular drive as she exits the private aviation terminal, the full-size Bronco is a beast restored to mint condition with every possible cutting-edge technology upgrade installed. *The thing could probably drive itself*, she thinks hopping into the back, pushing her bag across the seat next to her, "how you old men holding up?" she asks laughing.

"Just fine young lady," Jack says from the passenger seat, her dad just shakes his head dropping the Bronco into first gear and pulling out of the parking lot.

"You hungry Jess?" he asks.

Laughing, "you know it... where we eating?"

"Whatever you want honey, name it, except for KT's Jacks been banned – too many Pig Piles this month."

"Since when is four too many!" Jack retorts.

Jessie laughs, "let's do a pie at AJ's, besides they have that natural soda you like dad." Her phone starts buzzing before he can answer. "Holy shit!" she exclaims.

"What, what..." her dad asks.

"Umm, text message..."

"What's it say?" Jack asks.

"We need to talk – MK" Jessie answers.

"MK gotta be Kirilov, holy shit is right Jess," Jack says.

"You think it's really him?" she asks.

"Might be, not happy he was able to get that number though, let's get that pie to go and get to the office, Jack and I have some things we want to talk to you about anyway," Lou says.

"What kind of things, Dad?"

"Just some theories on this Azrael," Jack answers for him.

Jessie lets it go, let them have their secrets they would be at Paradigm's offices in twenty minutes she could wait.

They had killed a twenty inch "Italian Mamma" Jessie loved the mix of kale, Italian sausage, and onions, she nibbles on the last piece of crust as her dad finishes checking his email and Jack relaxes on the couch.

Lou looks over and shakes his head, "he has been spending a lot of time relaxing on that couch lately," he says to Jessie.

"Shut up, I'm an old man," Jack quips.

Jessie smiles at them, "so Dad, what are these theories you mentioned?" she asks opening another can of root beer and filling her Styrofoam cup.

"Well it's nothing firm," he says walking over to the conference table.

"Yeah, but tell her what you told me," Jack says joining them.

Jessie listens as her dad walks them through his theories on Azrael's identity and why he thinks it's possible someone already knows who he is. Jessie doesn't argue the point, it has occurred to her as well, especially after her last conversation with the director, but she still can't wrap her head around why anyone would willingly cover it up – she doesn't have the conspiracy paranoia her dad and Jack do.

"Ok, that all adds up dad, but why do that and who do you think is behind it anyway?" she asks.

Lou shakes his head looking out the windows, "I don't know, but none of this makes sense to me – the level of response is all wrong and think about it, no way we don't know who this guy is," he says turning back to the table.

"What do you mean, the level of response is wrong?" Jack asks.

"Well, think about it, super assassin magically comes into the most dangerous biological weapon the Russians have, he doesn't appear to be ideologically motivated which means anybody could be the target, and nobody seems to be doing anything about it. Oh, and nobody can find him... that sound right to you two?"

"Well, the Director did give me the file and free reign so it's not like we aren't doing anything..." Jessie says realizing too late how lame that sounds.

Jack pats her on the back with a smile, "I am sure you're completely underestimated young lady, but simple fact is the Agency should have mobilized a task force and the same with the Russians and every other major intelligence agency out there, but as far as we can tell everybody is just sitting on the sidelines, and that simply doesn't make sense."

She nods her head, "I guess when you put it like that... So, what do we think Kirilov wants and is he somehow involved?" Jessie asks

"Only one way to find out," Jacks says, "but he was Russian Intelligence and my guess is he is the one that gave you the tip on the Israeli..."

"Yeah well, that was a trap so clearly not cool there," Jessie scoffs.

"Hey, I didn't say trust him," Jack says defensively.

Jessie pulls her phone out and begins typing a text message. "Ok, let's see what he says!"

"Wait, you just sent him a message," her dad says incredulously, "what did you say?"

"I just said – 'thanks for almost getting me killed on that island – what do you want?'"

Jack laughs, "well that ought to do it!"

Jessie's phone is already buzzing before her dad can respond. She brings up the texting app and reads it off to them: "Sorry – need to meet – can you be in Kiev end of week?" Jessie looks at her dad, "what should I say?"

"Jesus, Jessie I don't know, I don't like it though, we don't know what this guy really wants or who he is in league with."

Jack smiles recognizing the fatherly concern in his old friend's voice, but he also knows that isn't the right answer, "Jessie we have to go... we don't have any other leads and Kirilov has good Soviet era connections we need to know what he knows it's really that simple, but I'm going with you."

"Makes sense sir, you think I need to let the Director know?"

"Fuck me, are you two out of your minds?" Lou explodes.

"Come on Lou, you know it's the right play, we aren't going to solve or stop this sitting safely here in your office, lend us that jet again so we can stay off the government radar though, I'm beginning to not trust our own folks..." Jack says looking his old friend in the eye.

"Dad he's right..."

"I know he's right, I just don't like it," Lou answers pacing. "Alright, the jets yours for as long as you need, I'll work that part out under Paradigm and let me get you new phones and Paradigm IDs from downstairs, since it's obvious someone has penetrated the Agency you can go as company executives."

"Penetrated the Agency?"

"Well, he had your phone number, didn't he?"

"May not have come from inside though, but I guess it doesn't really matter how he got it, does it?" she asks looking at the two men.

They both shake their heads looking rather grim.

"Okay, well let's get this party going then," she says.

Kiev

Mark guided the jet smoothly from the east into Zhuliany International Airport. The single runway made for a long taxi to the business terminal, but the upside was almost no traffic as most commercial airlines used the larger Boryspil International to the West of the Dnieper River on the Right Bank of the city. They had made the flight in three hops stopping only to refuel in Quebec then briefly in Reykjavik bypassing the larger Keflavík airport for the private charter field and a quick dinner and refuel before continuing on to Oslo in Norway for another refuel. The PC24 was versatile, but with that came a more limited range than found on the larger business jets most companies used. All told the trip had taken more than fourteen hours and you could see the strain on Mark's face as he dialed down the engines and began filling out the entry paperwork listing Jack and Jessie as Paradigm executives in Kiev on business.

Jessie sticks her head in the cockpit and hands Mark a SAT phone, "keep this handy and have us ready to leave in a hurry, okay?" she tells him.

"Sure, I'll get us checked out and refueled then I'm catching some sleep," he answers. "It would help if I knew what was going on," he says with a bit of an edge.

Jessie hesitates, "No it wouldn't help, just be ready to leave when I call," she starts to turn away. "Listen Mark, I trust you, but these are things I can't talk about…" she says a bit more gently.

He nods, "just trying to help, don't worry, I'll be ready." She gives him a smile and is gone before he can say anything else.

Jessie dressed in black slacks, a royal blue dress shirt, black pumps and light jacket, her back pack slung over her right shoulder – just another modern hip executive. Jack trails her, just an old man trying to keep up and pretty much failing. His demeanor was intentionally disarming but he had to admit to himself that the days of going toe to toe with the likes of Jessie were probably already in his rearview mirror. They entered the newly remodeled corporate jet center where a willowy young man dressed in a classic chauffeur's outfit held a sign with "Paradigm" printed in block letters. Kirilov's tradecraft hadn't slipped at all – no names to give anyone away just a normal business pickup.

The trip across the river and into the downtown business area takes twenty minutes, the car pulls up in front of a modern glass office building stretching twenty-five stories into the crystal blue air.

Kirilov met them in the lobby, looking the consummate businessman in a navy blue Italian silk pin striped suite that probably went for a couple thousand dollars on the row in Milan – the Santoni loafers probably added another grand to the total.

"So, I see business is good..." Jessie quips.

With a broad smile Kirilov answers, "a small indulgence for all my efforts! Style is important in this line of work, no?"

"And what line of work would that be?" she asks her sarcasm bleeding through.

He smiles but doesn't answer immediately, "I only supply what your country and others would sell anyway... we are not in business of people," he says with an edge.

"You sent that data to the Bureau, didn't you?" Jack interjects.

Kirilov hesitates, his finger on the elevator button, the doors slide open and he uses the biometric hand scanner to choose the top floor. "Yes, I did," he finally answers, "slavery doesn't interest me."

Jessie ponders that as the elevator starts to rise, *was there any difference in the arming of dictators that enslaved whole populations and the selling of a single human being into bondage?* It was too nuanced a conversation for an elevator ride, "no slavery but death is okay?" she asks without really meaning to.

The doors open on Kirilov's office, floor to ceiling glass panels form the outside walls, it's almost spartan in its simplicity but still elegant and functional. He motions to a pair of chairs by a massive mahogany desk as he brings three bottles of mineral water and glasses over from the bar in the corner.

"Miss McIntyre, aren't we all in death's employ?" He asks, quietly sitting behind his desk and leaning back in the leather chair, motioning around the office, "you dispatched Sokolov, creating this very opportunity I enjoy now, so let's not be disingenuous about what we do," he admonishes.

Jessie smiles and raises her glass, "well played sir, well played..."

Jack shifts in his chair not blind to the verbal sword play and underlying physical tension between Kirilov and Jessie. It was pretty clear the man was taken with her and why not after all, but it was time to get down to business. He clears his throat, "I'm sure we could spend all day comparing our kill lists, but Mikhail, tell us why I just flew fifteen hours to see you?"

Kirilov smiles at the use of his Russian name, "Jack, you invited yourself so no complaints about the jet lag... but let's just say I'm a humanitarian at heart and want to help with your Azrael problem..."

"Azrael?" Jessie says in a puzzled voice.

Kirilov breaks into a hearty laugh, "now Ms. McIntyre, let's not be coy, I know you've been hand selected to bring this assassin down, it's why I sent you the meet up with Ismael, I'm trying to help."

"Well, as much as I appreciate it, he was killed before he could give me anything, pretty much died in my arms," she replies.

"Damn," Kirilov mutters, "but you are okay, I wouldn't have put you in danger..." he stops leaning back in his chair, "tell me what happened."

Jessie looks over at Jack, he nods, and with a deep breath she tells how she met Ismael and how he must have seen something taking the bullet that was probably meant for her. She leaves out most of the details surrounding the night in the dive hut and getting off the island but Kirilov is still shaking his head.

"So, this storm, hurricane, you were right in the middle?"

Jessie nods, "I don't recommend it if you can avoid it, the sound of the wind is unbelievable, and it just goes on and on..." she falters thinking back on the experience.

"We don't have anything like that here," Kirilov murmurs, "amazing, just amazing... so Ismael told you nothing?"

"Not a word," Jessie says shaking her head, "what did he tell you?"

Kirilov looks at Jack before answering, "not much really, he was pretty upset but said something about being on the run from Azrael and that his own people were hunting him as well. I don't know what he expected but I think he wanted you Americans to bring him in and protect him, would have needed something to trade I guess."

"That's it?" Jack asks.

Kirilov hesitates before going on, "well not exactly no..."

Jessie leans forward, "well?"

Kirilov glances around, wondering if he is secure even in his own offices, "Azrael is ex-Mossad, a rogue agent... lost his family in a Hezbollah rocket attack, became their top assassin and then lost it when your President brokered the peace agreement, went off the deep end as you say and started picking his own targets."

"No shit, fucking Israelis," Jack exclaims. He turns to Jessie, "your dad figured they knew who he was, targets just didn't add up, son of a bitch though." He turns to Kirilov, "what about this VX17?"

Kirilov hesitates, but there's no turning back at this point, "comes out of Compound 19, you know this place?" he asks Jack.

Jack nods, "sure do, we used to call it 'DC' Death City."

Kirilov grimaces, "yes, yes, not much I can tell you, but if this Azrael has some then it's a very, very bad thing."

Jessie leans in, "Mikhail, I need a name, I need to know who Azrael is, can you help me?"

Kirilov knew this was coming, knew he was going to have to make a choice whether to get involved or not, he had known the very first text. This wasn't his job anymore, it wasn't his war, and when it came right down to it, this definitely wasn't in his best interest, but he also knew he was going to help Jessie if he could. It didn't make sense and he couldn't have explained it if asked. He looks her in the eye, "I'll do what I can."

She nods, "I hope so, I'll text you my new number, call me with anything." Jessie turns to Jack, "we good?"

He nods rising to his feet and extending a hand to Kirilov, "thanks for your help."

As they walk back to the elevator Jessie turns to Kirilov, "any idea why Mossad wouldn't just bring him in? They must know where he is, it's damn near impossible to really disappear these days."

"I don't know, I've wondered the same thing," he answers pushing the elevator call button. "There's ten billion people on the planet…" he says with a shrug.

"I get it, but this guy is traveling, he has probably either hacked our communications or has access to someone who has, top that off with significant financial resources – it just seems unlikely he could exist completely off the grid to the point that no one has been able to catch a whiff of him, I'm just not buying it," Jessie says. It's the first time she has really thought it through, but the realization points to a much scarier scenario than a lone master assassin.

The two men share a look, "what are you saying Jessie?" Jack asks.

She hesitates, looking from Jack to Mikhail, "well, I guess what I mean is maybe this is a lot bigger than we think it is?" She leans against the wall, "and that scares the shit out of me." The elevator doors open, but none of them get in. "Think about it, why would Mossad have been after Ismael? I guess now that I think about it maybe we shouldn't assume it was Azrael that took the shot?"

Kirilov motions back to his desk, "let me make a call, you have time, no?"

Jack nods, "all the time it takes, we are in no rush on this," Jessie nods her agreement as they all sit back down.

Four

Jason Sanderson had spent ten years as an officer in the Navy SEALs the last four as part of the legendary SEAL Team Six before an unlucky landing on a HALO jump had sidelined him with an uncooperative knee. He had taken a slot at the National Security Agency – NSA at Fort Meade in Maryland rather than ride a desk at Oceana Naval Air Station in Virginia. Three years of hardcore physical therapy and he regained full use of the knee, but by then it had been too late to rejoin his unit.

Recruitment into ALPHA team had come as a surprise, he had been having dinner with his old squadron commander, Ted Jeter at Paddy's a rundown Irish pub just outside the shipyard in Baltimore, not much to look at but Paddy O'Malley made his own corned beef and the biggest damn sandwiches you could imagine. Three beers in Jeter had finally got around to the real reason he'd made the drive up from DC.

He had left Team Six to sign on with the Defense Intelligence Agency (DIA) Special Ops Group shortly after Jason's accident, they had kept in touch, but hadn't seen each other since. Jeter had been asked to find a candidate for a new multinational team being put together, he hadn't said who had done the asking. They were looking for men that could be trusted without question and that shared a special set of skills - Jason's

Team Six experience combined with his three years of crypto work at NSA made him perfect Jeter had explained. There was more to it of course, the team needed access to NSA's intelligence and surveillance capabilities, but that was the quid pro quo for a chance to be "active" again.

He probably should have asked more questions, but the truth was he needed something more, needed to be part of an elite team again. The work at NSA was important no doubt about it, but they were a faceless, nameless, shadow team that worked from behind a computer screen; they were never going to have the wind screaming in the ears from a HALO jump, or waves crashing around them as they beach a RIB on some foreign shore with only the light of the moon to see; no, he needed something more.

Much to his chagrin the new assignment hadn't gotten him out of Fort Meade. In fact, they had insisted he stay in place - his current position providing the perfect cover. Two years in though he had reconciled himself to the reality of his new life and more importantly, he was all in on ALPHA team's mission. He had spent his entire adult life protecting his country and if it now meant orchestrating the acceleration of a million Muslims to paradise, well so be it.

"Four, do we have an update on the McIntyre girl?"

"Yes control, she took a private charter off St. Eustatius, spent one night in Miami before heading to her father's in Boulder."

"He runs Paradigm, right?"

"Yes sir, wired into the Defense Department, CIA, NSA, and FBI pretty deep – supplies encryption algorithms, some communications gear, and a new project dubbed NEO – I haven't been able to uncover much on that yet though." He hesitates, "it's a pretty good bet she's in Kiev right now, the plane she was using landed there this morning."

"Any confirmation she was on it, or why she might be there?"

"No sir, she wasn't listed on the manifest and Paradigm does do some business there, but the timing is convenient."

"Well, see what you can dig up, I want to keep close tabs on her, last thing we need is some Agency freelancer getting lucky."

"Yes sir, understand."

"If she's on that plane, we can arrange an accident to eliminate any loose strings. We're less than two months out so why chance it?" Five says his Russian accent giving him away.

"Doesn't she work for Director Simpson? Might raise more questions than we need right now," Six pipes up.

"Yes, let's leave it be for now, if she starts to make some progress identifying the asset we can deal with it then," Control says, "now let's move on."

They wrap up shortly after, but the casual discussion about eliminating an American bothers Jason. He brings up his station - logging in he begins a general search on Jessie McIntyre, most of the information he already has, but he uses a couple of backdoor hacks to access her files from the Rangers and the CIA – fact was there wasn't anything NSA couldn't get to if it wanted. He downloads everything to his local drive and erases his trail – it's as if he had never been there. He wasn't naive enough to think he could leave the building with any of it, the Snowden incident, even though years ago, had insured no one left with something as simple as a thumb drive or thumb tack for that matter – as a senior team lead he had his own office though and that was sufficient privacy to read the files, besides no one would question his running a deep background on a low-level CIA operative.

A server in the basement of Paradigm records Jason's keystrokes and IP address – Lou McIntyre may be a conspiracy theorist, but he is also a father and tech genius, and no one is going "check-up" on his daughter without him knowing about it.

The Keurig sputters as the hot coffee approaches the rim of Jason's cup, he blows on it gently before taking the first sip returning to his desk and the dual thirty-two-inch monitors displaying Jessie's files.

He pages through her West Point records and QUAL scores at Ranger School, impressive he thinks to himself. Moving on he pulls up the after-action reports from Panama, *damn Silver Star... maybe he had underestimated her. Hmm turned down twice for Special Forces, no doubt this one was a warrior,* he thinks. Leaning back in his chair he contemplates what this means, the McIntyre girl was clearly capable, but somewhat out of place in the clandestine world of the Agency and not your usual recruit. *So how had she ended up there*, he wonders, turning back to the screens he pulls up the FBI and CIA reports on someone named Sokolov.

Two hours later he pushes back from the desk, "Jesus Christ," he says to the empty office, *eight confirmed kills last summer including the top Ukrainian mob boss!* He was pretty sure how ALPHA Control was going to react to this, Jessie McIntyre's days were going to be numbered, he also knew they were going to want him to do it.

He looks at the screen again, *elite soldier and fierce as hell – she deserves better than this*, it didn't occur to him that he might not be able to take her down if asked. With a last look he shuts down his system and calls it a day, passing through security he exits into the parking lot, the sun is starting to approach the western horizon as the day wanes. He pulls the Jeep out of the lot heading West to the small home he had purchased in Norbeck several years ago.

Jason didn't have any particular cultural association with his African American half, his dad had never really emphasized his "blackness" preferring to assimilate as much as possible into the "white" man's world, but the fact that Norbeck had been settled by freed blacks prior to the Civil War appealed to him on a visceral level.

He leaves the Jeep running as he opens the front door, anticipating the two giant paws that pin him to the door jamb, King was a massive German Shepherd he had raised from a puppy, a gift from his squad while he was in rehab. He grabs the leash, not really needing it as they head back out to the car and the ten-minute trip to Rock Creek Park.

They would run the trails and King would pretend to chase the ducks until dark, it had started as a way to rehab his knee but had become their daily routine, a way to bleed off the stress of the job and keep in shape after sitting at a desk all day. This afternoon it also gave Jason time to clear his head and think through the McIntyre issue. King ran tirelessly in a figure eight around him occasionally brushing up against his legs playfully. He had worked up a good sweat and finally pulled up at one of the many benches sprinkled around the big lake, stretching as he glances at his watch, maybe another forty minutes of light. He should probably head back but opts to take a seat looking out across the water, King lays across his feet contentedly.

He knows what's right, knows what he should do, and with a deep sigh pushes himself up and heads back toward the lower parking lots at a slow jog realizing he feels more at peace than he has in a long time.

Jeddah

The passport said Karim Hamzavi and showed a clean-cut Pakistani national. It barely garnered a second look, although the agent still managed a rude sneer as David handed it to him. Jeddah was historically one of the worst airports in the world and even with the major upgrades over the past ten years it was crowded and chaotic. Attributes the international travel magazines were fond of berating the Kingdom for, but they just provided David additional cover and anonymity.

There were more than ten million foreigners in The Kingdom – the ruling family's efforts to achieve Saudization of many mainstream jobs had failed and the foreign professional ranks were swelling. Pakistani nationals represented more than two million of them – one more wasn't going to stand out. David spoke Urdu passably well, but fortunately English was the language of the educated in Pakistan and nobody was speaking to him anyway. He nods mumbling a quick thank you as he takes the passport back and heads into the terminal and the rail station.

Passports were the easy part, he had a dozen or more variations on this one issued from any number of major and minor countries sprinkled across the globe. The more difficult task had been creating the social, educational, and residential histories around these identities. When he had been Mossad there had been a whole department dedicated to the creation of alternate lives for each agent, but now he was forced to use the open market and although this level of hacking didn't come cheap it wasn't hard to find capable people amongst the company he had been keeping the past few years. To that end he had traded the elimination of a couple of "competitors" for half a dozen full proof identities a year ago.

This was almost the last trip - he had made a series of quick trips earlier; each one just a couple of days to complete the first series of inspections and secure a car which he had left parked at the airport. He had managed to sign on with the British firm responsible for the new pumping stations installed to handle the growing demands on the Zamzam Well – British Pump & Filtration (BPF). Access had always been the crux of the plan and the toughest challenge. His credentials had been impeccable, of course he had tailored them specifically to this project. BPF had needed Muslim engineers since religious restrictions prevented Non-Muslims from entering the holy city. He had been hired after a quick series of phone interviews and a brief meeting with a cantankerous overworked Brit ex-pat three weeks earlier. They had supplied him with a wireless tablet, water testing kit, and a complete set of schematics showing the pumps, filters, and piping. He had to smile at that, he had spent a large sum of money and untold hours procuring the very same plans now residing on his tablet, funny how things worked sometimes.

He would inspect the pumps and filters, then find a place to live. He only wanted to make one more trip bringing anything else he might need. The convoluted process of getting in and out of Israel and into Saudi Arabia was difficult enough for a normal traveler since you couldn't legally pass from one to the other even with stops in between. It required multiple stops and identities and he didn't want to do it any more than necessary. He had been using Cyprus, Turkey and a half dozen other countries to mask his final destinations for the past few months and each time was even more nerve wracking than the last.

Today would be spent ostensibly inspecting the new pump seals and testing the filtration systems. The well water was known to contain higher than normal levels or arsenic and bacteria, a claim disputed by the Saudi Royal Family, but a new filtration system had been quietly installed before this year's Hajj none-the-less. It was a balance between religious belief and public health, the very nature of the water many contended was what made it special.

The well itself was housed in an underground room below the Kaaba where the pilgrims performed the ritual of Tawaf, the Seven Rotations. The old electric pumps had been upgraded and now pumped the water through a series of inline filtration units before routing it out to the fountains and fill stations. It was in the last series of filters that David intended to disperse the VX17, insuring maximum distribution and potency.

In his new job he was performing weekly inspections and a monthly cleaning of the filtration system, giving him plenty of access and ensuring his presence would become ordinary and expected among the many guards surrounding the well room.

He shakes the plastic bottle, adding another two drops of liquid and checking the color against his chart. Filling two more vials he screws on the tops and labels them, these would go to the lab for testing. The armed guard checks out his clipped-on ID badge with the crimson BPF emblazoned above his name, the guard pretends to be disinterested even as his American made M16 is cradled and pointing David's way. Finishing up, he marks the results in the tablet and hits the upload button. He nods to the guard as he exits the pump room, it was time to find a place to call home for the next several weeks. He knew if his passport started showing up weekly on the Saudi immigration systems someone would start to ask questions.

He had been scouting the neighborhoods of Jeddah on the coast looking for a small flat that would serve as home. The city was perfect for his needs, as the gateway to Mecca it held the country's major airport and was also a major commercial seaport. A fact he had once planned on exploiting by signing on as a deck hand with of the commercial cargo ships when it was time to leave, but he already knew deep in his heart he wasn't leaving, he wasn't going to survive this and in moments of unfiltered honesty he had to admit he didn't want to.

The city reminded him a bit of home with its large contingent of foreigners and proximity to the sea. He had decided to stay centrally located in the Safa District lining up three flats a few blocks on either side of Al-Shakireen Road giving him easy access to Route Five and the new hi-speed rail stations linking Jeddah with Mecca. The area seemed to be mostly Pakistani and Indian families and although he knew how the Saudis felt about foreigners; he was disgusted at the undisguised disdain with which they treated their supposed Muslim brothers. He rented all three, planning on rotating one week at a time, minimizing the chance that someone might zero in on him.

Wedging into a too small spot he parks the car looking around for anything out of place, he takes the steps two at time to the third floor, his door is at the end of the hall, #319. He can hear the noise of televisions playing too loud and kids crying as he walks down the hall. The smell of curries and simmering meats permeate the building. It's not unpleasant but brings a tear as he thinks about these young families - and the loss of his comes roaring back at him before he can suppress it.

The flat is only two rooms and a small kitchenette, someone had hung multicolored curtains over the single window that looked out on the back alley and a rickety folding door separated the bathroom and shower stall from the rest of the space. The late afternoon sun was slanting through the bottom of the curtain and warmed his arm as he lay on the thin mattress, there wasn't a box spring or frame, a small couch, forlorn armchair and small desk was the extent of the furniture. Still in this neighborhood it was what passed for a furnished flat and he was sure many a small family had found a way to make this home for a time. The young man that had rented it to him had been in a hurry, as if he couldn't wait to get out of the building, but he had shown him around extolling the place as if it was one of the royal palaces - he had been particularly proud that the water was almost "always" on.

A soft knock on the door startles him, he had decided not to carry a weapon in the Kingdom, not that he needed it to defend himself against most threats, but a knock on the door the same afternoon he had "moved" in was unexpected. Standing to the side he inches the door open, a short plump Indian woman in a brightly colored sari with two toddlers in tow smiles shyly at him, she offers up a covered plate of something smelling delicious. With a brief nod she hands him the food before retreating up the hall, the toddlers look back with wide eyes as they try to catch up with their mother. David is stuck in the doorway trying to assemble his thoughts, the kindness of strangers was an experience he had expunged from his consciousness.

Night had fallen on Jeddah and the building had grown quiet as the normal cycles of life had unwound and succumbed to the night. Still David lay on his thin mattress the amber rays of the street lamps slipping under the thin curtain covering the window. In the distance he can hear the whine of some young sheik's Lambo advancing through the gears, he takes a deep breath working through the details of the plan once again. It was an unnecessary exercise at this point, but it kept him from focusing on the aftermath, the death, the black pit of horror he would be responsible for opening up in the world. It was nothing though, compared to the hole left in his world by the loss of his girls. There wouldn't be anything left after this, would there? It was a question he knew the answer to but couldn't bring himself to acknowledge.

Uncle Yuri

Mikhail looks over the desk at Jessie and Jack as he dials the number, "unlikely he will talk to us on the phone," he murmurs.

Jessie mouths to Jack, "Who?" He just shrugs in return.

"Mikhail, how are you nephew?" The voice booms from the speaker.

Kirilov holds his finger up to his lips, "I'm good uncle, very good, you have a few minutes?"

"Of course, always for you."

Jessie smiles in spite of herself, she can imagine it's the same way when she calls her father, doesn't matter what he is doing or how busy he always seems to have been just sitting around waiting on her to call.

"Uncle Yuri, I need to ask you about the VX and Azrael again, I know you said to leave it alone, but there are things I must know..."

The silence stretches out, "Mikhail I cannot talk of this, believe me there is nothing more you should know, this is bad very bad to talk about."

"Please uncle, I wouldn't ask if it wasn't important."

"More important than your life Mikhail, than my life?"

"I think it might be uncle, more important than many lives."

Maybe it's their relationship, or the tone of Mikhail's voice, or just the gravity of the question. The old man sighs audibly, "ok Mikhail, but I hope you are careful, there are rumors here of a secret group – they call it 'ALPHA'. You know how it is though, here there are no secrets even among my men and one of my Captains, he is in this group. Of course, they think no-one knows but how can this be?

"I don't know uncle, what have you heard, what does this 'ALPHA' do?

"Mikhail, it is rumors only, vodka inspired tales, you know how it is!" The old man sighs again, "I don't know any more than this, but I hear things and I watch, there are always whispers in the dark, nods and murmurs when taking the steam… we Russians are only small part of this."

"Uncle, it is our weapon! How can we be only a small part of this?"

"Come now Mikhail, you know better – it is not the weapon but he who wields it that is important."

"Ok, Ok, of course you are right uncle, and Azrael wields this weapon?"

After a long pause, "yes, he does, but Mikhail, only one thing more I will say, maybe this Azrael is also a weapon… you need to know who wields him, more I cannot say nephew." There is a soft click as the phone is hung up.

The three of them look at each other, none willing to break the silence.

Jessie looks across the desk, "Uncle Yuri?"

Mikhail smiles, "He is Major General in Russian Spetnaz... head of the garrison at Center Nineteen," he says with a grin and a shrug.

"Well, there ya go, I guess," Jessie says.

Jack finally clears his throat, "ALPHA group?" He leans back in the chair, palms pushed together a frown on his face, "I don't like it, nope, not at all," turning to Jessie, "this what your father was worried about."

"Your father?" Mikhail asks.

"He was my partner back in the early days," Jack says by way of explanation not willing to reveal more about Lou. "He felt like there may be more to this than just a freelance super assassin, if your uncle is right... then this is a lot more complicated."

"Uncle Yuri is very conservative, if he told me that much then it's much more complicated as you say."

Jessie gets up pacing around the office, Jack and Mikhail watch her. Jack holds his hand up to the other man, "father does the same thing, helps them think, give her a second," Mikhail nods.

"Fuck me dead," she mutters shocking the two men, "what?" she asks, noticing the looks. "Sorry old habit, but I'm just thinking your uncle said 'we Russians', which of course means the Russians are only a small part of ALPHA. So, shit," she says pursing her lips, "so who else does that mean?" she asks turning back to the desk and sitting down.

"Probably us and the Israelis if I had to get guess," Jack answers turning to Mikhail, "what do you think?"

"Yes, makes sense, a group like that would have to be small, but I think you are missing the important question."

"What?" They say in unison.

"Why… why form this secret group and what did my uncle mean that Azrael was the weapon, I think that was the most important part, but it doesn't make sense to me."

Jessie wasn't entirely comfortable being this open with Kirilov, the man wasn't exactly on the right side of the law or what passed for it, but that didn't seem to be dissuading Jack from confiding in him. She was going to have to ask him about it later, but for now she was following his lead.

Jessie plunges forward, "I guess I have two questions, maybe three. If Azrael is the weapon, does he know it? Meaning he is working in collaboration with this ALPHA group, that seems unlikely to me on the surface of things, but either way what is the objective?" She thinks back on her Ranger training, there was always a mission objective, but that objective didn't always reflect the larger picture either. She was used to thinking tactically, but this required a more circumspect strategic viewpoint – a skill set she was still developing.

"I don't know the politics of the West so well, but in Russia there would have to be a significant payoff strategically or economically for us to be involved," Mikhail says.

Jack nods, "it's not that different for us, we tend to cloak things in moral outrage or the defense of democracy, but there is almost always an economic or strategic factor somewhere in the mix." It was a cynical but unfortunately true reflection of things - the realities of a global economy often forced a country's altruistic ideals to the back of the bus, not that any politician worth his salt would ever admit it.

"Well, that makes sense if we are only talking about us and the Russians," Jessie adds, "but what about the Israelis? Unlikely they are economically motivated."

"True," Jack murmurs, "but you don't procure a vial of this VX stuff just to put it on the mantle, there has to be an end game here – I just don't understand giving it to someone as unpredictable as this Azrael seems to be."

"So, we are back to square one as you Americans say."

"I guess so," Jack laughs grimly, "we have a super assassin, a biological weapon, a shadow group, and no idea what any of it means!"

"Well, we've got more than we had yesterday," Jessie quips, "but it's still pretty disconnected. What do you think," she asks, turning back to Kirilov.

He spreads his hands, "I don't know, I'm going to be in Moscow this weekend, I will see my uncle. Maybe he will have more to say in person, it is dangerous for him though."

Jessie hands him a card – it's blank with the exception of a string of numbers across the center. "What I really need is a name, call me at this number any time, no one but Jack, my father and you have it so guard it closely."

He takes the card and nods, "it is safe with me, I will only call if there is something worth telling." He leads them to the elevator, "my driver will take you back to the airport," he hesitates extending his hand, "thank you for coming..." he pauses, "and trusting me."

Kindling

The number twelve had not been chosen at random, the symbolism was meant to further mock the Shia - the Twelvers - the minority - an esoteric insult magnifying the bloodshed. Each young man had been chosen for his fervent devotion to the Caliphate and its leader Al Zarwari Ahmad, who preferred his men call him Aza, this was to be their coming out party.

The humiliating defeat of ISIS a decade earlier and the recent annihilation of the Syrian government had provided the kindling needed to restart the flames of fanaticism. The Western powers seemed intent on ignoring the simple fact that the harder you squeezed in this part of the world the less grip you had. There were thousands of years of history testifying to this simple fact, still, it seemed to keep eluding the supposedly enlightened governments of the West.

Aza had combined the fervency, thirst for bloodshed and grand theater of ISIS and Al Qaeda forming a group willing to exploit local fear and intimidation while paying homage to the elders by targeting the West as well. Of course, until this morning that had all been talk, plans, impassioned speeches and a lot social media chatter.

The vests had been packed with explosives and ball bearings insuring maximum carnage and all twelve had managed to extinguish themselves within a minute or two of each other. They worked in twos; and had chosen their targets for maximum media impact: the two main refugee camps in Syria, the market district in Tel Aviv, a busy coffee shop in Munich, the central train station in Tehran, and in Jeddah a playground outside a school for foreigners.

It was a quarter past nine as David sips the hot coffee next to him and takes another bite of the sweet cream filled pastry, putting the final touches on the pumping station status report he prepares to hit send - the double whump of explosions rattles the windows and seems to set off an immediate cacophony of sirens. He doesn't panic, he is familiar with the sound, closing the laptop he rushes outside with the rest of the crowd. He isn't worried, but to have not reacted would draw attention he wasn't looking for. *Savages*, he thinks, *why this incessant need to kill each other?*

He doesn't follow the crowd, opting instead to head back toward his apartment. He knows what shrapnel riddled bodies look like, and he is all too familiar with the wailing of mothers as they cradle their broken children or the vacant stares of children whose parents won't wake up. He doesn't feel anything for them, after all, these are the people that support the criminals responsible for killing his precious girls, even if it was just with their apathy, their unwillingness to stand apart from their fanatical brethren. In his mind it made all of Islam culpable and the time was coming when Azrael would make them pay. Oh, would they pay!

It was the twenty-first of June, a day without any particular significance, but today's body count topping more than a thousand souls with a particularly large number of children and young people would insure it was added to the growing list of dates to be remembered.

Aza was already claiming responsibility and touting a new wave of terror shepherding in the resurrection of a new Caliphate and the push for a consolidated unified Islamic nation committed to the most stringent interpretation of Sharia law. It was hard to believe that someone could sound more fanatical than the early years of Al Qaeda and ISIL but Aza's speeches and ramblings had the ring of true madness.

ALPHA Control had initiated a call shortly after the news reports had started flooding in, there wasn't a great deal of additional data to share, but they all agreed this inflamed the situation and that wasn't necessarily a negative development. Four would keep tabs on anything new coming into the NSA on this Aza and develop a profile for the group. The Mossad contingent wasn't particularly happy about the bombing in Tel Aviv but agreed as hard as the sacrifice was, ALPHA needed to stay clear of this and focus on the larger mission.

No one mentioned the coincidence that two of the attacks had taken place only blocks away from where Azrael had set up his safe houses. Accidentally losing the asset wasn't something any of them wanted to consider this late in the game.

By mid-afternoon the major media outlets were running loops of the massacres while the talking heads repeated the oft used mantras of how radical Islam did not represent the broader Muslim community and how horrific it was that a small group of criminals could perpetrate such terrible deeds. None of this of course kept them from replaying Aza's handiwork for all the world to see on an endless loop.

The governments of the Western powers once again vowed to renew their efforts to eradicate this new strain of terrorism. Their serious faced representatives hitting all the major news outlets decrying the loss of life and pontificating about pursuing these terrorists no matter who they were. It was the same tired rhetoric that had been bandied about for decades, a strategy that failed to address the root issues with no real way to achieve a lasting victory as if that was a real thing. There was always going to be another Aza and everyone knew it, but it wasn't politically correct to admit it.

In many respects it was the core belief that the civilized world was in an unwinnable war with fundamentalism that had created the conditions allowing a group like ALPHA to even exist. The plan to set the Middle East on fire was a brand of Western fanaticism rivaling even most radical Jihadists, no one thought it strange how the cloak of "government action" could so easily legitimize genocide.

But for David none of these thoughts concerned him, rationalizations weren't necessary or needed, he was simply focused on applying the cool salve of vengeance to his pain, the sirens screaming in the distance were the perfect playlist for his final preparations. With only weeks left, he had only one more trip left, a final farewell to his girls. He knew it was a risk he shouldn't even consider but he also knew the chances of making it out of the Kingdom were pretty slim and he wasn't willing to end it all without saying goodbye, kneeling at their graves, feeling the earth of his homeland beneath his feet one last time.

Moscow

Kirilov didn't wait for the weekend, he had downplayed the call to the Americans, but his uncle's words had him more than a little anxious, he had decided to fly out this afternoon for Moscow. It wasn't that he was hiding anything, but he knew Yuri well enough to know there had been plenty he hadn't shared on the phone. Whether it was simply the older man's intuition, or he truly knew more than he was saying – it had been obvious to Kirilov his uncle was holding back. The revelation that there was a multi-national team orchestrating who knew what was concerning enough, but Azrael as a weapon of some misguided political agenda had ramifications that went well beyond his or his uncle's personal wellbeing and that couldn't be ignored.

He hadn't intended to involve himself and his uncle in anything this serious, *that's what getting distracted by a pretty woman does for you – should have just stayed out of it*, he thinks packing up his briefcase and calling his second to come up to the office. But he was involved now, his uncle was involved, his country was involved – Mikhail wasn't mercenary enough to just pretend like it didn't matter.

The elevator door slides open as he places the pair of CZ75 9MMs and two extra clips in his briefcase, he had always loved the Czech made pistols and carried them everywhere.

100

"Dmitri, I'm headed to Moscow for a few days, probably through the weekend, keep track of things here, make sure the shipment to Burundi leaves on time and no bullshit on the payment — no gold, no guns, understand?" Dimitri just nods, Kirilov looks up to make sure he is listening, "call me anytime if something comes up," he says without preamble. He had been supplying small arms to a resurgent NLF in the small African country for about eighteen months, it was obvious the funding was coming through the CIA, but more often than not it was being diverted and he was left trying to collect from some self-styled freedom fighters with no resources.

The two men head down the elevator to the basement garage, Dmitri would drive him out to the airport in one of the black Land Rovers, Kirilov didn't mind treating himself to the luxuries his business could afford and the Land Rovers and Gulfstreams were evidence of that.

Jack and Jessie had taken off a half hour earlier starting the long journey back to Boulder as Kirilov pulls up to the private hanger his company keeps the pair of jets in. He would be in Moscow in under two hours and then another forty minutes to the dacha his uncle kept outside the city. He was coming unannounced this afternoon's call had him nervous, that combined with a heightened sense of paranoia and his GRU training had that little voice in his head telling him he needed to be careful.

He realized it wasn't Azrael that worried him, not that the assassin wasn't deadly, but misguided governments with unlimited resources were far more dangerous when it came right down to it. Of course, none of this explains why he is getting involved – he was sure the Americans had been pretty close to the mark this afternoon, but it was clear to him that whomever was running this black op wasn't going to tolerate Jessie McIntyre interfering even if she hadn't figured that out for herself yet. He didn't owe her or Jack Hardy anything, the Sokolov situation had been mutually beneficial, but in his heart, he was a patriot and the thought of his country participating in something – *participating in what?* He had to admit that was the part that he just wasn't able to wrap his head around, *what the hell were they up to?* Well, whatever it was it involved a deadly biological weapon and the world's foremost assassin. That wasn't a positive combination, no matter how you looked at it. The McIntyre girl... there really wasn't any reason for it, but he didn't want to see anything happen to her either.

He nimbly climbs the steps, the jet's engines already spinning up. Shrugging out of his jacket he tosses it across the first seat and loosens his tie. Gone were the girls and the trappings of the Sokolov days, his operation mirrored the discipline of his military background. He tightens the belt and signals the pilot to get them on their way, he's in a hurry – not knowing what's going on has him unsettled.

Four hundred miles to the West Jessie drifts off to sleep, Jack looks over and smiles, *the girl could sleep anywhere*, he unbuckles and heads forward to the cockpit. "Mark, right?"

"Yes sir."

"You okay son, I know we pushed pretty hard to get here."

"Yes sir, caught a nap while you were out, can't go further than Oslo without some sleep though, hope that's going to be okay?"

"Sure, no problem, what time does that put us back in Boulder tomorrow?" Jack was anxious to get back, but also knew he couldn't push his pilot past the point of exhaustion either.

"If we can get an early start probably just past midday with the time changes, that going to be okay?"

"Yep, that's fine, mind if I sit up here?" Jack says pointing to the second seat.

"Not at all, be good to have some company," Mark answers.

The Gulfstream lands at Vnukovo Jetport southwest of Moscow. Sheremetyevo would have been closer but Vnukovo is the only airport discreetly catering to corporate clients allowing plane-side private car pickup, and discretion is worth paying for in his business. The Mercedes S series is a couple of years old, but the big engine purrs contently as he heads down A101 before taking the A107 North. His uncle's place, a rustic cabin set in the diminishing fir and aspen forests West of Moscow is about an hour's drive.

He hasn't bothered to call ahead, Yuri would just have told him not to come, and he didn't want to argue with his uncle, but he needed the whole story and this was the only way to get it. The satellite radio is replaying a BBC feed on the morning's terror attacks, Mikhail switches it off not needing to hear another regurgitation of the latest madman's venture into the death game. He pulls a CD out of the console and slips it into the player, singing along to Boy George and "Karma Chameleon" he takes the exit for his uncle's cabin. The road is paved but narrow enough that his sedan takes up most of the road, it's only his quick reflexes that saves him from the head on collision as the black SUV comes barreling over the short rise, he slides sideways on the shoulder narrowly missing a large tree before bringing the car to a stop. He gets out as Boy George launches into "Do You Really Want to Hurt Me", he has to smile at the irony of it. The car is fine with the exception of a blown right front tire, he pulls back onto the pavement setting the hazards and popping the trunk. It's been a long time since he's had to change a tire.

Forty minutes later with nothing worse than a skinned knuckle he pulls into the long drive heading up to the cabin. Its dark by now, but there are no lights on. He smiles at the red LADA 4X4 parked out front, his uncle insisted on buying Russian and driving himself everywhere, he loved the little SUV and refused the official car and driver his rank came with.

Mikhail parks next to the vehicle running his hand over the hood out of habit - cold - his uncle must have been home for at least an hour. Maybe it's just instinct, the lack of lights, or the stillness, but he pulls the CZ from his pocket and creeps quietly toward the front door, the speeding SUV from earlier now seems even more out of place.

He pushes the front door open, already knowing what he is going to find, no way his uncle would have left the door unlocked. He stands inside the entry letting his eyes adjust to the gloom. Yuri is face down in the living room and his blood has soaked into the red Persian carpet, one of the few positive things he had brought back from Afghanistan in the '80s. Mikhail doesn't touch anything, the nubs of his uncle's fingers tell the tale – they had tortured him, but no way Yuri would have given anything up – there wasn't anything they could do that he hadn't seen or experienced tenfold already. He does a quick search of the house, no one there and nothing obviously missing, whatever they had come for they either had or had been irretrievably locked in his uncle's head.

Mikhail stops in the small room off the kitchen that served as his uncle's office, everything seemed in order, his laptop was on the docking station, the large monitor Mikhail had given him for Christmas was dark. He taps the keyboard more out of curiosity than anything else, the screen glows to life, showing an unaddressed email the icon still blinking. Hmm, no subject, just two words in the body: "David Eisen" nothing more. He'll have to think about that later, he steps out the front door leaving it unlocked, he has already stayed too long, *what now* he muses?

Orders

Jason dials the encrypted line which is routed to an empty office in DC and goes "black" from there. He waits as the rest of ALPHA team logs in. He is a few minutes early today, not really anxious but not happy about what he has to tell the team. He had held off updating everyone on the McIntyre girl, the suicide bombings had derailed their normal agenda items, but he really had no choice now.

Control brings them online – "Five, why don't you give us an update on General Semonovich."

"Yes, well the General will no longer be listening at the door," Five answers.

"What does that mean? Who is this General?" Jason asks.

"The General was the unit commander for Compound Nineteen, he was asking too many questions about the missing vial and Azrael, we think he might also have sniffed out this group." Control shares, "we couldn't take a chance…"

"Well, you're going to love this then," Jason adds. He proceeds to give them a run down on Jessie McIntyre, including her background and a brief summary of the events of the previous summer, "it seems we may have underestimated her a bit."

"But she's not an experienced intelligence agent," Six adds dryly.

"No," he admits, "but she is a highly capable soldier and that actually might be more dangerous right now. besides she is working with Jack Hardy and from what I can tell the bastard is a living legend."

Three lets out a low whistle, "he taught at The Farm, I was in one of his classes..."

"Where is she now, Four?" Control asks.

"I don't know, if she was on that Paradigm jet then she left Kiev yesterday and is probably back stateside today."

"Do we know who she met with in Kiev?" Five asks.

"No, I don't have that kind of access and no way to re-task resources for that without having to answer too many questions," he answers the frustration bleeding through.

"Okay listen, let's stay focused – Four, find McIntyre then we can decide what to do about her – obviously she poses a threat and will have to be dealt with. Five, see what you can dig up on the General: who he might have been talking to, anything that seems important I don't care how small I want to know about it. If you have contacts in Kiev see what you can find on who the McIntyre girl met with – someone has to know, everyone clear? We are almost there, people."

Jason signs off and leans back in his chair, he twirls it around thinking, *this has turned into a serious cluster fuck – what the hell? Now we are killing Russian Generals, never mind CIA operatives?* Control might have soft pedaled the McIntyre situation, but it was clear as day as soon as they had her location she was marked, and he was the only stateside resource they had.

The knock on the door startles him, he motions the Section Director in, not that she needed his permission. She sits down in the chair next to his desk, "Jason, I need a full work up on this Aza guy and the bombings yesterday, and I need it now. The President is pissed we didn't see this coming and somehow warn them."

"With all due respect that's bullshit, we did a whitepaper on this guy a month ago..."

"Well, that didn't help yesterday morning now, did it?" she answers.

"No, I guess not," he says with a sigh. "Okay, I'll get it done, can I have a couple of guys?" he asks, motioning to the group of cubes outside his office.

"Sure, whatever you need, just get it done," she looks around the office again, "you okay?"

"Yeah why?"

"Nothin', just checking," she says as she leaves.

Christ on a cross, he thinks, *what the fuck was that about, am I okay?* He didn't need the Director poking around and starting to ask questions, he was starting to wonder what he had gotten himself into, he was going to have to be a lot more careful moving forward. He was worried, if some General in Moscow could figure out what was going on, it stood to reason his superiors at NSA might also be picking up some signals. *No way we are just going to erase that, unfucking-believable,* he wasn't naïve but *Jesus, killing a fucking Major General cause he might know something, the fuckers act like this is some fucking spy novel?*

He spends the rest of his day ramping up the two analysts on Aza, pulling the earlier white paper and instructing them to have a draft ready for his review in the morning. "Details, details, details, and cross reference everything, I don't want any assumptions!" he tells them. The United States was in the business of retaliation these days, sentiments had changed a couple of administrations ago – Trump had made sure of that.

He posts up a standard monitor and track or M&T as they called it – on Jessie McIntyre and Jack Hardy. It was a simple electronic tracking tool that would look for any incidences of their name, credit cards, social security numbers, passport, driver's license, any identifying information that triggered an electronic signature would be routed to his desk. It was a passive tool, so no one else would be notified and no physical assets would have to take any action, but if she so much as used a debit card to buy a pack of gum he would know where she was. He wasn't willing to go any further tonight, but if this didn't locate her he would have to move to tracking her cell phone signals and tap into the facial recognition tools that were wired into every law enforcement and municipal video system in the country. Of course, that would probably raise some red flags and set off bells here that he really didn't want to explain, either way though the net was going to close on her pretty quickly.

It was several hours later after a long run with King, grilled steaks for both of them and a couple too many beers that his phone starts chirping. He checks the number and murmurs "Fuck me..."

"Four here," he answers, hoping his words aren't slurred.

"Have you located the McIntyre girl yet?" Control asks.

"No sir, but we will, I've got tracers up on her and Hardy now, it's just a matter of time."

"I'm afraid we are running short on time, I... we need her found and neutralized."

"Neutralized sir?" he asks, not sure he had heard correctly, "you mean like the General sir?"

"Yes, like the General, is this going to be a problem for you? Do I need to bring in other resources?"

"No sir, I can handle it, what about Hardy?"

"Secondary target, if you can do it fine, if not we believe his effectiveness without the girl is minimal."

Jason almost laughed at that, but he bit it back, "time frame?"

"Now."

"What's changed sir, this morning we didn't seem to be in such a hurry," he was stepping out on a limb asking any questions at all, but damn if he was going to target a US soldier, especially one of her caliber without some type of explanation.

Control hesitates, "we think she may have the asset's name and location, turns out the General had been talking to his nephew in Kiev earlier in the day."

"No shit, sorry sir."

"His name is Mikhail Kirilov, that ring any bells with you?"

It did and if he didn't have a few too many beers in him it would have all made sense, "I don't think so sir, I'll run it on this end though."

"Okay, let me know when it's done, and be careful, I don't care how you do it, but the preservation of our mission and team is your first priority... clear?"

"Yes sir." Jason hangs up the phone and looks at King, "it's not good," he says rubbing the dog's head. There wasn't going to be anyway to get out of the office without a lot of questions, this was going to have to wait for the weekend, which gave him two days to plan, probably not enough, but what choice did he have.

He pulls up his laptop and books a Southwest flight out of BWI to Denver for Friday night, he doesn't have confirmation yet, but odds are pretty good that's where she's at and he doesn't want to chance not getting a flight. *What a mess, it's not like I can just walk up to her in the street and gun her down, or maybe it was that simple. Goddammit though, he was a SEAL, there wasn't any honor in this – FUCK,* his mind rages as he drifts into an uncomfortable sleep.

Vendetta

Jessie and Jack had landed in Boulder late Thursday afternoon, Jason and ALPHA group had already decided to eliminate them and Mikhail's uncle had been dead for thirty-six hours. The time zones had events chasing each other, Mikhail was in the air heading towards the US, his Gulfstream didn't have the range restrictions the Paradigm jet did, and he would be in Boulder shortly after Jessie, even having left a day later. He was as off the grid as was possible but heading into the US and in particular, Jessie's backyard, was taking a serious risk. Two days ago this had been a bit of a dalliance for him, sure national pride was at stake, but he had been intrigued by Jessie McIntyre and that was the greater truth. Now it was personal, they – whoever they were – had murdered is uncle, his family, his flesh and blood, and he wasn't going to let that stand – Jessie had a new partner, want it or not.

Lou sits behind his desk listening to the debrief from Jessie and Jack, she probably should have called this in he thinks, and was going to need to, but he didn't trust his own government right now. He hadn't shared with them yet the NSA hack, well monitoring program.

"So, what do you think Dad?" Jessie asks.

"Uh, what do I think?" he had been caught.

"Yeah, about this ALPHA group, you weren't listening were you," she says pointedly.

"Of course, I was," he says emphatically waving her off, "it's as I suspected."

Jack gives a "hmmmphh," from the couch. Drawing a warning look from Lou – Jack smiles as he fishes another potato chip out of the bag and takes a long sip of his root beer, "what?"

The buzzer on Lou's phone goes off before he can respond, he picks it up, "what? I said no interruptions…" He listens for a moment, "are you sure?" He looks over at Jessie and Jack before swinging his computer monitor around, "recognize this man?" he asks Jessie. She just nods, Kirilov is staring back at her, "Ok, bring him up… no just do it," Lou says hanging up the phone. "Want to explain that to me?"

"I honestly don't know dad, we left him in Kiev two and half days ago, said he was going to visit his uncle this weekend, Jack?" she says, turning to the other man.

He just shrugs, "apparently things have changed, pretty damn nervy showing up here though." There's a knock on the door before he can say anything else and one of the security detail shows Kirilov in.

No one says anything for a moment as Kirilov looks around the room, Lou finally breaks the silence, walking over with his hand extended, "Lou McIntyre, welcome to Paradigm."

Kirilov takes his hand firmly, "Mikhail Kirilov, thanks for letting me up…" he looks over at Jack and Jessie still gripping Lou's hand, "hello again."

"Come on in, can I get you a drink?" Lou offers leading him over to the couch.

"No thank you," he turns to Jessie, "they killed my uncle," he says simply as he sits down next to Jack.

"Who killed your uncle?" Jessie asks softly.

"My guess is this ALPHA group, but…" he doesn't finish.

Hold on, hold on… someone start at the beginning…" Lou interjects.

"You really weren't listening were you," Jessie admonishes him. She starts at the beginning again falling back into her straight forward almost clinical style of recitation. The men listen without interrupting, when she finishes she turns to Kirilov, "why don't you fill in the rest for us, I thought you weren't going to Moscow until this weekend?"

He nods, "well, I figured my uncle was holding back; he is so old school…" no one corrects his tense. "Anyway, I decided to head there right away and see if he had anything more, maybe something he wasn't comfortable sharing on the phone, someone got there before me. The bastards tortured him, cut his fingers off, but uncle Yuri wouldn't have told them anything."

"But we don't know that for sure," Lou cautions.

Kirilov looks him in the eye, "yes we do, my uncle fought in Afghanistan saw and experienced things you can't imagine, if I tell you he didn't say anything then he didn't say anything," his voice rising.

"Okay, Okay, I didn't mean any disrespect," Lou says holding his hands up. He looks over at Jack, "what do you think?"

Jack purses his lips before answering, "well, neither one of us would give Jessie up and my guess is Mikhail's uncle was the same way, so whatever secrets he had probably died with him. Doesn't matter though."

"What do you mean it doesn't matter?" the other three ask in unison.

"Well, two things actually... one ALPHA already knows everything it needs to, maybe not the details, but how hard is it going to be to track down Mikhail? Not very hard, and my guess is they already know all about Jessie, won't take but a couple of keystrokes to know Paradigm had a jet in Kiev this week... two and two always makes four, this isn't rocket science, so we need to be a lot more careful than we have been."

"What's number two?" Mikhail asks.

"What?"

"You said two things, what's number two?"

"Oh, it doesn't matter cause your uncle didn't give us anything more..., sorry, that sounds bad, but you know what I mean," Jack answers.

"Well, not quite true… do any of you know the name David Eisen?" Mikhail asks spelling it out.

"No but Eisen is a common Jewish name," Jack answers, "Why?"

"Found it on my uncle's computer, no explanation, just the name."

"Dad, can we run it through NEO?" Jessie asks.

Her dad gives her one of his looks, it's clear he thinks she is sharing too much.

Too late though, "NEO?" Mikhail asks.

"It's just a computer program that matches things up," Lou answers, playing it off, "no reason not to try though I guess," he says, picking up the phone and dialing an extension – "run this through NEO now: DAVID EISEN – send the result to my desk, thanks. Ok, that's going to take a bit but let's see what we get."

"Thanks dad," Jessie says, "Mikhail you never said why you are here though…" she says turning toward the couch.

He speaks directly to Jessie, "You came to me for help," he holds his hands up before she can interrupt, "I know I sent you the message, but you came. I admit at first I was just curious, and even after it was clear this was bigger than just Azrael, well I wanted to help but only to a point, sorry but you know what I mean this wasn't my uh what is phrase? my fight I guess."

"And now it is?" she asks.

"They made it personal, they killed my uncle, you know they are going to come for me and you too… they have to…" He looks at Lou, "let me help, I can do things maybe you can't, I have contacts all over the world that won't talk to you but will do uh business with me."

Lou looks skeptical, but he knows Jessie well enough to know she isn't going to listen to anyone on this but he has to try, "Jess listen to me on this, I think you need to run this up the flag, you need to bring Director Simpson in on this…" He knows that's going to fall flat, "Mikhail is right though, they are going to come for you…"

"Dad, we don't know who we can trust, and think about it, if the Director was serious about this, I wouldn't be the only one trying to track this maniac down, you said it yourself."

Mikhail stands up offering her his hand, "you can trust me…"

She looks at Lou and then Jack, she can't read either of them, she takes Mikhail's hand, "alright, but I call all the shots period no questions asked, got it?" He just nods with a smile.

The computer screen on Lou's desk pings and flashes up a file icon, before anyone can say anything he clicks the file, scanning the screen, "Shit… hope you're ready for this…"

Simpson

Vance Simpson had been appointed Deputy Director of Operations during the last administration and had been asked to stay on with the new one, he had been a career operative in Western Europe and the Soviet Union, finally coming home after the fall of the Berlin Wall and had taken progressively more advanced management opportunities until finally reaching the top spot in Ops.

It was late, well past nine thirty and he should have been home two hours ago, the halls were quiet, only the overnight analysts left in the building many floors below him, the executive floor was empty. He looks out the window but there isn't much to see this late in the evening, a thin line of turquoise and purple marks where the sun had set an hour ago, and the bright white of the LED lights in the parking lot illuminate the few dozen cars sprinkled about. He turns back to the file on his desk "AZRAEL", they hadn't even bothered to code it, choosing to use the assassin's moniker instead.

Simpson had two problems, and no idea how to deal with either of them, he hadn't heard from the McIntyre girl in four, no five days – she had missed her last update – he wasn't so much worried about her, she was clearly capable of taking care of herself, but she was basically off the books and working AZRAEL covertly for him. That made him smile, *a CIA operative working a CIA case covertly for the CIA, what a fucking tangled web*, he laughs to himself. His bigger problem was the call earlier this afternoon from the DNI – Director of National Intelligence - Moyer.

Moyer was a political appointee, as a Cabinet level slot he worked directly for the president, but Simpson knew the career guys over at the DIA – Defense Intelligence Agency had his ear, and although their missions were ostensibly the same, the folks at DIA had developed a more radical interventional approach to handling things over the past couple of decades. Bottom line was Moyer had called and told him to drop the AZRAEL file, and specifically to pull McIntyre out of the field – and no he wasn't going to discuss it. It wasn't that unusual for the groups to step on each other a bit, but a call directly from the DNI, well that simply didn't happen, and why pull McIntyre? It was one operative, not a whole team and she was basically operating without any support and how did he even know about her?

There weren't any answers lurking in the dark outside his window and McIntyre hadn't picked up when he had called her, *fuck me what the hell are they up to*, he thinks putting the file in his safe and turning the lights off. He nods to the guards at the security station on the way out and double clicks the key fob unlocking the Lexus as his phone begins to beep.

"McIntyre, where the fuck have you been?" his frustration boiling over.

"Sorry boss, got tied up, couldn't call in," she answers clearly not sorry.

"Fine, where are you?"

"Really rather not say sir, do you want an update on the Azrael situation?"

He takes a deep breath, leaning back in the soft leather, "you'd rather not say? Are you serious?"

"I'm sorry sir, but things have changed, and I don't know who I can trust at this point."

"Jesus Christ McIntyre, I'm the Deputy Director, I put you on this file..."

Silence fills up the line, "can I ask you about that sir? Why me, why not a whole team, if this guy is really such a threat and has this VX17 stuff why not our most experienced people..."

"Wondered how long it was going to take you to ask that question," he answers softly.

"Well sir? It doesn't make sense..."

"McIntyre, it doesn't always have to make sense, there is a bigger picture at play here..." it's a weak answer and he knows it.

"That's fine sir, I've been putting my life on the line for my country for a long time now, but this is the first time I can't figure out why."

"Because that's the job," he says with a sigh.

"With all due respect sir, that's bullshit."

"Alright, alright, Jesus you're a pain in the ass... listen no one wanted to touch the AZRAEL file, I thought you might have some success working independently, doesn't matter now anyway."

"What do you mean, it doesn't matter sir?"

"We've been pulled off, shutdown, whatever you want to call it, I'm supposed to bring you in and sit you at a desk."

Jessie bites her lip debating whether she believes him or not, "sir tell me about ALPHA Team..."

"ALPHA Team, what the hell is that?" he responds without hesitation.

It's a gamble but at this point Jessie doesn't have very many options, "doesn't ring a bell, sir?" she asks with just a touch of sarcasm.

"Look McIntyre, don't play games, we don't have an ALPHA Team and you know that, what are you talking about?"

"Sir, I don't have a lot of data on these guys, but we're talking about a small team, multinational – either working with AZRAEL or at least using him... really don't have more than that, but looks like it probably includes us, the Russians, and maybe the Israelis – and you're telling me you honestly don't know anything about this? Sorry sir, but that seems pretty unlikely..."

"Listen to me very closely McIntyre... burn this phone, stay off the grid, do not under any circumstances come back to DC – I swear to you I don't know anything about this, but if it's true, and that's a big if, then you're no longer safe, and I can't protect you. Call me when you have a new phone, I'll see what I can dig up."

"Thank you, sir... and uh sir, be careful, okay," she says before clicking off. Jessie looks around the office, "what do you think?"

No one speaks, her dad is standing by the windows watching the sun set over the Flat Irons, Jack and Mikhail are on the couch. Lou clears his throat, "hate to say it, but I believe him and that isn't a good thing, if this is bigger than the Deputy Director well..."

"I've known Vance a long time Lou, he was in the field when we were, I don't believe he would be part of something like this, I agree with you he's telling the truth, or at least what he thinks is the truth," Jack says.

"What he thinks is the truth, what does that mean," Mikhail asks.

Jack turns to him, "just that even folks at the top aren't immune to making assumptions or only seeing what they expect to see, it's a variation of hiding in plain sight if you will... feed someone what they expect, and they rarely ask any questions."

"So where does that leave us?" Jessie asks.

124

Lou sits back down at his desk, "well, let me walk you through what we have on this David Eisen and then we can figure out where to go from here, I think we have some outside confirmation on this ALPHA group too."

"Confirmation?" Jessie asks.

"Yeah, whoever pulled your Army jacket and the FBI and CIA files on the Sokolov case is probably part of ALPHA, fits the model," he looks over at Kirilov. "Mikhail I'm going to have to trust that this all stays here, we clear?"

"Clear," the man nods.

"Do I want to know how you did that?"

"No, you don't Jess…"

"Jesus Dad…" she keeps forgetting what a total bad ass her dad is.

"Alright Lou, drop it on us, what are we dealing with here, super ISIS assassin or rogue Mossad agent, or something else entirely?" Jack says with a smile.

Active Shooter

Jason had caught the last non-stop out of BWI from Denver. He was supposed to take off at seven but the everyday summer thunderstorms had delayed him a little over an hour, and it was after ten in Denver when he landed. Duffle at his side he makes his way to the East Hourly lots, checking his phone again he looks for Row R - Slot 17, the grey minivan is right where it should have been. He pops open the door and pulls the visor down, the keys drop in his lap. He pushes the start button and adjusts the AC, he looks in the back seat - the long black bag is on the floor. He doesn't bother to check it already knowing it contains an AR15 with bump stock and four boxes of rounds.

The stocks had been outlawed fifteen years earlier, but you could still buy one in the parking lot of any gun show. Gun control in the states was no further along now than it had been after the Vegas concert and Florida school massacres – they had tried, but when, a few years later, two good old boys in Iowa had used their ARs to hold off six well-armed MS13 gang members intent on stealing the gate receipts from the Iowa State Fair, well the NRA had their poster boys, literally. The whole mess had re-inflamed the immigration issue and given the politicians just the thing they had needed to re-direct the public's myopically short attention span.

Jason pulls into the Quality Inn just south of Boulder on the Turnpike, he checks in using the ID that had been in the glove box of the van, Terry Jackson of Detroit, he didn't appreciate the stereotype, but it didn't really matter did it? There had been a driver's license, Visa card, five hundred in cash, and a clean satellite phone, more than enough for the couple of days he planned on being there.

Settled in the room with two Big Macs a large fry and two bottles of water, he zips open the bag, extracting the rifle and boxes of rounds, working the action a couple of times he sets it down and loads up four thirty round clips. He rarely ever indulged in fast food but that first bite of special sauce, pickles and onions with the salty beef – too good! He had a weakness for Big Macs and well if things went to shit this weekend it wouldn't much matter would it, he thinks stuffing four of the hot salty fries in his mouth.

He didn't have much of a plan, he knew where the McIntyre house was, he had thought about approaching from the West and taking them by surprise at the house itself, risky but contained. Would have been easier with a sniper rifle and scope but that would have narrowed his options to just one. He had the layout of both the house and the Paradigm offices on his laptop, he brings them up again. The high-resolution satellite views provided a clear layout of both properties, the Paradigm offices are out of the question, the security layout is tighter than most government installations and there are no approaches that don't have line of sight visibility to the security cameras and guards. Paradigm was locked up tight.

He turns his attention to the McIntyre place, if he came in from the West crossing the river and following the shallow crease toward the house he could probably approach to within a few hundred yards before he would be out in the open. It meant driving out probably six or seven miles and hiking back in from the edge of the National Forest nothing he was uncomfortable with though. He calls it a night deciding he will scout it out tomorrow before executing on his plan early Sunday morning. If he could hit the house before dawn on Sunday odds are everyone would be sleeping, and he could be in and out before sun up. If everything went right he would have at least twenty-four hours before anyone came looking for the McIntyres, and he would be back in Maryland at his desk by then.

Even for June it was chilly before the sun was up to warm the thin air, Jason parks the minivan in the picnic pull off he had found yesterday, he looks around to confirm he is alone before extracting the backpack and rifle. He had put the three extra clips, two bottles of water and a banana in the backpack before leaving the room – he had left his ID and credit card there it was standard operating procedure not to carry any identifying information. He's wearing jeans, a dark blue and green plaid flannel shirt and hiking boots. He had chosen a combination of dark clothes to help hide his approach but nothing that would arouse suspicion if he ran across someone unexpectedly. It was about two miles as the crow flies, he had hiked most of it yesterday and figured it would take about forty-five minutes or so. He hadn't crossed the stream, but it hadn't looked more than two or three feet deep. Even in the dark that shouldn't pose a problem, fact was this was a walk in the park compared to his SEAL training. He checks his watch; the faintly glowing numbers tell him it's time to go - he was finally back in the field.

Mikhail stands in the kitchen wearing his boxers and a CCCP Hockey T-shirt, he waits for the blue light to start flashing on the Keurig, he had to get one of these for his office, perfect coffee one cup at a time, he loved it. He hadn't been able to sleep, a combination of jet lag and something he couldn't identify, maybe it was just nerves – he was back on a team and it was a bit disconcerting to be working with the Americans. They were well trained, highly intelligent, but impulsive and that was taking some getting used to. He hadn't turned on the kitchen lights, the soft glow from the embers of last night's fire still cast enough light to see into the kitchen and the sky was starting to brighten in the East. It was that quiet time of morning before anyone is up and the night creatures have already bedded down for the long sleep of the day, but the morning has yet to rouse those who call the day theirs.

He sees the motion, a shadow darker than the background coming up the far side of the yard in the long brush that leads down to the stream Lou had shown him yesterday. He doesn't react at first, still in that morning state that recognizes things, but doesn't ascribe any importance to them. It's only when the shadow shifts the rifle off his shoulder that Mikhail realizes what he is looking at, the man is within a hundred yards by then and moving fast.

Mikhail doesn't hesitate, there's no time to wake the others, he turns and pulls the pair of CZ-75s from his duffle sitting on the floor in the living room and begins to move back to the kitchen when he hears the crack of wood, the man has forced the back door open. Mikhail is in the entry way to the kitchen a pistol in each hand as Jason rounds the corner the rifle lowered toward the floor. It's only an instant but Mikhail opens up with both pistols, as Jason is raising the rifle and pulling the trigger. The house erupts in noise, the flashes from all three muzzles illuminate the kitchen for a brief moment. Mikhail exhales as his slides rack open, he can feel a warm trickle of blood down the side of his face.

Jessie comes down the hall in a tank top and underwear, Kimber at the ready followed by her father in a black silk robe emblazoned with a huge dragon his shotgun cradled in his arms, he holds her back with his hand as he flips the lights on. "Mikhail," he calls out.

"I'm okay, I think," Mikhail answers shakily.

Father and daughter come around the corner, guns still at the ready, Jason is on the tile floor, at least a dozen rounds in his chest he isn't breathing and a crimson puddle is following the grout lines in the tile - neither give him a second look, before moving toward Mikhail.

"You ok?" Jessie asks, "looks like you got a graze wound up top," she says wetting some paper towels in the sink. "Here let me take a look," she says wiping the blood off his face, "not too bad, you'll live," she says suppressing a smile and handing him the paper towels.

"What the hell happened?" Lou asks, bending down to examine the body? He checks the pockets and back pack, "nothing on him." He turns to Mikhail, "nice shooting."

Mikhail sits down at the kitchen bar holding the paper towels to his head, "thanks, was making coffee," he points to the Keurig, "just happened to see him making his way from the river, he hit the door before I could wake you, I grabbed my pistols and made it to here as he came around the corner." He looks at Jessie, "just got lucky, he wasn't expecting anybody, I fired first and well, I just kept firing till I was out."

"Close combat's a bit different isn't it?" she says.

"Yes, I'd forgotten, it all slows down and then speeds up while you're trying to catch up."

"Well Mikhail you did good, saved all of us, that's for sure," Lou says.

"Who is he?"

Lou looks up, "no idea, American though, and see this tattoo?" he holds the man's arm up, "that's SEAL Team Six, nobody else has those."

"Shit, what do ya think Dad, ALPHA?" Jessie asks leaning in to look at the tattoo.

"Makes sense, and timing is right, only question is, what are we going to do now? We can call in the locals, but it's going to generate a heap of questions."

"Now we're going to see where the Director really stands, that's what," Jessie says heading back to her room. She returns a few seconds later wearing a robe and dialing her phone. She waits as it connects, "Director Simpson, sorry to call so early, but I've got a bit of a situation here, going to need some help." She explains in her standard clipped and precise manner, leaving Kirilov out of it completely. She hangs up and turns to the two men. "He is calling in a favor with the FBI in Denver, they should have a team up in less than an hour." She sits down next to Kirilov, "Dad you think we should call Harrington have him check it out just in case we're getting set up?"

"Yeah, honey I do... let me call him." Lou heads up the hall to grab his phone.

"Jesus, I need a drink," Jessie says opening the fridge and pulling the orange juice out, she takes a long swig from the bottle before holding it out to Mikhail, he just shakes his head trying not to stare and points to the Keurig, the blue light blinking.

FBI Favors

Special Agent in Charge, Tim Harrington likes to be up early on Sunday mornings, he walks down to the end of the drive retrieves the New York Times and scurries back to the porch where he savors a cup of French press coffee and works through the crossword puzzle. On a good Sunday he can finish in just under three hours, today wasn't one of those days, he picks the phone up with his left hand – glancing at it briefly – pencil in his right hand still hovering over the paper. "Before you fuck up my day McIntyre: bagel topping six letters, second letter is a 'C'."

"SCHMEAR" Lou answers without hesitation, "are you serious?"

"Jesus, how could I not get that," Harrington says mostly to himself.

"Cause you're from Boston, asshole," Lou answers with a laugh.

"What do you want Lou, you're going to screw up a perfectly good Sunday aren't you?"

"Sure am buddy, but I need your help and unless I'm way off here, this might make the Sokolov mess look like kid's play."

Harrington sets the paper down, "okay, what's going on, give me the scoop I'll do what I can."

Lou walks him through the events of the morning, leaving Kirilov out of the story, and taking responsibility for the shooting himself, he briefly sketches an outline of what Jessie has been working on without any real details and no mention of ALPHA team. "I'm calling you Tim cause I don't know who we can trust and honestly, it looks like a black op type job, which means someone in our government now thinks it's okay to come after its own citizens – which I think would bother a fella like you."

"So clearly you are leaving plenty out of this and only telling me about ten percent of the truth... which is pretty typical for you spooks, and yes, that bothers the hell out of me - is your girl okay?"

"Yeah Tim, she is fine, but thanks for asking. You know I'm limited in what I can say, especially on the phone, but can you call the Denver office and make sure whoever is headed this way is on the level and maybe keep your finger on this?"

"Sure Lou, in fact I'll do you one better, let me make a couple of calls, I might be able to wrangle this under our continued cleanup of the Sokolov mess, who's to say the shooter isn't tied to what went down last summer? Might be I can have everything funneled through my office, give me about thirty minutes and I'll call you back."

"Thanks Tim, really means a lot, I'm going to owe you one after this..."

"You mean another one, don't you?" Tim says with a laugh.

"Right, that's what I meant," Lou laughs as he hangs up. He turns to Jessie and Mikhail, "listen this is going to get dicey in the next hour or so. Jess get dressed and take Mikhail over to Jack's place, I want him out of sight." He pauses for moment, "Mikhail, those pistols registered anywhere?"

"Registered?"

"Can they be traced back to you somehow?"

"Oh no, not at all, as far as anyone knows they are in a Russian warehouse," he says with a smile.

"Ok, take the shotgun," he says picking it up off the counter, "get all your stuff." Lou turns to Jessie as she returns wearing sweats, a Tom Petty T-shirt and running shoes, "be careful, no way to know if this guy was acting alone or not, as soon as you are in the car give Jack a call and let him know you're on the way."

"What about you Dad? We haven't heard back from Harrington yet, what if these guys from Denver..."

He gives her a hug, "don't worry, I can handle myself, if Tim says its thumbs down, I'll head out the back and call you to pick me up... now get out of here," he says guiding her to the garage and handing her the keys, "take the Beast."

"You serious?" she says incredulously.

"Yep, go on now," he hands the shotgun to Mikhail, "don't let anything happen to her – understand?"

Mikhail takes the gun with a nod, "understood," he says as the men exchange a look and in that instant Lou knows Mikhail would give his life for Jessie.

Lou's phone is ringing as he watches Jessie drive out the front gate, "yeah Tim what have you got for me?"

"Alright Lou, two agents headed your way from Denver: Peterson and Davis should be there in about twenty minutes, don't touch anything, I have a crime scene van about ten minutes behind them. We are going to black this out, no press, no announcements, nothing. I've taken charge of the investigation from here and if this is what you think it is, I want to keep it dark as long as possible. Any identification on this guy?"

"No, that was the tip-off actually, well, he also has a SEAL Team Six tattoo on his left forearm."

"Fuck me, well that's a pretty small group of guys, should be fairly easy to identify him, prints will be in the national database. Listen Lou, we are going to need to talk about this, when can you be in DC?"

"Well, I don't want to leave here till I'm sure we have this under control, how is Monday late afternoon?"

"Make it Tuesday morning, I'll see if I can round Albert up, might need Justice on this," Harrington replies. Alberto Jimenez was the Deputy Attorney General and had played a big part in the resolving the Sokolov mess last summer, the man was animated to say the least, but he was also one of the sharpest men Lou had ever met.

"Good idea on Albert, I better bring some donuts, your office, say nine o'clock?" Lou asks with a laugh.

"Perfect, call me if you need something."

Lou grabs a dishrag from the kitchen drawer and sprays an ammonia glass cleaner on it and wipes down the two pistols, when he is satisfied they are clean he takes one in each hand and racks the slides making sure his fingerprints are clear. He then grabs a box of 9MM rounds out of the hall closet and loads one in each pistol. He doesn't have much time, but he is far enough out of town so he isn't worried about drawing any attention. Walking onto the back deck he fires one round from each pistol into the soft ground.

Satisfied, he returns inside, he wants to make sure his story is full proof, now his prints are on the guns and if tested the agents will find powder residue on both his hands. He sits at the bar ignoring the body lying on his floor, it's just a matter of waiting. He reloads both clips and slams them home hoping he won't need them.

He thinks about all those years ago standing in this room making French toast of all things, and hearing the screams from the bedroom, he had lost the love of his life that morning but gained a precious daughter. Now, thirty plus years later, he had almost lost her, would have lost her if it hadn't been for an ex Russian intelligence officer turned international arms dealer, you almost had to smile, *you can't make this stuff up,* he thinks.

He is interrupted by a sharp knock on the front door, he picks up one of the pistols, chambers a round and heads that way. Standing to the left of the door, "who is it?" he asks.

"FBI... agents Peterson and Davis," a deep voice answers.

"Gentlemen, the door is unlocked I am going to ask you to open it and come through single file with your hands locked behind your head, is that clear?"

"Excuse me sir, but that's not going to happen," says a second voice, this one a woman.

"Agent did you speak with Special Agent Harrison?"

"Yes sir," the woman answers.

"Then you know what happened here, I'm not going to ask again and you're not coming through that door if I can't see your hands."

Lou can't make out the words, but it's clear the agents are having a heated conversation. "Coming through now sir, hold your fire." The door pushes open slowly, the first agent can't be more than five five with blond hair and fierce blue eyes, her hands are locked behind her head. Behind her the young man must be six five with red hair, freckles and a scowl. "Satisfied sir," she asks.

"Not really, down the hall in the kitchen, keep your hands locked please," he motions with the pistol and falls in behind them dialing Harrington's number with his other hand. "Tim can you describe Peterson and Davis to me..." He clicks the phone off and lowers the pistol, "Ok, you check out, sorry about that, but can't be too careful," he says holding out his hand, "Lou McIntyre, glad you're here."

"I'm Agent Peterson, what did Harrington say," she asks taking his hand.

"You don't want to know," he says with a smile.

"Probably not," the taller agent says, "sir, can you give us a run down on what happened? The crime scene guys will be here in about fifteen minutes, but maybe you can walk us through it?"

Lou gives them the run down, basically replacing Kirilov with himself, explaining that he hadn't been able to sleep and had come out to the kitchen to make a cup of coffee.

"You always carry two loaded pistols with you to make coffee sir?" Peterson asks pointedly.

Lou gives her a smile, "pistol's not much good if it's not loaded, but no, I keep them in the living room, which is why he made the door before I was able to get here," he points to entry way.

"You mind if I take a look at those," Davis asks pointing to the pistols. Lou drops the clips and ejects the round in each breach before handing them over. "CZ75s nice piece, tough to get one of these," the agent says looking up.

"Don't I know it," Lou responds.

Peterson looks around, Lou can see she is measuring the distances in her mind, "anyone else here sir?"

"Just my daughter, but I've sent her to a friend's."

"Going to need to talk to her also then."

"Yeah, that's not going to happen, so..."

"Look sir, you're not exactly cooperating here, we're trying to help you," she says.

"Are you? Do I look like I need help? No, so let me be perfectly clear – you're here because the Deputy Director of the CIA and Special Agent Harrison sent you here, not because I need you, so let's drop the pretense and you can quit with the standard revolving interrogation techniques as well, we clear?"

Lou is interrupted by a sharp knock on the front door, he reaches for the nearest pistol slamming home a clip, "you two don't get it do you? This was an assassination attempt," he motions to the body, "he wasn't stopping by for coffee..."

Peterson nods, drawing her Glock she motions for Davis to get the door. The younger agent pulls his pistol as well and heads down the hall. A minute later three men dressed in the traditional FBI wind breaker follow him back carrying two tackle box looking cases and a body bag. "Jesus, what a mess!" one of them remarks.

Lou moves to the living room, as much to get out of their way as to reflect back on the morning trying to put the pieces in place. He had expected ALPHA to move against them, but this happened quickly, which had to mean the order had gone out earlier than they had thought. He comes back into the kitchen as the agents are finishing up, the body has already been moved out and one of the techs is taking a few more pictures. Turning to Peterson and Davis, "listen, I've been thinking about this, come out on the back porch with me," he leads them through the living room and out the glass sliders. Lou points to the break by the stream and the hills beyond, "he had to have come cross country from that direction, there really isn't any other way in here without being seen. My guess is you'll find a car couple miles out that way, there are a ton of cut outs and picnic pull offs on the canyon roads." Both agents nod, "and I would check the motels from here to Denver as well - someone probably saw this guy."

"Okay sir, we got it from here," they respond in unison.

Lou shakes their hands and thanks them again as they walk out to the driveway. Once they are gone he heads back inside. *What a mess! You never saw the cleanup after the cops leave in the movies* he thinks, grabbing a bucket and mop from the laundry room. He fills it half way with hot water, dumps in some pine scented cleaner and begins mopping the floor. It's a strange experience cleaning another man's life off your tile, even if he had meant to kill you.

DNI Moyer

Director Anthony Moyer was having a Monday, an epically bad Monday; it had started with his morning NSA briefing and progressed from there. He had expected an update on Aza, but after twenty minutes of hemming and hawing the NSA folks had finally come clean explaining that the senior man putting the intelligence estimate together had gone missing and couldn't be located, senior level NSA employees don't go missing.

Moyer had been one of three men involved in hand selecting the ALPHA team and now one of them was missing, plausible deniability had meant disengaging and letting the team operate independently, but Moyer was beginning to wonder if that had been a mistake.

The briefing over he retreats to his office and closes the door, dialing the memorized number he waits as the encrypted connection goes through. "Hello, please verify you have confirmed my voice print identity."

"Yes sir, I have to advise you sir this call is outside the established communication protocols for this number, how did you get it?"

"Seriously Control, did you think I was going to let this team operate completely outside of my sight?"

"Yes sir, that was the whole point, wasn't it?"

"Don't you lecture me; our man is missing and I want to know why? NSA doesn't lose people, there'll be an investigation, we don't need anyone asking questions."

"Your man?"

"Yes dammit, Four is missing," Moyer shouts into the phone. There is no immediate answer, "well?"

"Sir I have no independent confirmation, we've been handling some potential leaks, he was asked to address one there in the States, I'm sorry but I can't really say more than that."

"Potential leaks, you can't say more than that, are you serious?"

"Yes sir, we discussed this, I told all of you when we built this team our chances for success were limited, there was always the possibility this would get out, that was the whole point in isolating you from the team."

"Wait a minute, are you telling me you asked him to....to.... to take out a U.S. citizen?" Moyer sputters.

"I'd rather not say sir."

"Who was it, tell me now," Moyer asks his voice rising.

"Sir, I think we should wait for Four to check in, there are any number of reasons he could be delayed."

"I need the name, it appears to me that you are losing control of this situation."

"I'm sorry sir, but this operation is beyond the black flag point, we are a go," Control hesitates for a moment, "sir, I am going to ask you not to use this number again," he says hanging up.

Moyer stares at the phone, this wasn't happening, this couldn't be happening – "Laura, get me Deputy Director Simpson over at Langley on the phone," he says into the intercom. Setting the phone down, he can't help but think about the decisions they had made almost, what, two years ago now, it had all seemed so simple. Create a conflagration in the Middle-East that would let civilized nations step in and take over. It had taken too long though, this administration was almost over with an election looming in the fall that could go either way if you believed the polls, not that anyone did, but still. God forbid this came out! They'd be, no not they, he, would be lucky not to end up in jail.

His contemplations don't get any further as his phone starts buzzing, "Vance, just wanted to confirm you pulled McIntyre in."

Simpson decides to play along, it doesn't make sense that the DNI would personally involve himself in the assignment of an operative, even one with a profile like Jessie McIntyre. Her story was well known inside the intelligence community but that didn't explain this. Something else was definitely going on, "she is taking some leave sir, spending some time with her father in

Colorado I believe..." He doesn't ask the obvious question, but it's there.

"Her father's Lou McIntyre, the fella that owns Paradigm, right?"

"Yes sir, that's correct... sir, what's going on?"

"Going on? What do you mean Vance?"

"With all due respect sir, it's not every day the DNI bothers with one of my operatives in the field, why the interest if you don't mind me asking?"

Moyer pauses before responding, he was going to have to answer, but Simpson had some nerve questioning him, "Now Vance you know the Middle East is heating up again, this Aza character with the suicide bombing has got folks here worked up. You add this Azrael into the mix and well, we can't have any missteps, I've got a group working on it, just want to make sure we don't complicate this mess."

Simpson decides to push a little, "Does it make sense to have McIntyre join your team sir, she has been working on Azrael for more than six months..."

"No, no that won't be necessary I think we've got all we need for now, but good suggestion. Listen Vance I appreciate you taking the call, I'm sure you've got plenty on your plate, keep me in the loop if anything changes." He hangs up before the CIA man can respond, *that was a disaster* he thinks.

Simpson hangs up the phone, *what the hell is going on, clearly the DNI was fishing but for what*? He needed to talk to McIntyre again, she had dropped the ALPHA group thing on him and then forty-eight hours later someone tries to eliminate her, and in the middle of it all Moyer is asking questions that don't make any sense. Moyer was definitely involved - but involved in what was the question. It was Vance's job to manage clandestine ops outside the US, and his people didn't know anything about this, and worse than that Moyer had basically told him to mind his own business, *well fuck him, this was his business.*

He picks up the phone and calls the logistics office, "how quickly can you have me in Boulder Colorado?"

"Hold on sir, let me see what's available, when you do you need to be there?"

"I need to be there now..."

"Alright sir, Air Force has a bird going to Colorado Springs, leaves in two hours, about a two-hour drive North, I can have a car there for you when you land, will you need a driver?"

He makes a note on the pad next to his phone, "that's fine, I'll need a driver to take me out to Andrews, but not on the other end, just have a car ready."

"Yes sir, give me about ten minutes to get a car out front for you."

He hangs up, calls his wife to let her know he will be out of town for a few days. He keeps a couple spare changes of clothes in his office closet, not so much cause he travels unexpectedly, but there were enough nights when he didn't make it home and he would change in the basement gym, catch a quick shower and at least have a fresh suit to wear. His next call is to Lou McIntyre, its two hours earlier in Boulder, but he figures eight isn't too early.

"Mister McIntyre, it's Vance Simpson, sorry to hear about the trouble yesterday, listen I'm flying out to Colorado in a couple of hours can we get together in your office this afternoon? It's pretty important."

"Let me see what I can do, I'm supposed to be in DC tomorrow morning for some meetings. Would it be easier if I came to you?" Lou isn't really sure he wants a Deputy Director of the CIA in his office, beside Harrington had done him a solid.

"Really don't think this can wait, like to have Jessie and Jack Hardy there as well if possible."

"Ok, Ok, give me about five minutes to make some calls and see about rescheduling my meetings, what's the best number to reach you at?"

"I'm headed to Andrews, call me on my cell," Simpson gives him the number - hangs up and heads down to the lobby his suit bag slung over his shoulder, it had been a long time since he had felt like he was heading back into the field.

Lou hangs up and looks over at Jessie, Jack, and Mikhail – "well, that was interesting."

"What?" Jessie asks.

"Your boss is on his way out here and he wants to meet with the three of us this afternoon." Lou turns to Mikhail, "can't tell you what to do Mikhail, your call if you want to sit in or not, I think you're probably okay, but I can't really protect you."

"Dad, I think you should call Tim and see if maybe he wants to come out also, let's get everyone we trust in one place."

"I don't know Jess, the Bureau and the Agency aren't known for playing well together, what do you think Jack?"

Jack shrugs, "this is pretty unchartered territory, I think we need all the help we can get. I prefer to meet here on our turf at least if they're all in the same room we might have a better chance of controlling the situation... maybe."

"Alright, I'll make the call," he says, picking up the phone and dialing. Tim Harrington picks up on the third ring, "Tim, Lou here, listen, just got a call from Deputy Director Vance Simpson over at Langley, he is headed out here says he wants to meet..."

"No shit, you're serious?"

"Yeah I'm serious, any chance you and Albert hopping a jet out here, sure would like you two here if possible, besides, if he can shed some light on who the hell sent this asshole maybe it will help us figure out whether there is something for you."

"Okay, makes sense I guess, I can do it, but I'll have to check with Albert not sure if he has anything that can't wait, give me about ten minutes I'll call you back."

"Sure, no problem, appreciate it. Oh listen, if you need transportation I can have a jet pick you up at National."

"Seriously? We are paying you way too much, but shouldn't be a problem, call you back."

"You and your jets Dad, geez," Jessie says with a laugh.

He is about to retort when the phone rings, "Lou McIntyre."

"Lou, it's Vance, we on?"

"Yes Director, give me a call when you land and we can figure the rest out then."

"Great thanks, see you this afternoon."

Lou hangs up and looks at the others, "Well, there we go, this should be interesting."

"You don't think we should have told him about the others Dad?"

"Better to ask for forgiveness than permission in this case," Lou responds.

"Well, what's for lunch then?" Jack asks, "I'm thinking it's not too early for a Pig Pile..."

"Let's order in okay? I want to review the data we have on David Eisen before everyone shows up this afternoon."

"Tell you what Dad, Mikhail and I will run out and pick up lunch then you can brief us all while we eat."

Lou nods, "okay, sounds good," he turns to Jack, "you can help me sort through this while they're gone." With everyone's order in her phone Jessie and Mikhail head out. Lou turns to Jack after they leave, "what do you think that's about?"

"I think it's about lunch, lighten up, Jess can take care of herself."

"I wasn't worried about her..."

"Uhh right."

"You're no help at all old man, you know that?" Lou laughs.

It's just past eleven in DC when Anthony Moyer slips out of the office cancelling his afternoon appointments, he blames a sinus headache and allergies, but the truth is this disaster of a Monday has him on the verge of an anxiety attack and he is having trouble catching his breath, maybe a couple of drinks on the back porch will take the edge off he thinks driving out of the city, it won't.

The Meeting

Tim Harrington and Alberto Jimenez were able to catch one the FBI jets out of National to Boulder, the direct flight and proximity of the airports gave them a couple of hours lead on Director Simpson. Lou had their security passes ready and waiting when they arrived at Paradigm and they were shown up to his office where the "Paradigm Team" as they were now calling themselves had been reviewing the data they had on Azrael.

Lou handles the introductions, "let me introduce you fellows to Mikhail Kirilov, a business associate of ours in from Kiev..." he turns to Mikhail, "this is Special Agent Tim Harrington from the DC field office, and US Deputy Attorney General Alberto Jimenez," the men all shake hands.

Tim turns to Lou, "business associate?" Lou just nods with a grin. He turns back to Mikhail, "Mr. Kirilov, I don't suppose you know anything about an anonymous data dump my office received last year, the name Sokolov ring any bells with you?" Tim asks a bit forcefully.

Mikhail just nods, "you're welcome, hope it helped."

Albert lets out a loud laugh, "well, there ya go Tim," he says, slapping the other man on the back, "what you want to do with that?" He turns to Mikhail, "sir, I don't know why you're here, but turning all that data over might have bought you a little credit but don't push it." He looks around, "got anything to eat here Lou, the FBI doesn't know how to treat its guests..."

Lou laughs, "I'll have some sandwiches sent up, we've got a first-class cafeteria here, drinks are in the fridge over there," he says, pointing as he picks up the phone and orders a sandwich platter and chips.

"Thanks, I appreciate it, beautiful place by the way."

They move to the conference table where they exchange news, Tim has been working his way through the data Mikhail had sent him, he grudgingly admits it's been extremely helpful. The FBI has managed to recover a number of missing teenagers and unfortunately in other cases given families closure where their children had been killed or died. It's a difficult task and the stories are filled with unspeakable horrors, but every rescue makes it all worthwhile, Tim explains solemnly. He turns to Mikhail, "you know there are still a lot of details I bet you could help clear up for us?"

Mikhail just nods, "I don't think there is very much more I can do for you," he says softly, holding the other man's eye.

"Would a grant of immunity from the US Attorney General's office change that?" Albert interjects.

Mikhail doesn't answer right away, "it's something we can discuss after this business is complete," he answers.

The sandwiches show up and Albert helps himself to a piled high roast beef and then adds a ham and swiss on rye, Tim takes the egg salad on sourdough. "That all you having Tim?" Albert asks.

"Just keep an eye on Jack, we've got him on a diet," Lou says.

"Shut up Lou, I'm in perfect shape!"

"Perfect for lying on my couch..."

"Sorry guys they're like an old married couple," Jessie says.

They are just finishing up when Lou's intercom buzzes, Deputy Director Simpson has arrived. "I'll go get him," Jessie offers. Jessie brings him up to the office and introduces him to everyone. Simpson is a tall angular man with greying hair and a runner's physique.

Introductions completed Simpson eyes the remaining sandwiches, "mind if I have one?" he asks, "just had a protein bar and some coffee on the way out this morning, didn't think I would be halfway across the country by lunch time."

"Help yourself, drinks are in the fridge," Lou offers pointing.

They are seated around the conference table, as an awkward silence develops, Lou looks at Simpson, "Director..."

"Call me Vance, rather keep this informal if we can," he says.

"Okay Vance, of course you know Jessie and Jack, let me give you a brief background on everyone else," Lou offers.

"No need, I'm pretty familiar with everyone - DC is a pretty small town when it comes right down to it, nice work cleaning up that Sokolov mess Tim, and Albert, good to see you again," he looks directly at Mikhail, "I've got to say I'm a bit surprised to see Europe's top arms dealer here though."

"I can explain…" Lou starts to interject.

"No, it's okay Lou, the CIA is a very good client of mine, pleasure to meet you Director Simpson," Mikhail says extending his hand.

Albert lets out a soft laugh, "the balls on this guy, I love it."

"Touché, Mister Kirilov, touché," Vance says with a smile, "but I am still not sure I'm comfortable openly discussing some of this…" he falters. "There really is no good way to say this, but we are talking about highly confidential and I would say even matters of national security."

"Vance, I think we all understand the sensitivity of what we are dealing with here, why don't we start with what's already out, let Jessie and Mikhail give us an update on what they have and then you can decide how much to share if anything," Lou interjects.

Jessie gives a concise review of the events leading up to her meeting with Ismael on St. Eustatius including the cryptic text message she had received that prompted the meeting. She turns to Mikhail, "I think this might be a good time to fill them in on your dealings with Ismael and your uncle."

Mikhail takes a deep breath, "I know my business might seem, what is word, criminal to you, but I am only fulfilling a need your country and others can't, won't, or in many cases don't want to be seen doing. I am not human trafficker that Sokolov was, I do not sell people!" He pauses, "just want that to be clear." He tells them about his dealings with the Israelis, and Ismael in particular, how the man approached him many times about Azrael becoming more and more irrational with every meeting till he finally asked Mikhail to reach out to the CIA and Jessie in particular. "By the way he had your phone number so not sure how he got that but clearly your system is not as secure as you think it is."

"Go on Mikhail, tell them about your uncle..." Jack prompts him.

"Yes, yes, my uncle is... Major General Semonovich, he was the senior officer for the garrison assigned to Compound Nineteen." Mikhail explains that he had spoken to his uncle a few times about Azrael and VX17 mostly because he was concerned about his own exposure after Ismael's strange behavior. "I reached out to Jessie after the Ismael call hoping for more information." The explanation falls flat, but none of the men comment, "Jack and Jessie met me in Kiev and we had a conversation with my uncle. I could tell he was holding back, but he warned me of a top secret multi-national team code named ALPHA – he said they were somehow connected to Azrael."

"Wait a minute," Vance turns to Jessie, "you and Jack were in Kiev, and didn't tell me?"

"You said whatever means necessary sir..." Jessie says somewhat defiantly.

"Let the man finish his story..." Albert butts in, "go ahead Mikhail what is this ALPHA team?"

"My uncle didn't share very much, just that one of his senior officers was part of this group that was somehow involved with the VX17 and Azrael, my uncle was cryptic, but I could tell he was very concerned about it. I decided to go see him in Moscow, hoping he would share more with me in person." He pauses clearly upset and trying to compose himself, "I never got the chance though, I found him in his home, tortured and murdered... the bastards cut off his fingers!"

"Jesus Christ," Tim says, "why?"

Mikhail looks at him grimly, "I can only guess they knew he talked to me, or at least that he had learned about them, anyway I flew directly here hoping to help, it's personal now."

"Tell them about the name Mikhail," Jessie says gently.

"Yes, my uncle left a name on his computer, David Eisen, I think this is Azrael..."

"We ran it through NEO, pretty definite it's Azrael, and that's not the worst of it I'm afraid..." Lou says.

"We can't be talking about NEO like this..." Vance exclaims, "that's a highly classified system."

"It's Paradigm's system, Vance and we need to talk about what we found," Lou says pointedly.

"Fine, but I'm really not comfortable with this..."

"Is NEO the system you showed me last summer, Lou?" Tim asks.

"Sure is, but we've made some improvements since then."

"Look, before we talk about this David Eisen, can you walk me through what happened Sunday?" Albert asks, "I didn't really get the whole story."

"Let me ask you a question first Albert," Lou looks over at Mikhail, "does the US prosecute foreign nationals that break the law in this country?" The question is a giveaway, and Lou already knows the answer, but wants Mikhail to hear it from Albert directly.

"Honest answer is we don't, ICE can detain someone for up to three months or so depending on the severity and then deport them, but their home country would have to choose to prosecute. Hell, we could try to extradite them back here to face trial, but that's rare and most countries aren't inclined to send their citizens back where we still have the death penalty... so simple answer is not much." Albert gives Mikhail a look, "why, what did you do?"

Jessie answers for him, "he saved our lives…"

Mikhail breaks in, "I couldn't sleep, it was probably five in the morning, still dark but just starting to lighten up, I was in the kitchen making a coffee in this Keurig machine, amazing machine! Anyway, I was waiting while it heated the water, looking out the kitchen window…" He tells them how he retrieved his pistols and was just coming back into the kitchen when the man breached the back door. "I think we must have fired almost at the same time, but he had a rifle and I had surprise, no contest," Mikhail says matter-of-factly.

"Jesus Christ this guy fits in perfectly with the rest of you!" Harrington exclaims. "Anyway, the Denver office identified the body this morning, Jason Sanderson, retired Navy SEAL, currently working as a Senior Section Chief at NSA. Agents tracked down an abandoned van about three miles from your house Lou, looks like he stayed in a motel outside of Boulder Friday and Saturday night. If I had to guess I would say he is part of this ALPHA group you've been talking about."

Vance shifts in his chair uncomfortably as everyone looks his way, "What?" he says, "Oh fine, fine, I'm sure you're right Tim, Moyer – the DNI…"

"The what?" Mikhail asks?

"Director National Intelligence, the top guy in US Intelligence answers directly to our President, asked me to pull Jessie off the Azrael case, and ordered me to stand down on anything to do with Azrael." He looks around, "I'm telling you that just doesn't happen, no way he gets involved on individual assignments or bypasses protocol to tell CIA Ops to stand down, there has got to be something else going on. I don't know anything about this ALPHA thing, but it seems to fit, big question is what the hell are they doing and what can we do about it?"

ALPHA

ALPHA Control didn't wait for the regularly scheduled update, the fact that the US bureaucrat Moyer had bypassed communications protocols and contacted him directly was worrisome, but his attempt to take them offline and black flag the op was even more concerning. Top that off with their US team member missing – and there was plenty to be wary of. Theirs wouldn't be the first black ops group to suddenly disappear at the whim of some politician with cold feet, and what the hell had happened to Four? All he was supposed to do was eliminate one low level CIA operative.

The team was going to expect an explanation, no one had ever missed a called meeting. They may be anonymous to each other, but that didn't mean they weren't a team. They had even developed camaraderie over the past couple of years. He had expected it to be the Brit but Five asked before the others – the Russian might be the brusquest of them all, but Control had wondered on more than one occasion if it wasn't a bit of a façade to throw the others off.

"Where is Four," the Russian asked?

Control had hesitated just a micro-second too long, a normal person might not have noticed but these were all highly trained intelligence officers and some half-baked story wasn't going to float, he would have to come clean or risk losing their trust. "Four has not checked in − at this point we may have to consider that he's been compromised or..." he doesn't finish everyone knows the alternative. He takes a deep breath, "I was contacted by one of our sponsors, they want to shut the operation down." He waits, wondering if anyone will speak up − they don't, "I advised them that this operation has moved beyond that point - the asset is in place. I think at this time though Five and Six, you should go offline, the rest of us will deploy to the field in support of the mission, any questions."

"Yes, I have question," Five breaks in, "I have information on the General's nephew a Mikhail Kirilov, black market arms dealer in Kiev, he was meeting with the Americans the day we interviewed the General, do we pursue him?"

Control hesitates, an interesting development but at this point there really wasn't any where to go with it, "no, we stay on course with the asset, the Americans and this Kirilov are too far behind the curve to pose a threat at this point." A mistake, but maybe one that could be forgiven considering the situation and that they still didn't know what had happened to Four. "One, I want you to keep an eye on his place in Tel Aviv. Two, you head north to Nahariya. Three, you and I will head to the Kingdom − remember our only concern is making sure nothing happens to him − he has to complete this mission. Once the VX17 has been released terminate Eisen with extreme prejudice. If we miss him in Jeddah it will be up to the rest of you, clear?"

Six clears his throat, "is there any chance at all he knows about this group? I'm not excited about the prospect of this lunatic showing up on my stoop one morning... we need a way to know you've taken care of the situation."

"Yes, have to know you succeeded," Five agrees.

Control pauses, "Okay, no way he knows about us, but if it makes you feel better, when it's complete – who ever does it, send a coded message to the others..." He hesitates, "send – *They have bowed and fallen but we have stood upright.*"

"What is that?" Six asks.

"It's part of Psalm 20 from King David, fitting, I think," Two replies.

"Yes, it's a song of victory," One adds.

"Sometimes I think we must all be crazy," Five murmurs, "I don't think your God will have anything to do with this..."

They wrap up shortly after, Control sends a message to the three Israelis setting up a face to face later in the day. They are all based in Jerusalem, and although they know each other they have kept the pretense of anonymity intact, the time for that has passed.

They meet in a small café, four friends after a long day of work sharing a laugh and a cigarette, casual and at ease with each other no different than a thousand others - no one gave them a second look they were invisible, but these four hold the fate of a million or more souls in their hands. Their laughter rises and falls in tune with the others and as the night deepens they make their plans, final decisions, sealing their commitment with a look, a nod, a melancholy smile.

Rina would take Tel Aviv, Neil to Nahariya to keep a graveside vigil, Daniel and Mitch would fly into Jeddah just two more of the millions heading that way in pilgrimage. It was unlikely these four would ever see each other again, success wasn't guaranteed and the odds of getting out of the Kingdom were slim. It didn't bother any of them, they had all signed on for this and the exchange of one or all of their lives in the service of their country and their God wasn't a cause for hesitation - they had always been ALPHA team's true warriors.

The irony of it all wasn't lost on Daniel, he had operated as ALPHA Control for more than three years overseeing their evolution from a team intent on destroying David – his brother – to the four remaining members ready to give their own lives to protect the man. This was a Biblical moment – "Old Testament style" – as the Brit had been fond of saying, and in a way, he was right - they were going to unleash a modern-day plague that would have done Moses proud. He would try to get Mitch out, but he had already reconciled himself to the fact that he wasn't going to survive – David was simply too good – it hadn't occurred to him that David had no intention of getting out. He kisses his boys as they sleep, before slipping into his own bed, he listens to the soft breathing next to him, God he was going to miss them he thinks, unable to turn his thoughts off.

Several hundred miles away David stares at the ceiling of his apartment as the air conditioner labors in vain to cool the small room, with less than a couple of weeks left, if he was going to make a final trip home it would have to be soon. The traffic had picked up substantially in the past days as many pilgrims had already started flooding into the Kingdom, he had taken to walking through the city in the early evening wondering what would become of the sea of faces he passed without really seeing them. He was on autopilot at this point, becoming numb to the horror he was going to create, he had honed his pain and loss to the point where they eclipsed any other feelings. *Soon, very soon* he whispered to the dark, *I'm coming home my sweet girls...*

Right & Wrong

David Eisen — decorated soldier, top Mossad agent, husband and father - the man had been the indisputable poster boy for Israeli success. It had all unraveled in a long night of rockets and mortars and when the morning light had dawned upon the death of his wife and daughter the foundation for Azrael had been laid. David wouldn't embrace the moniker Azrael for a number of years, but he was subconsciously assembling all the pieces and like all stable equations it would take an outside catalyst to start the chain reaction that would ultimately culminate in Azrael.

The group has relocated to the executive conference room of Paradigm where they are reviewing the timeline and major milestones in the evolution of Azrael — as the images flash across the displays the progression seems so obvious and simple. There is a sober silence in the room as Lou reviews the data driving the displays from his virtual keyboard, he senses the tension and pauses, looking around the room — Jessie, Jack and Mikhail are heads down at the far end of the table comparing notes while Tim, Albert, and Vance are pensively looking at the four high-resolution screens built into the wall.

"You know this guy was everything you'd want in an operative," Vance says mostly to himself.

"What do you mean?" Albert asks.

"Well, he has all the training you want, military background is a plus, could pass for any number of nationalities, and has a family."

"I would think having a family would be a liability..." Tim says.

"Definitely not, operatives with families are significantly more stable, it has something to do with being anchored — gives them a reason to come home."

"I disagree," they all look down the table at Jack, "it just gives you a reason to be too careful, to over think things, hard to be all in when you know you have people at home counting on you..." No one says anything it's difficult to argue with a man like Jack. "Not saying those other attributes aren't important, I got my start in the Marines for that matter, I just don't think the family part necessarily applies, but clearly for this guy losing his family broke something inside."

Vance nods, "I see your point Jack, and you've spent more time out there than any of us, what's your take on this man?" he asks, nodding toward the screens.

Jack leans back in his chair, a thoughtful look on his face, "he's lethal, I mean extremely... part of Mossad's Kidon unit if I had to guess, best training in the world, probably well financed considering his history of targets — no question he got paid well..." He leans forward, "I don't know though, probably half a dozen guys like this in the world." He doesn't say it, but everyone in the room knows that Jack is probably on that list himself.

He stands up moving around the table to stare at the screens, a candid picture of David and his family glow on the far right, Jack pauses in front of it.

"What is it Jack?" Lou asks softly.

Jack turns back with a grim smile, "I've studied people my whole life, always had a knack for knowing what motivates them, how to manipulate that if you will, you know what most people really want at the end of the day?" He looks around the room, "love, real simple they want to love someone and be loved by someone... most people think it's about money, sex, or power but deep down under all that, hidden away love is the one thing that trumps all... and you know what – someone took away the thing this man loved more than life itself... his family." He looks over at Jessie and then back to Lou, "If someone ever took you or Jessie from me, well, there isn't anywhere on this earth they could hide..." he says softly sitting back down. It's a stark admission from a man that works hard to seem impervious to emotions.

No one says anything, it's a sobering moment, "but to answer your question Director, this man has all the tools and motivation to achieve something truly catastrophic, what I can't figure out is who is he most angry with – us for brokering the peace, his country for accepting it, or the whole of Islam for killing his wife and daughter, or maybe it's all of the above..." Jack looks back up at the screens, "my guess is whatever this is he doesn't expect to or maybe even want to walk away from it... and that makes him even more dangerous, a man who accepts death as his fate doesn't have any real boundaries."

"Let's not forget this ALPHA group either," Vance chips in.

"Right I think it's a good bet whatever he has planned is either supported or maybe even being orchestrated by this group, anybody think they are actually working together?" Lou asks.

Tim shakes his head, "one of the things the Bureau is really good at is profiling folks, I don't think this fella is interested in working with anyone, this is a personal mission, not a cause. Mikhail you mentioned this fella Ismael a couple of times, seems like he probably knew this David, may even have known he was Azrael... and for that he ended up dead, no way this guy is looking for partners."

"I agree Tim, when nations orchestrate these types of ops it's almost always a matter of putting assets in place or creating conditions that push events in a certain direction, normally we don't work with uncontrollable outside resources, just too messy honestly," Vance adds.

"Jesus..." Jessie says a touch too loudly. The men all look her way, "sorry I'm still getting used to the backroom aspects of this, too many years on the tip of the spear I guess," she says with a sheepish grin.

"No, you're right," surprisingly, it's Mikhail that speaks up.

Vance leans back in his chair with a sigh, "sad but true, it's too easy to pretend we aren't talking about actual people, to convince ourselves the needs of the nation outweigh the needs of the individual..."

"Fucking opposite of what our founding fathers intended," Albert adds in his immutable way. "Built a model with checks and balances, purposely constructed to constrain the power of the government and yet here we are not only exerting our will on our own citizens but everywhere else in the world as well..." He takes a deep breath, "and you know what - I'm not sure if we are right or wrong, did we create this need or are we really defending those democratic ideals we claim to hold so dear..."

Lou claps him on the shoulder as he walks to the end of the table, "I don't think there is a singular answer to that Albert, it's not as simple as right and wrong, good and evil if you will..."

"You're wrong dad," Jessie says softly, "politics, government, religion, none of it matters at the end of the day its simply about doing the right thing, following that moral code that runs through everything – there is a right and a wrong, and we all know it." She points to the screens, "what happened to this man's family was wrong, but what he is doing, or will do, that's wrong as well, we can rationalize it as justice, vengeance, or whatever this ALPHA group thinks benefits our countries, but it's still wrong. Sometimes doing what's right has a cost, it doesn't advance your own agenda, but that doesn't mean you don't do it... so we need to figure out what he is planning and we have to stop it... someone needs to stand in the breach and this time it's us."

"We don't live in a world of moral absolutes Jess..." her dad says quietly.

"No, we don't Dad," she says defiantly, "but right now, right here we can decide what we stand for and I don't know about the rest of you, but just because the rest of the world has grown comfortable equivocating about what's right doesn't mean I have to!"

"I don't think that's what we're saying Jessie," Vance interjects.

"Yes, it is... she's right and we all know it," Albert says, shaking his head, "like it or not I can't walk out of here knowing what I do and convince myself it is what it is..." Jessie smiles at him, appreciating the moral support.

The message icon is flashing on Lou's display, he clicks on it while the others continue talking, "son of a bitch..." he exclaims.

"What is it Lou," Jack asks.

"Well, part of what we do with the new NEO algorithms is take all the data points gathered in the initial run and feed them back through, a second iteration if you will... allows the matching programs to build exponentially on the last set of data."

"And what the hell does that mean?" Albert asks.

"It just means we have a lot more data to use... but look at this," Lou moves the cursor around and punches up another image, a pic of an ID badge with a crimson BPF pops up on the center screen.

"Is that this David? Looks like him." Mikhail asks.

"Yes, that's a British Pump and Filtration badge," Lou answers.

"I'm still not following this?" Albert quips.

"Hold on Albert, just a sec and this will all make sense..." Lou moves the cursor rapidly around clicking on documents and finally bringing up a corporate profile and press clipping on BPF. "Alright, look at this. BPF is an international supplier of large scale water pumping and filtration products," he points to the profile with a laser pointer, then switches to the press release, "these guys have been retrofitting the wells and pumps in Mecca in preparation for this year's pilgrimage, what's it called Jack?"

"The Hajj, fuck me there'll be two plus million Muslims in one place, got to be coming up too."

"Less than two weeks from now actually," Vance says, "we've just authorized about half a dozen operatives hoping to pick up a few of this new Jihadi group... you don't think?" He looks around the table not happy about the grim nods the others give him.

"Has to be... too many red flags, too perfect to pass up..." Lou says.

Jessie breaks the silence, "Now what?"

Politics & Politicians

Anthony Moyer was on his sixth scotch and water sitting on the deck overlooking his back yard as Monday slipped away, each drink with progressively less water, he had waved off dinner two hours earlier settling for some cheese and crackers which sat mostly untouched on the plate next to him. The ability to think clearly had started to fade with the fourth drink and he found himself stinking of scotch and wallowing in self-pity – the bombastic patriotic demeanor exhibited on the Sunday news shows was nowhere to be found. He considered ending it all, but courage was pretty far down his list of personality traits, never mind not having anything but his father's service revolver and his old hunting shotgun in the house and in his alcohol induced haze he wasn't even sure if he had any shells. Left with the only thing he was truly good at – deflection and politics – he takes another long sip and begins to wonder whose fault he could make this debacle. The answer is easy he smiles not sure why he hadn't thought of it earlier - CIA Ops and the oh so famous Jessie McIntyre and why not she was already a bit of a loose cannon and the CIA was always an easy target. He wanders off to the guest room to sleep the dreamless slumber of the morally bankrupt.

A scalding hot shower, two cups of a bold Columbian coffee he has personally roasted in a specialty shop on one of the side streets in Georgetown and four Tylenol later Moyer is headed into the office. Most of the previous night's remonstrations have faded, but not whose fault this mess is. First order of business was to find Jason Sanderson, he knew the identity of ALPHA Four - no way he was going to let the U.S. ALPHA team member remain anonymous, but now he needed information and who better than an actual ALPHA team member - NSA had to have located him by now.

He settles in behind his desk with the third cup of the day, "Laura, Laura…"

"Yes sir," she says sticking her head around the door jamb into his office.

"I need to see a Jason Sanderson as soon as possible, he is a Middle East Section Chief over at NSA, track him down and see how soon he can be down here."

"You want to personally see him here sir?"

"Yes, isn't that what I said?" he says dismissively.

"Yes sir," she says retreating.

Now how to make this Simpson's and by extension the McIntyre girl's problem, he thinks leaning back in his chair. He doesn't get very far solving that puzzle before his phone starts to buzz, "Moyer," he says picking up the handset.

"Sir this Deputy Director Terrence Peters at NSA, your office called looking for Jason Sanderson?"

"And..." Moyer asks, slightly irritated, *why couldn't anyone just do as he asked?*

"Sir, Sanderson has not been in since last Friday and didn't notify us that he would be out, we ran a basic trace on him this morning..."

"Well, what did you find?" Moyer asks his irritation growing.

"It's strange sir, only thing that flagged was a fingerprint inquiry from the FBI field office in Denver, otherwise nothing, I've dispatched two officers to his home, but since your office had called I wanted to get back to you as quickly as possible, is there anything I can assist with?"

"Uh, no, nothing - he was working on some things for me, keep me up to date," he answers awkwardly before hanging up. *What a fucking mess, Jesus wasn't the McIntyre girl in Colorado?*

"Laura! Get me Vance Simpson on the phone!" he yells from the office.

Laura Dalrymple has been an executive assistant in DC longer than most politicians have been in office, and has no trouble recognizing when her boss is losing his shit – her favorite expression - this was going to be a long day. "Sir they say he isn't in the office, and isn't expected back today..."

"Are you fucking kidding..." he says, mostly to himself, "where is he, I need to talk to him now!"

"Sir, they have him logged out as of yesterday afternoon, flew out of Andrews to Colorado Springs on an Air Force transport, what do you want me to tell them sir?" She asks.

"Get me a phone number where he can be reached, this is ridiculous!" he thunders.

Laura brings in a sticky note with a phone number a few seconds later, "this is his cell phone number sir, do you want me to try to reach him for you?"

"No, no I'll take care of it, sorry for the yelling, it's been a morning," he says morosely. Laura doesn't answer, just nods and heads back out to her desk, she knows he doesn't really need or want an answer and he isn't sorry either.

He starts to dial the number before setting the phone back in its cradle, *FUCK!* – Vance Simpson was a professional, had spent years in the field himself, he was going to have to think about this a call now might tip him off – he was pretty sure the man wasn't buying his story from the other day. Why else would he be in Colorado other than to meet with the McIntyre girl, and what the hell had Sanderson been doing out there? Too many questions with no answers, what he really needs to know was why the FBI had run Sanderson's finger prints – the last thing he needed was those fucking Boy Scouts at the FBI sniffing around.

The DNI looks out his office window, he hadn't reached this position by panicking, he was a skilled negotiator and had played the DC political game for a very long time, it was his ability to work with people that had led the President to nominate him for this job in the first place. He takes a deep breath, time to slow this down – there was no controlling ALPHA anymore and this lunatic Azrael was going to do whatever he wanted anyway, he realizes in a moment of clarity, so why not sit back and let it happen? He needed to make sure Sanderson was out of the picture, but the man was a Navy SEAL and a patriot, no way he was going to talk to anyone – so that left Simpson and McIntyre and he was pretty sure they didn't really know what was going on. Still... Vance Simpson wasn't just going to drop it - Moyer needed to develop a narrative that made enough sense to sideline the CIA man for a couple of weeks.

Once Azrael unleashed mass murder in Mecca the Middle East was going to go up in flames and no one was going to be looking in his direction. Sure, they were going to take some hits for not having seen it coming, but who could predict the actions of a mad man after all? He would do all the requisite interviews, striking a balance of remorse and horror, but still reminding the viewing public that once again this administration had protected them – after all as terrible as it was it hadn't happened here. Even if they needed to expose Azrael as ex-Mossad – hadn't this holy war been going on for thousands of years – this was just another chapter. Now all he needed was a bit of a goose-chase to keep Simpson and McIntyre out of the way – this was going to work.

Pulling up the synopsis from Monday's security briefing he begins to page through looking for something that he can use. *Ahh, there it is* – NSA had picked up some low-level chatter indicating London was a potential summer target for terrorist activity. Not a real stretch since most of the major European metropolitan centers were permanently on this list. It didn't matter though it would be enough combined with the information ALPHA had developed on Azrael early on – before they had gone dark – there was no way to know if it was still accurate – but did it really matter? Moyer didn't think so... as he dials the number Laura had given him, he leans back in the oversized leather chair slowly spinning from left to right and back again as the phone cord stretches.

It was just before eight AM in Boulder, the Paradigm team as they were now calling themselves had been up late and were meeting for breakfast at the Parkway Café a place both Jack and Jessie had been raving about the night before, the two of them seemed to be in a serious eating contest most of the time... Vance was pretty sure Albert was going to give them a run for their money though. He takes a tentative sip of his coffee, hoping not to burn his lips when his phone starts ringing.

"Vance, glad I caught you, been thinking about your offer on McIntyre, I think I can use her after all."

Simpson holds his hand up to silence the others, "good morning sir, catching a quick bite to eat want me to dial you back when I am in a more secure area?"

"Not a problem, we've developed some intel placing Azrael in Israel with London as his next target – call me later today and I'll brief you in..."

"Ok sir, will do," Simpson hangs the phone up shaking his head.

"What?" Jessie asks before the others can.

Simpson looks around, "this really needs to wait for a better place to talk, too many ears here, but short version..." he hesitates a moment, "well the DNI wants to send you after Azrael... in London," he says to Jessie.

"London?" Jack asks.

"Yeah, London – it's got to be a diversion – no way London is a target. Lou, can we can we impose on you again?"

"No imposition... we need to decide what's next."

They spend the next forty-five minutes finishing up breakfast and making small talk, but no-one has much of an appetite, except Albert, who inhales his huevos rancheros and tacks on a short stack of pancakes slathered in butter and syrup.

In DC, Moyer dials a number not listed on any of the published contact lists, "Who do we have in London, we have a rogue asset that we need handled."

"Sir I have multiple options, I recommend…"

"I don't need to know, I'll transmit the dossier you handle the rest."

"Yes sir, time frame?"

"The asset isn't in country yet, sometime in the next three to five days," and just that easily Jessie was a target again.

The US had sworn off assassination decades earlier, now it was just framed as targeted elimination and mostly handled with drones or smart bombs, but the inclusion of American nationals was a new development the last administration had justified internally – claiming it was necessary to fight the growing domestic terror threat with a very loosely defined set of rules.

Et tu, Brute?

Simpson was arguing forcibly with Lou, Tim and Albert, "I can't just ignore Moyer, this is a Cabinet member we are talking about, he answers directly to the President for God's sake!"

"I don't care if answers to Christ himself, my girl isn't going to London, these fuckers have already tried to take her out once, now you want to serve her up on a platter, are you out of your fucking mind?" Lou exclaims rising from his seat.

"Look Lou, no one is suggesting we serve Jessie up..." Tim says trying to calm him down.

"Yeah, whatever, not the first time I've heard that," Lou snarls, as he walks over to the windows and gathers himself together, "hey, hey sorry Tim, you know how I am, that's my kid we're talking about." Tim doesn't respond, it wasn't that long ago he had used Jessie to draw out Sokolov.

"Dad, I'm not a kid and don't worry, I'm not going to London, that isn't where Azrael is, and it isn't where he is targeting either so there isn't any issue here," Jessie says calmly. She turns to Simpson, "sir, I know you are caught in the middle here, tell Moyer whatever you need to, I'll take the consequences for not doing what you instructed, what's the worst they can do?" she says with a smile.

"It's no laughing matter Jessie," Simpson says seriously.

"I know sir, but I'm not going to London… so call it insubordination or whatever you have to."

She turns to Albert and Tim, "we know this is a setup, and we know there was an attempt on me and my father that probably came from this ALPHA group or maybe even higher, can't we do anything about that?"

Tim looks at Albert before answering, "what do you mean Jessie?"

"I mean it can't be legal to put a hit out on a civilian like my dad or probably even me for that matter, so isn't that something the FBI would investigate?"

Albert breaks in before Tim can answer, "it's not quite like that Jessie, it's as much political as it is criminal. We don't know how far up the chain this goes and that makes it potentially very political. Normally investigating something like this has to come out of the Senate Intelligence Committee or even from the Attorney General himself and would involve appointing a Special Counsel to undertake the investigation. Hell, it could take months to even get off the ground."

"So, there's nothing we can do?" she asks.

"What about just investigating it as a home invasion and attempted murder?" Jack asks, "maybe if we make enough noise we can force someone's hand on this…"

"Well, we would have to have some rational for the Bureau's involvement," Tim answers pressing his hands together.

"Actually, Lou you are a high-level contractor with us, why don't we leave Jessie out of it for now and say we are investigating based on sensitivity of the victim," he pauses, "that will fly all day, have to explain my involvement, but I can say you called me, which you did... yeah this could work."

"As soon as you make the NSA connection I'll approach the Attorney General and see if he will get Justice involved," Albert offers.

"I like it, keeps Jessie and the Agency out of it, you okay with this Lou? Puts you front and center..." Simpson asks.

"Well I guess so, but doesn't really address this ALPHA issue or the fact that Moyer is neck deep in this mess does it?"

Albert shakes his head, "No it doesn't, but once we have a Special Counsel in place we can start feeding them everything we have, hard part is creating enough noise to force Justice to act, after that it's pretty much Pandora's box – don't you remember how crazy Mueller got a few of administrations ago?"

"Who doesn't, Jesus, what a fucking mess that was," Jack laughs, "what was it, six years?"

"Seven, thirty-three indictments, two convictions, and who really knows how many millions of dollars..." Albert answers, "pain in the fucking ass is what it was."

"How quickly can we get this underway?" Lou asks.

Tim drains his coffee, "well we have the body, we have an ID, your statement and a ton of evidence – enough to start an investigation. I can assign a couple of agents from DC to work with the two in Denver you met already. From there we can start ringing some bells at NSA, see what that kicks up. They aren't going to tell us anything, but we can make enough noise to draw some attention," he turns to Jessie, "that should give you some time to disappear and go after Azrael. After that I don't know, this will probably get kicked up the line pretty quick, that's where you come in Albert – you gotta be ready to whisper in some ears."

"Don't worry, I'm a professional whisperer," Albert says with a smile. "Mikhail, you need to be long gone when this all starts to hit the fan, ok?" he says looking down the table.

Mikhail nods in response, "I'll leave today, not to worry."

"How are we going to handle this at the Agency?" Jack asks looking at Simpson.

"I think you two need to accompany me back to DC, we'll outfit you like you're heading to London, identifications, cash, plane tickets - the whole works then you need to disappear – Moyer probably has someone waiting for you on the ground there and no doubt he has eyes and ears inside Langley so we have to at least make it look like you are headed that way," Simpson answers. He turns to Lou, "I don't want to know how, but can you make it look like they are on a commercial flight, checked in, TSA the whole thing?"

"I'll take care of it," Lou says with a nod, "you just get me the names, passport numbers and flight info."

"You don't want to know how many laws that breaks," Tim laughs.

"No, we don't!" Lou says with a grin, "consider it a security test, cause that's what I'm going to say if anyone ever asks." He turns to Jessie and Jack, "After DC I'll have Mark fly you wherever you think you need to start, but based on what we have so far we need to find David Eisen as soon as possible and that means either Jeddah or Israel, anybody disagree?"

"Maybe we should split up, I can take Jeddah and Jessie you take Israel," Jack offers. He can see she is about to protest, "look before you say anything Jess, it's simply a cultural thing, harder for a woman to move around in the Kingdom..."

Jessie just nods, she knows she isn't going to win this argument and it's not that Jack is wrong, but even the inference that there is something she can't do as a woman irritates her. "I get it," turning to her dad, "going to need new phones, probably want to give everyone here one too."

Lou nods, pressing the intercom on his desk and making the arrangements. "Takes about twenty minutes to set one up with our new encryption, they'll be preloaded with everyone's number and are tasked to our satellite test channels. They piggy back on the military's LEO satellites so you should have coverage anywhere."

"What the hell is a LEO satellite," Albert asks.

Lou smiles, "low earth orbit, without getting too technical, these are satellites that orbit at a lower altitude than normal telecom satellites and provide greater coverage and speed, but they're expensive so the commercial carriers don't usually use them - but no question it's a better option."

"Uh ok, sorry I asked," Albert laughs.

The phones show up shortly after and everyone gets a quick tutorial from Lou. "Ok, real simple, these babies are just like any other normal phone with a few exceptions – first they have our latest encryption so should be completely secure, especially when talking to each other – second we have loaded the Azrael hi-lites from NEO on here." He shows them how to access the data and use the basic functions, "most important though if you press the star key and then six, six, six the phone will wipe all data, history, everything, obviously you only want to do this in an emergency. We can also do it from here if you somehow manage to lose it, but don't, any questions?" There wasn't.

Vance joins Tim and Albert taking them up on their offer to share the jet back to DC. Jack and Mikhail camp out in the conference room discussing lunch options as Lou and Jessie retreat to his office.

"Listen Jess, I know you have to do this..." he struggles for the right words, "this isn't like last summer – this is guy is a pro not some street thug – just be careful ok..."

"I know," she doesn't bother to tell him not to worry, he will, and she knows better than to patronize him. "Dad, we didn't really talk about ALPHA again, what do you think their involvement is?"

"Well, it's like Vance was saying, probably orchestrating circumstances to fit their agenda..." he trails off – saying it out loud it doesn't seem right.

"Dad, that's bullshit, these guys sent someone to our house! They're not standing on the sidelines."

"I don't know Jess; the whole thing is just crazy honestly... I mean what motivates someone to kill millions of people?"

"I don't know dad, I can't wrap my head around it, but listen, can you keep working on ALPHA and the Israeli connection? If I can crack that, maybe, just maybe, it's a way to get to Azrael – I'm worried if we don't get to him before this Hajj thing it will be too late."

Lou wraps her up in a hug, "I will honey, you guys need to get going, bigger head start you have the better, and I still have to figure out how to make you magically appear on a flight to London."

"Ok dad, I still can't believe our own country would target us..." she says quietly, "Et tu Brute, et tu..."

Count Down

There are three bottles of water, a jar of green olives, two eggs, and a container of hummus in David's refrigerator. The old unit barely cools enough to keep the food from spoiling, not that it mattered, he had no intention of eating any of it. The only thing of any real importance was the vacuum sealed tube of VX17 buried deep in the hummus. He had been surprised at how small it was the first time he had held it, clear tempered glass in a removable thin metal wrapper it was only about three inches long and the circumference of a shotgun shell.

There were some nights he would gingerly extract the vial, rinsing it in the sink careful not to drop it, the danger was psychological the hardened glass was made to withstand a small blast – dropping it in the sink wasn't really an issue. There was a morbid fascination with holding the fate of millions in your hand, he had expected something more menacing, but the pink liquid reminded him of the Shirley Temples his daughter used to love so much.

The instructions had been simple, almost too easy… release the liquid in an aerosol spray or directly into a water source, the live virus would take care of the rest, and of course don't expose yourself and end up patient zero. He had smiled at that, the great Azrael... a victim of his own carelessness, the irony would be too great to bear.

The concentrations were so potent that even with the massive flow being pumped from the well there would be millions of virus cells per cubic meter of water. The Saudis had installed a sophisticated system of filters and ultra-violet irradiation units to combat bacteria twenty years early and BPF had upgraded the carbon cartridge filtration systems just that year, but none of these were capable of filtering or eradicating a virus – a viral contamination was something that simply wouldn't happen under normal circumstances.

Never-the-less David had planned on releasing the VX17 in the last set of filters before the pumps carried the water to the public fountains and filling stations. He figured he would have somewhere in the neighborhood of six hours to make his way out of Mecca and into Jeddah before the first cases started to display systems. The virus was deadly, rapid, and easily transmitted once contracted, the spread was going to simply overwhelm those consuming the water and the secondary impacts in Jeddah would be widespread in less than forty-eight hours.

Sitting at the rickety card table staring at the pink liquid slowly flowing from side to side as he tips the vial left to right, he thinks about how or whether to leave the city. He had no conscious wish to die, but he was tired, oh so tired, and what future could there really be after this horror. Vengeance for its own sake wasn't going to bring his girls back, the realization doesn't dissuade him – he had reconciled himself to this fact a long time ago. He sighs, replacing the vial in the hummus and sealing the container. It didn't really matter, he would have his revenge. Whatever happened after he would leave in God's hands, as if God had anything to do with any of it. The tribes of Israel and the nations of Islam had been justifying their behavior with "God" for all of recorded history, it was no more rational now than it had been at the beginning.

He washes his hands in the sink, letting the tepid water run through his fingers. Water, the sustainer of life, the life blood of the earth would be the sword of Azrael's wrath. That was the real irony he thought – God had sent an angel – Gabriel the scriptures said to save Ishmael, Abraham's son bringing forth the life sustaining water and now he, David, son of Benjamin, a descendent of Isaac – the Angel of Death - was going to use it to kill millions of his cousins.

He gently shuts the faucet off not bothering to dry his hands on the perfectly folded dish towel sitting on the counter. He lies down on the lumpy mattress, hoping for a few hours sleep before the sun resumes its relentless march across the sky, but as the dawn approaches he finally drifts off, tossing and turning, fitfully tormented by dreams he can't escape and won't remember.

Daniel and Mitch had landed in Jeddah late in the evening, their flight out of Mumbai India had been delayed, not unusual for those flying out of Shivaji International, their passports identified them as Saudi nationals. Mossad had been creating identities in the Kingdom for years and kept a number of safe houses in both Jeddah and Riyadh. If anyone had bothered to check the men were posing as buyers for a string of electronics stores and were in Mumbai to meet with their tech support call center. The flight had been mostly businessmen returning home and neither man had garnered a second look.

The safe house was an apartment strikingly similar to David's and only about half a dozen blocks away, there were four million people living in the city and another million or more descending for the Hajj — although he wondered if the Russian's casualty estimates might be on the low side. Daniel wasn't worried about accidentally running into David, he and Mitch had grown their beards out and would be wearing the traditional robes of Arab men making it unlikely even a chance sighting would expose them.

They were running a bigger risk than he was willing to admit, until the VX17 was disbursed his only directive was to keep David alive — which meant he couldn't defend himself. It was a difficult thing protecting a man you knew would kill you if he was able — it didn't help that just a few days later you would be hunting him, at this point if he was honest his only motivation was to try to stay alive long enough to get home to his boys. Mitch taps him on the shoulder whispering, "let's go, there he is," he says nodding up the street.

The men pull out following half dozen car lengths back, there is no need to worry about losing Azrael, his routine is set in stone and he hasn't deviated from it in weeks. Mitch had asked why he didn't vary things to avoid being noticed, Daniel had laughed, "it's a technique they teach at the American CIA – they call it hiding in plain sight, show people what they expect to see and nobody will ask any questions."

Mitch shakes his head, "seems risky to me..."

Daniel gives him a sideways look, "it is risky, you have to become the person, every detail, every action – the stress is incredible."

"You've done it?" Mitch asks.

"No, not really – never spent very long in the field honestly," Daniel answers.

Mitch is silent while they drive through the crowded streets the heat already permeating the thin metal of the car, the air conditioning barely keeping up, "what happened to him?" he asks quietly, "we all looked up to David, he was bigger than life..."

Daniel smiles, he knows what Mitch means, the younger Mossad agents had come up watching David take the most dangerous missions, the most difficult kills, things other people simply couldn't or wouldn't do. "I don't know, something died inside him I guess, I considered him my brother though..." he trails off.

Neither has noticed that they are now within just a few car lengths of David and he has been watching them in his mirrors, realizing too late Daniel slows down, letting a number of cars pass them by, he wonders if this is the mistake that will cost him his life. "Enough talk now, pay attention, the turn off to the highway is coming up..."

Azrael whispers to himself, "what took you so long... Daniel my brother, I knew it would be you..."

London

Jack and Jessie landed in DC early in the evening, after checking into the DoubleTree they wandered over to Rasika's on D Street, the aroma of Indian food greeting them on the sidewalk made Jessie's mouth water. She had the Kadai Gosht, a lamb dish cooked in a spicy tomato sauce seasoned with coriander, Jack stuck with his tried and true Tandoori chicken; they shared an apple beignet with two scoops of cardamom ice cream for dessert. The conversation had mostly covered what they knew about Azrael and possible scenarios explaining ALPHA, sipping on her sweetened espresso Jessie leans in, "how the hell are we going to handle this London situation? If we don't show it definitely tips our hand, doesn't it?"

Jack purses his lips, "yeah, I can see what you're saying, but a decent sniper can take you down as you walk out of Heathrow, that's not going to go over well with your father," he says with a smile.

"We need the director to pop some smoke for us," she says, reverting back to her Ranger days, "let him tell Moyer I am going end of the week alone…" she takes another sip, "think you can find whoever it is that's supposed to take me out?"

It was too matter-of-fact for Jack, "Jesus Jessie, what if I don't? Never mind that we might be talking about one of our own..." He sucks in his breath not waiting for an answer. "Fuck me... I guess I could leave tomorrow, should give me a couple of days – not much time Jess, we are going to need a plan B if I can't get it done."

"Come on Jack, you know there isn't a plan B, I'll have to take my chances, we're down to days on this – go big or go home at this point."

"Yeah well, I'd rather not go home in a box if I can avoid it. Come on, let's head back," he says, picking up the check, "I need to make some calls tonight – time to wake some people on the other side of the pond up," his British accent perfect.

Jessie smiles at him, "amazing."

They part ways in the lobby, upstairs Jessie slides out of her clothes, rolling them up and putting them back in her suitcase, it was a trick her dad had taught her, they were more compact and didn't get as wrinkled. She dons a pair of sweats and a T-shirt, and dials her dad on the SAT phone, "hey dad, just finished up dinner at Rasika's anything new there?"

"Lucky you, let me guess Jack get the Tandoori chicken?"

"Of course, turn anything else up on Azrael or ALPHA?"

"Not really Jess, just full background on Eisen from the Mossad files – it's uploaded to your phone, but I think we already know where this is all going..."

"Yeah, I guess, so how do you think he's going to do it?"

"Well, got to be an aerosol or water source – which actually probably makes the most sense with the BPF job, gives him access to everything." He pauses, "problem is when and where, even if we knew, how do we get to him – no way we can line up that kind of security access this quickly."

"We could tip off the Saudis," Jessie says softly.

"I thought about that too," Lou answers, "but we don't know what game ALPHA is playing and who knows what kind of assets they have in play – two big problems one it implicates our government – and two he is an Israeli - we're finally making some progress in the Middle East hate to see it all undone if we can avoid it."

"I'm worried dad..."

"I know Jess, I'm pretty scared too..."

"No dad, I'm not scared, I'm worried - worried I won't figure it out, won't find a way to stop him..."

"Jess, honey we will figure it out, we have to..."

"Love ya dad..."

"Love you too honey," he answers as she hangs up.

Jessie tosses and turns unable to sleep; the six o'clock wake-up call ends her struggle as she makes her way down to the gym and then a quick shower. She doesn't notice the blinking message indicator on her phone. She hits the lobby by half past seven finally seeing the waiting message, punching up the vmail she listens.

"Jessie, I'm catching the eight AM to London, going to get started on what we talked about, try to give me till Friday if you can, catch up later... I'll be staying at the Kensington Arms, I'll text you the room number, cheerio!" The message is short and to the point and Jack had used his best British accent. *Damn*, she thinks, *how am I going to explain this to the Director?*

The valet brings the car around, she tips him five bucks and heads out to Langley thinking about how to spin this in a way that would make sense.

Jack slung the backpack over his right shoulder carrying the compact umbrella in his left hand, this was London after all, he had taken a much-needed nap in his room before catching the train a few blocks from the inn. He disembarked at the Kensal Green Station. It was already late and the small neighborhood station was empty, he makes his way three blocks over on Harrow and knocks three times on the nondescript door next to the Portuguese Deli.

"We're closed, come back tomorrow," the gruff voice projects through the door.

"Open up Salazar, I don't have time to argue with you old man..."

The door opens slowly spilling light onto the sidewalk, "Jumping Jesus Christ... didn't know you were still in the game Jack," the old man says closing the door quickly behind them.

"Well, semi-retired old friend, hope this is the last time for me, your boy still working with you?"

"Yes, he runs the deli, but he'll take this over too, soon enough."

"You still have my box tucked away somewhere?"

"Of course, this way..." he turns and leads Jack into the back of the deli. "Wait here, not room for both of us," he says opening the walk-in freezer. In the back he pushes the glowing thermostat, silently a false wall slides aside revealing a row of foot locker sized boxes with digital key pads. He grabs the third one from the right and trundles it out to the stainless prep table. "Too fucking old for this," he grumbles, "the cold kills my arthritis."

Jack pats him on the back, "how bout something to drink?"

Salazar nods, knowing Jack is just being polite, "sure."

Jack watches him walk to the drink cooler in the front. As he punches in the code 1923 the double locks click, and he opens the chest. Salazar hands him a Fuller's Porter, they clink bottles as Jack takes a long pull... "Nothing like a Fuller's," he says setting it down next to the chest. He reaches in and pulls out two stacks of hundred-dollar bills, two Springfield XD pistols, with attached suppressors, two boxes of 45 caliber rounds, double rig shoulder holster, and two passports. He pushes aside an HK machine pistol, two knives, and several boxes of rounds, before pulling out a wire garrote, he stuffs everything in the backpack and turns to Salazar. "Old friend, I won't be back, but I'm passing the baton on to a young lady – McIntyre – American, and she'll have my code - I expect you to take care of her, understand?"

"Yes of course," the old man answers.

Jack places a hand on each shoulder, "she doesn't have my sense of humor, so be careful." He extends his hand with ten of the bills folded in it, "for your trouble and discretion - been a pleasure, take care of yourself." The old man closes the door softly behind him, pocketing the bills and debating whether to make the call he had been told to.

"Are you going to call them father?"

Salazar looks up, his son is standing in the shadows, "I don't know son," he hangs his head.

"What happens if we don't?" the younger man asks.

"Better question is what happens if we do..." he turns to his son, "never heard of anyone that crossed Jack Hardy and lived to tell about it, and that bit about the McIntyre woman was just to let us know she would take care of it if something should happen to him. No son, I think we'll keep our own counsel on this."

"Ok, but he didn't seem all that... I don't know some of the ones that show up are downright scary... he was normal I guess."

His father gives him a look, "I haven't taught you anything have I? He is the scariest of them all son, and the fact that you can't tell proves it."

Jack catches the train back into central London, he still had a few stops to make, there were only a few people in London that were capable of taking on a hit like this — normally the challenge would be finding someone willing to tell him who it was, but Jack had been in the game a long time and his network was as well placed as it was extensive. He had cultivated the cogs in the machine, the overlooked people, the ones that knew everything — because they did the all the real work — Harriet had been the London Station Chief's admin for as long as anyone could remember, she was British Intelligence and they had a thing years ago. He had kept her confidence and she his; it didn't hurt that she knew things long forgotten by most everyone else.

The pub was dark and busy, he sat at the end of the bar on a swivel stool, if this had been a spy movie he would be in the last booth watching the entrance — it wasn't. The foam settles on his pint of Guinness, as he takes the first sip a lady in a plaid rain jacket with the harried look of an overworked clerk on her way home takes the stool next to him, he doesn't bother to acknowledge her, this isn't that kind of pub. She places her cell phone face up on the bar and signals the keep, she must be a regular — he is already headed her way with a pint of a light ale. Jack memorizes the text on the phone, it's just a name and address and is gone as the phone's screen goes blank. He drains his glass, leaving a few bills on the counter and makes his way out. He smiles to himself, today's technology made things much simpler in some respects, thirty years ago that would have been a lot more difficult.

He sits on the park bench watching the late-night wanderers come and go, he knew the name – which didn't really bother him – it was just a matter of picking the right time and place, the man was a professional he wasn't going to just walk into it. With a sigh he pulls his phone out and dials, "Lou…"

Smoke

Jessie spent the morning at Langley working through the logistics of traveling to London, a new passport, plane tickets, hotel reservations, scheduled meetings at UCL the top university in London – her cover as a linguistics professor at Georgetown still intact. She finishes up around eleven and heads upstairs to meet with Director Simpson, she only has to wait a few minutes before being ushered in.

He nods to the chair in front of his desk, "where's Jack?"

"I need to talk to you about that sir," she hesitates, "he's in London..."

He looks up from his desk, "London? I thought we decided you two weren't going to London..."

"We did sir, but after talking through it last night, we think if I don't at least land in London and check in with the Station Chief it's going to tip off the DNI we need to remain under the radar as long as possible. If he thinks I'm in London maybe they won't expect us in Israel and the Kingdom..."

"I guess that makes sense, but Jessie, what if they are planning to take you coming out of the airport, we don't know how far this ALPHA group or Moyer is willing to go..." he stops as if having just heard her, "wait, did you say Jack was already in London?"

"Yes sir…"

"I don't want to know do I?"

"No sir… I don't think so."

"It's a big risk Jessie, what if Jack… I mean he is good but…"

"I know sir," she breaks in, "he's more than good sir, he's the best," she says calmly, "I'm betting my life on it."

He swivels his chair around and looks out the window, "alright, I don't like it, but you're probably right, what do you need from me?" he asks, turning back to face her.

"I need a smoke screen sir, I need you tell Moyer you're sending me to London on Saturday. Tell him I'll check in with the Station Chief when I get in for instructions." She pauses thinking, "if I don't check in they will think their man was successful even without confirmation, so it should buy us a few days."

"Actually Jessie, it will buy you more than that, Moyer can't admit he put a contract on you, so without confirmation he has to sit on it and play along – who is he going to say anything to?"

"Makes sense sir, so only challenge is actually surviving London…" she says with a smile.

"Not funny, but yes," he answers matter-of-factly.

"Anything else sir?" she asks getting up.

"No, that'll do it, I'll call him in a few minutes, but listen, be careful and only communicate with me on the SAT phone, no official channels until this is over…" She nods and heads for the door, "good luck… we're all counting on you."

She pauses at the door and looks over her shoulder, "thank you sir, I won't let you down."

"I know," he says to the closing door, he picks the phone up dialing Moyer's number, "Vance Simpson sir, just wanted to give you an update…" He lays the smokescreen down praying the man doesn't ask too many questions.

"So, she'll be in London on Saturday?" Moyer asks.

"Yes sir, she is taking a commercial flight, should be there Saturday night, I've told her to check in with the Station Chief for further instructions."

"Okay, why Saturday? Would have preferred to have her there sooner, we don't want to miss this guy you know."

"Yes sir, I know," Simpson answers, ignoring the obvious lie. "My fault on that, took a day to track her down in Colorado – she was hiking or something, by the time I got her back here, briefed and setup, Saturday was the earliest flight available. Didn't think we wanted to draw attention by putting her on a special transport, you want me to change that sir?"

"No, no it's fine, I'm sure you're right, don't want to tip our hand unnecessarily… good work Vance listen keep me posted personally on her progress okay?" They both know the other isn't telling the whole truth but neither are in a position to say so.

"Yes sir, will do," he says hanging up and staring at the phone, the audacity of the man amazes him. He picks his SAT phone up and texts Harrington and Albert, "we are in play..."

Jessie pulls to the curb in front of the townhouse that serves as her DC home, she sits in the car for a minute contemplating the call she needs to make to her dad, she probably should have told him the other night, but he wasn't going to understand her walking into a trap.

She loves him more than anything, and there are moments like these where she has a hard time reconciling the life she has chosen with the fear her dad has of losing her. She hadn't fully understood it until last year during the Sokolov mess, it made sense now – he had never gotten over losing her mother and when he had said she was his whole world it wasn't just a sappy cliché. She grabs the veggie wrap and Diet Coke she had picked up for dinner and heads into the house debating how to tell him she was going to London.

Her phone begins to vibrate as she unloads the food into the refrigerator, "Hey dad."

"Hey honey, how you holding up?"

"I'm fine dad, but I need to talk to you," she says anxiously, now that there's no avoiding it.

"Look Jess, before you say anything listen to me okay."

"Sure dad," figuring there's another safety lecture coming.

"You can drop the tone young lady, I'm still your dad," he admonishes her, "I just hung up with Jack a few minutes ago and as you probably can guess I'm not real enamored with the idea of you heading to London, but I get it." The vagaries of three time zones had allowed Jack to brief Lou in even before Jessie could get to him.

"You spoke to Jack?" she asks, confused.

"Just a minute ago, it's after ten there," he tells her.

"Oh, right time zones, sorry should've caught that."

"You sure you want to take the commercial flight over, seems like an unnecessary risk coming through Heathrow."

"I know, I thought about that, but there's no way to know how deep this goes and what tip-offs there might be along the way, don't want to be done before we get started. Did Jack talk to you about, you know – how we plan on doing it?" She didn't have any qualms about shooting people – particularly people who were intent on killing her, but it was still difficult to discuss casually in conversation.

"Yes, he's identified their person over there and will be neutralizing that threat before you get there, I'm still not sure you should go to the Station Chief though... if they're in on it then you are just exposing yourself again."

"I know it's a roll of the dice, if we knew when and where they were planning to hit me," the words give her a chill, "we could play it out a little more..."

"No way to know that Jess and we're already taking a pretty big risk. I'm going to have Mark fly over tomorrow with the Jet, that way you guys have transportation out of there that's off the books and you can leave at any time... Jess, don't push a bad situation."

"I won't dad, you think I should call Jack?"

"Yeah, I'll let him update you on everything else... be careful kiddo – dad loves you."

"Love you too dad," she says hanging up. She smiles thinking about the conversation, she was always going to be his little girl, really didn't matter if they were tracking down international criminals or the world's foremost assassin – and the truth was she didn't want it to be any other way.

She dials Jack's number, "see you spilled the beans to the old man..." she says with a laugh.

"You know the rule Jess, no secrets between us."

"I know, it's all good, I was about to call him and break the news anyway."

"How did it go with Simpson? He pitch a fit?" Jack asks.

"Not really, he's worried – but doesn't want to know the details – typical. Said he would lay down some smoke for us though."

"Cut him some slack Jess, Vance is one of the good guys, and there are damn few of those left, he'll cover us if he can."

"I know, you all set on that side, we know what we are dealing with yet?"

"Well, I know who we are dealing with, real pro, but I think that plays to our advantage – predictability is something we can use to tilt things in our favor, have you heard from Mikhail?"

"No, we all kind of left in a hurry – feel like I didn't thank him enough, if that makes any sense."

"It does, but I talked to him before he left – he knows trust me."

"I guess, feel bad about his uncle – should never have been mixed up in this – gotta tell you I was pretty surprised when he showed up in Colorado."

"He made his own choices Jess, and if you don't know why he showed up in Colorado you haven't been paying attention."

"What's that supposed to mean?"

"You know exactly what it means, don't play coy with this old man, you've been in his head ever since you got the drop on him in Odessa, don't act like you haven't noticed," he admonishes her.

Jess laughs, "okay, maybe a little but seriously there's nothing happening, believe me."

"I know that, and he probably does too – but Jess, Mikhail is a dangerous man and he isn't necessarily living by the same rules we are so watch yourself."

"Yes dad..." she says with a grin.

"Alright, I'm just callin' it the way I see it, let's touch base tomorrow around six your time, I want to make sure we are on the same page for Saturday."

"Okay, I'll call you then, anything changes shoot me a text."

They hang up and Jessie drains the last of the Diet Coke before crumpling up the wax paper that had encircled the wrap, tossing it in the recycle bin she thinks about Jack's warning. He was right, she had noticed Mikhail's interest, but hadn't really given it any thought, men were always interested - she didn't pay it much attention. Mikhail was different though and it was true he lived by a different set of rules, she appreciated him in a professional way and didn't want to disrespect him – she was going to have to think about this.

Choices

David preferred to park in the public lots at the east end of the Kuday Ajyad tunnels – two underground thoroughfares that led directly to the hotel complex outside the walls of the Great Mosque. The bus ride in allowed him to prepare himself, it was a perpetual test of his ability to remain in character, and exactly what a poorly paid Pakistani engineer would do. All of the research and practice he had completed preparing for this part had made him ready for the daily interaction with people – what he hadn't anticipated was the very strange dichotomy this holy place presented.

There was no denying the spiritual presence here it was real and inhabited the very earth beneath him, but the contrast with the ultra-modern trappings the Saudis had built was difficult to assimilate – it wasn't just the enormity, but also the ornateness of the surrounding Mosque, combined with the tremendous amount of construction dedicated to the comfort of the crowds – it all seemed at odds with the underlying story. Hadn't Hagar and Ishmael been alone, dying of thirst and at the end of their hope in this very place? He had listened to the stories as a child, studied the Torah as an adult – he didn't attempt to reconcile the underlying hypocrisy that the Jews and

Muslims had sprung from the same source – shared the same God.

He sways with the bus holding onto the overhead grab handle as the fluorescents flicker by, he has learned to ignore the mix of diesel, sweat, and food smells that mix in the close quarters.

He had started exploring other areas of Mecca during his down time, the Mosque itself was huge and beautifully ornate, but the tent city of Mina was the most intriguing. A few weeks earlier he had taken one of the bright green trains that ran from the Mosque out to the center of Mina. The Saudis had only recently completed this last section of rail and during the Hajj it was the busiest metro rail in the world.

He had ridden out before the real crowds had arrived – the train had dropped him in the middle of the city - thousands of tents stretching in every direction, the sheer size of it was amazing. David hadn't known exactly what to expect; the Saudis claimed it could hold more than three million pilgrims but seeing the photos and satellite pics didn't completely prepare you for how big it really was.

Even without the crowds that would fill it in the next couple of weeks there were already thousands of people there. He had known immediately this was going to be the epicenter of the spreading contagion – the pilgrims would drink the water in the Great Mosque but the volume of people in close proximity to each other in the tents was going to make this an inescapable horror show. They would suffer and die in the shadow of Mount Arafat; he knew the story, the hill was where Adam was supposed to have received God's forgiveness and the Prophet had delivered his farewell sermon – now it would stand in witness to Azrael's judgement.

David finishes his inspections, nodding to the guards who continued to ignore him, he was part of the routine and they no longer gave him a second glance. He uploads his report before heading out to the Makah Mall, there was a little Pakistani place on the third floor he had actually come to enjoy for lunch, although experiencing the noon prayer in the mall setting with thousands of others had been a bit disconcerting the first time, it had become part of his routine though. Today he opts for Burger King, he would never admit it, but he really loved the overly salty fries, and the charbroiled hamburger loaded up with extra pickles. He takes the greasy bag and sits on one of the many benches built into the support pillars stretching down the central aisle of the mall, he watches the crowds pass around him as he unwraps the burger and takes the fries out of the bag.

He squeezes the ketchup out of the foil pack onto the limp fries appearing to concentrate on not letting it get on his shirt – he had picked Daniel out of the crowd pretending to shop in one of the many stores, what he was looking for now was the man's number two. Mossad was predictable – they always worked something like this in pairs — he wondered who it would be.

He waits until Daniel is turned the other way before deftly slipping behind the pillar, dumping the remaining lunch into a nearby trash can. Masking his movements with the lunch crowd he is behind Daniel before the man realizes he has left the bench. He gently places his hand on the center of Daniel's back and whispers in Hebrew, "Daniel my brother — go home," before quickly disappearing back into the crowd.

Daniel is a trained Mossad agent and no stranger to combat and stressful situations, but he can't help the cold knot of fear that rises inside him at the whispered words and soft but firm touch, looking quickly around he sees what he thinks is David's back receding in the crowd. He doesn't even try to catch up, why give the man a reason to kill him. Making his way over to the bench David had just been sitting on and collapsing, he tries to suppress the tremors assaulting him.

"Daniel?"

He can't answer immediately and just shakes his head, "we must go now, can't stay here," is all he manages to get out.

Daniel leads them back to the bus stop and the tunnels, hoping David isn't waiting for him. They had followed him as far as the public parking lots earlier but opted to wander the mall until he had shown up at lunch time. Since their only focus was generally keeping track of him until the VX17 was released there hadn't been any urgency to track his every move. In a moment of clarity Daniel realizes David probably believes Mossad has sent them here to eliminate him – he doesn't know about ALPHA – which means they are in serious danger.

As they approach the parking lots he makes a decision, "Mitch we need to disappear now, stay on the bus – we will circle back and take a taxi back to Jeddah, I need time to think."

The younger man just shrugs, "whatever you say."

Daniel looks around, the bus is mostly empty, "you don't understand, we are dead! We can't go back to the car, the apartment, we have to disappear."

"No, I don't understand, he doesn't know where we are, how could he?"

Daniel looks around, "we can't talk here, but if I have to explain it to you..." he doesn't finish. "Let's go." He says disembarking from the bus and make his way to the Taxi stand. Opening the door to the nearest one he rattles off an address in Jeddah, they agree on two hundred-fifty riyals and are off. It's an hour and a half before they are dropped at the airport's North Terminal - Daniel hasn't spoken a word the whole trip. He turns to Mitch, "we need a car, rentals are this way," he says leading the way.

Forty minutes later they drive out of the terminal in a non-descript Toyota sedan and blend in with the rest of the traffic leaving the airport. Heading through the city to the coast they take Corniche south along the Red Sea, Daniel finally pulls over into one of the many empty parking spaces. The area is mostly deserted as the summer temperatures average above ninety degrees and the humidity can be oppressive, that suits him just fine he doesn't want anyone overhearing their conversation.

He leaves the car running, air conditioning on high, he looks out over the Red Sea, "Mitch, I'm sorry about what happened back there, I couldn't take a chance that Azrael was waiting for us." He has switched back to Azrael – he can't afford to think about David as anything other than an assassin at this point.

"Ok, but what happened, I thought you were ill or something?"

Daniel shakes his head and explains how he had been shadowing Azrael as he ate lunch. "I looked up and he was just gone, next thing I know he is behind me whispering in my ear and then just disappears again."

"You're serious, what did he say?" Mitch asks incredulously.

Daniel turns to him, "he said go home…"

Mitch gives him a strange look "what…" he never finishes, the safety glass of the window explodes around him the tiny pieces twinkling like a thousand crystals in the bright sun. Azrael is moving almost too fast to see and has his hands on Mitch's

216

chin and head snapping them in opposite directions so quickly the man is dead before he even knows what is happening.

"Out Daniel... now!"

Daniel doesn't see a weapon, but he knows that doesn't matter, Azrael can just as easily kill him with his hands. He opens the car door leaving it running and steps around to the front resigned to his fate, time seems to slow down. He can hear the gentle waves lapping against the concrete sea wall, the cry of gulls on the salt air, and the jarring traffic sounds in the background. He waits for the blow that will end all of this, but it doesn't come.

"Daniel, I don't want to kill you..."

"David or should I say Azrael... you'll forgive me if I don't believe you..." he answers mustering his courage and turning to face the man that had once been his brother.

"It doesn't matter what you believe Daniel," the man says with a pained expression, "go home to your boys, leave me to this..."

"To what David, leave you to what?" He already knew of course but he was buying time, he didn't necessarily believe David was really going to let him leave alive, but he didn't want him changing his plans even if it meant his life.

"Soon none of this will matter, go home Daniel... please," he pleads.

"Let me help you," Daniel answers.

David moves in close to him, their faces inches apart and maneuvering Daniel up against the hood of the car, "I said go home, I won't ask you again," he says in a low voice, eyes flicking over to where Mitch is dead in the front seat, the message is clear – leave or die.

David turns and abruptly walks away as Daniel slumps against the hood letting his breath out in a deep sigh. *Now what the fuck am I going to do,* he thinks, looking over at the younger man lying lifeless in the front seat. The answer was simple enough though – *go home.*

Salazar

Jack got off at the South Kensington Station his shabby rain coat wrapped around him the garrote buried deep in his left pocket and the twin pistols snug in the shoulder holster, it was probably too warm for the jacket but like most older people he had overdressed. Leaning on the long umbrella like a cane he limps down Pelham and over to Walton, this was one of the nicer areas of London — he wasn't surprised death paid well in today's world.

He easily finds the address shuffling by without looking up and continues down the block; it was late afternoon and he had been wandering around the neighborhood for a few hours. Jack didn't like putting things together this quickly, there wasn't enough time to work out all the variables — success was driven by planning, by accounting for every potential variation. This wasn't that, he had landed forty-eight hours earlier and Jessie was already in the air — this was improvisation pure and simple.

Jessie shifted her legs looking out the window of seat 23A, the United 757 had a three and three configuration, she normally chose an aisle; but it was easier to sleep by the window. Two rows from the over-wing exits was her preferred location, she had read somewhere, or maybe it was in one of the trainings, that if you were within five rows of an exit your chance of surviving a plane crash increased eighty-five percent.

She smiles to herself, remembering trying to convince her dad of that, he had just shaken his head and said, "people don't survive plane crashes." Of course, that wasn't entirely true, and she had spent the next two years sending him clippings via email till he had finally conceded the point, but only to get her to stop. They would be landing in a few hours, she was supposed to find a bar in the airport and hole up until Jack contacted her – it felt like hiding and she wasn't real fond of hiding.

Jack looks up at the building again, the light is fading and most folks are sitting down to an early dinner or preparing to go out for the evening, the street is quiet. *Maybe I should just knock on the door and start blasting away? No, this guy is too smart to open the door to anyone, least of all an old man he doesn't know.* Staying in character, he moves to the end of the block sticking to the deepening shadows, *the garrote would be the quietest method but the man had a good twenty plus years on him* – it would be risky and he wasn't sure he was strong enough anymore.

"What am I missing?" he murmurs to himself. "The car, I am missing the car, Fuck, me dead..." he says with a smile. Jack heads back up the block, parked in front of the door is a silver Mercedes sedan, he hopes he isn't too late as he bends to release the air in the rear tire, the hiss sounds like a jet engine in the deepening night. All he needs is a moment's hesitation, enough of a distraction to fire a couple of quick rounds and retreat into the shadows, just another old man out for an evening stroll.

Jack hears the footfalls a few seconds too late, the voice rings out from above, "what are you doing old man?"

He doesn't hesitate reaching inside his jacket for the pistol he falls forward against the car and rolls onto the sidewalk bringing the 45 up in a two-hand grip, there's an instant of hesitation not wanting to shoot an innocent, it's enough to give the younger man time to pull his own weapon. Jack's first round catches the man in the chest angling up forcing him back a few feet. Just as Jack feels a searing in his side he pulls the trigger again, this time the round enters under the man's chin snapping his head back.

Jack rolls again into a kneeling position, he can feel the blood seeping down inside his shirt - *fuck me* - he thinks feeling the area with his right hand, *in and out* he concludes finding the exit wound a few inches further back, *lucky but not that lucky*. Decision time, he can't show up in a London hospital with a bullet wound – there wouldn't be any explanation that would serve and although suppressed the shots aren't silent – there's a better than even chance someone may have heard them. He needs to get somewhere he can get this cleaned up and sewn back together.

Removing his jacket, he ties the sleeves tightly around his waist applying as much pressure as he can and knotting it off. He starts off toward the train station not looking back hoping he has at least a few minutes before anyone stumbles upon the body. He is just turning the corner on Pelham when he hears the first sirens, "going to be close," he murmurs to himself. He pushes into the public restroom, grabs a handful of paper towels and locks himself in a stall. Stripping off the holster he hangs it on the coat hook and removes his shirt. Jack knows that more than ninety percent of fatalities in the field are from bleeding, he has to at least slow it down. He shoves the paper into both the wounds trying not to cry out from the pain, then ties his shirt tightly around his waist and shrugs back into the holster. With the rain jacket back on he looks in the mirror, *not ideal, but maybe it will be enough* he thinks, tying the raincoat's belt as tight has he can stand. Taking a deep breath that sends a searing pain through his side he washes up in the sink and limps out onto the platform. He sits on the far side of the station holding the phone with one hand while texting Jessie the address, hoping no one notices the red bloom starting to seep through his shirt.

Jessie pays the taxi getting out and looking up and down the dark street, this didn't make any sense – Jack had sent the address an hour ago but nothing since and here she was on a dark neighborhood street with no weapon and no idea what was going on. She looks around again, it's quiet – knocking on the door she takes a step back and to the side, no point and giving someone a point-blank shot at her. The door is opened by a man about her age, he doesn't say anything just motions her in.

Jack is lying on a stainless prep table in the back room of the deli with his shirt off and a lot of blood everywhere, Jessie stifles a cry rushing forward past the younger man. There is an old man weaving a curved needle in and out of Jack's side - he looks up and nods. "Hey Jess," Jack croaks, "meet Salazar Hernandez..."

She ignores him, "is he going to be okay?" she asks the man.

He pauses and looks up at her with a shrug, "maybe lost a lot of blood before he got here," he says going back to work.

She hesitates a moment debating what to do, taking her phone out she punches up the speed dial menu and picks the third entry, "Director Simpson... it's Jessie we need some help."

"What's going on Jessie, I'll do what I can."

"I don't know exactly, I landed a couple of hours ago and well Jack sent me a text with an address, I just got here..." she catches her breath.

"And... Jessie what is it?"

"He's been shot sir, looks bad, definitely alive... well I've seen worse, but he's lost a lot of blood, needs a hospital soon as possible." She has reverted to her training and is inspecting Jack closer now, the old man has done a nice job cleaning the wound and stitching it back up. It's still oozing blood a bit but the two men are applying gauze pads and taping them in place.

"What should I do sir?" she asks.

"Send me the address, I'll make some calls to see what I can do, we have good support services there, you don't have any idea what happened though?"

"No sir just got here, I'll work on that, and thank you sir."

"No problem Jessie, Jack is one of ours and an old friend besides, let me get on it, you sit tight okay..." he says hanging up.

The old man is wiping his hands on a clean towel having rinsed them off in the large sink against the wall. "Salazar Hernandez," he says rather formally holding out his hand. "This is my son," he nods to the young man helping Jack sip some water out of a plastic bottle.

"Jessie McIntyre, pleased to meet you sir, thanks for helping him," she says taking his hand firmly. "Jack, you okay?" she asks turning back to the table.

"Going to be," he says with a wince, "fraid I'm not going to be much help to you though." He attempts to sit up, but grimaces and leans back on the table, "was that Simpson?"

"Yes sir, said to sit tight going to send some help, might be a while though," she says moving over to the side of the table.

He grabs her hand, "you can't stay Jessie, you gotta go..." he grimaces again, "look we don't know who's going to walk through that door, you can't risk it." He turns to Salazar, "bring my box old friend."

"You don't think we can trust Simpson?" Jessie asks.

"It's not that, I don't know who we can trust here anymore, not much they can do to me, but you gotta go – can't compromise our end goal Jessie – you know that."

"Jack, I'm not leaving you behind, I don't leave my men behind…" she says her voice rising.

"You listen to me young lady, this isn't the Army you understand? You have a job to do…" he says sternly. He looks down at his side, "I did my part now you have to do yours, I can't help you anymore."

Salazar trundles the box out of the walk-in and sets it on the counter. Jack leans in and gives Jessie the code, "open it up Jessie, take the cash, knives, and hand me the HK and a couple of clips okay."

She punches the code in and opens the box, pulling out the HK and two loaded clips she hands them to Jack. She slips three stacks of hundreds and two stacks of fifty Pound notes into her backpack along with a tactical knife, and two boxes of 45 rounds. "Jack, I'm taking the pistols," she says, shrugging into his shoulder rig and tightening it.

"Of course, Jess I want you to call your dad, you need a way out of here that can't be tracked, get that flyboy Mark over here as soon as possible and then disappear." He turns to Salazar, "one more favor my friend, can your son drive her out of town, I'll give you the address?"

"Yes of course," Salazar answers, pulling a set of keys out of his pocket and handing them to the young man. "Take her wherever he says son."

Jessie grabs Jack's hand, "you be careful, I can't lose you old man, we clear?"

Jack pats the HK on his lap, "don't worry, nothing's going to happen to me, now get out of here – I'll call you later... and Jess, be nice when you get there, okay..." he says with a wan smile as he lays back on the table.

"Where am I going?"

Jack just waves her out, turning she follows the young man out the back, "what's your name?" she asks him.

"Salazar," he says solemnly.

Jessie nods, *what else would it be* she thinks.

Going Home

Salazar had cleaned up the blood as best he could without moving Jack, he hadn't known what to do when the man had knocked on his door; clothes soaked in blood clutching his side. It had been his son that had jumped into action carrying Jack to the table and urging his father into action. They had done the best they could, with what they had.

"Jack, I need to tell you something..." the old man says softly.

"What is it my friend?" Jack whispers.

"I uh, I was supposed to call a number if you showed up, a man called, he used all the right passcodes, wanted me to let him know if you came here... I'm sorry..."

"Did you call him?"

The man hesitates, "no, no I didn't..."

"Why not?" Jack asks.

"Well, I..." Salazar stops and smiles, "honest answer, you scare me more than they do..." he says, trailing off into silence, "just thought you should know."

"You're a wise man, my friend... give me the number," Jack says leaning up to look him in the eye.

"Jack..."

"Nothing for it now my friend, give me the number."

Salazar recites the number and Jack enters it into his phone adding a few more lines and hits send. "There, no harm see..."

Salazar doesn't answer he just continues to clean up wiping over the table and rechecking Jack's bandages. Jack lays back on the hard table trying to get comfortable, it's almost an hour before there is a sharp knock on the door. Jack picks up the HK, cycling the slide and chambering a round, he nods for the old man to open it up. Neither of them is ready for the two US Air Force corpsmen that enter carrying their EMT gear. Jack hands Salazar the HK as they quickly start an IV on him and rebandage the wounds.

"Hang on to that for me old friend..." Jack says.

Without another word they trundle him out the door to the backseat of the standard Air Force issue sedan waiting outside.

"Who are you guys?" Jack finally asks.

"352nd out of Mildenhall, sir," the driver answers.

"Well, thanks fellas," Jack says still a bit surprised.

"No problem sir."

Jack leans back, *someone must have dropped some serious favors to pull this off, CIA pretty much never exposed its people and there was no precedent for involving the military in something like this. Well, never look a gift horse in the mouth* his father had always told him. *Things had really gone to shit this time though, first time he had caught a bullet, definitely not something he wanted to do again, damn it hurt.* He drifts in and out coming awake as they slow down and stop.

The car pulls up to a security gate and Jack looks around, this is clearly not the main gate of the base, must be one of the side gates he figures. The driver flashes his ID and is waived through with barely a nod, "taking you to the infirmary sir," he says looking straight ahead.

"Then what?"

"Above my pay grade sir, Captain told us to fetch you here, his problem after that," he answers with a touch of a smile.

"Well, I guess I don't need to tell you I was never here then," Jack says with a laugh, "oh man, that hurts..."

They pull up in front of a single story white building and they all jump out. Two additional corpsmen are there waiting with a stretcher, they strap him on and wheel him into what would be a typical bay in any emergency room in the States. "Take care sir," the driver says on the way out.

Jack leans back on the clean white sheet and reflects on the last few hours, it was surreal, and he had to admit he was probably getting too old for this. He had gotten lucky tonight, a few inches to the left and he would be a corpse on a London sidewalk, not how he wanted things to end. Time to come in from the field, his head and heart could keep up, but tonight had shown him he just didn't have the physical edge needed – it was a hard pill to swallow.

"Jack Hardy?" The man was wearing blue scrubs and had pushed the curtain aside and started pulling the tape and gauze away from the wound. "I'm Captain Williard, let's see what we have here."

"Pretty sure I got lucky, think it went right through..."

"Looks like it, but still need to make sure nothing else going on in there and get some antibiotics started, who sewed it up? Nice work."

"An old friend... can't really say more than that, Sir I gotta ask..."

The Captain pauses, "Mister Hardy, if that's really your name, no question this is way out of the ordinary, but Vance Simpson is my father-in-law and he says you're a national asset so here you are." He applies some disinfectant to Jack's side and reaches for some clean gauze pads, "but honestly the sooner you're out of here the better." He pats Jack on the shoulder, "you're lucky, this could have been a lot worse, I'll be back to check on you."

"Thanks Captain," he replies as his phone starts to buzz. "Hey Lou, you heard from Jessie?"

"Yeah, you ok? I was afraid you wouldn't pick up..." There's a moment of silence between the two friends, there really aren't words to describe what they mean to each other; they are as close as brothers maybe closer.

"I'm okay Lou, but it was close, close as I've ever been..." he pauses before going on, "getting too old I guess, made a mistake and almost paid dearly for it, wouldn't have happened in the old days..." he trails off.

"No, it wouldn't have cause I would have had your back..." Lou tries to stifle the emotion in his voice, but it shows through. "You need to come home, I'm sending the jet for you, should be there in the morning."

"No Lou, Jessie is going to need it..."

"She doesn't want it, wouldn't tell me what she's planning, you know how she gets, told me to worry about you, something about not leaving a man in the field..."

"Lou, she's a tough kid, she'll be alright."

"I know, I know, just drives me crazy when she clams up and goes all combat focused on me, I'm her dad for Christ's sake."

Jack's laugh turns into a groan, "don't make me laugh dammit, she only does it cause you're her dad, you know for a genius you don't get it sometimes."

"Jack, I don't think I'll ever get used to this, damn thing is she seems happy!"

"She'll be okay Lou, never seen anyone with instincts like hers, she's better than you and I ever were... and she's a quick study for sure - don't worry... You remember Harriet?"

"Sure, pixie of thing loved to dance..."

"Well she is MI6, never told you that did I? Well anyway Jessie will be safe with her and she can help."

"Yeah for now, but this guy she's hunting — you said yourself only a couple people in the world like this one." He doesn't wait for Jack to answer. "Anyway, the jet will be there in the morning, I have a flight medic coming with them just in case, want you back here as quick as possible, so don't hassle anyone you hear?"

"You got it Lou, and thanks, I appreciate it, oh we're going to owe Vance one too, turns out his son-in-law is stationed here taking good care of me."

"Will do, now get some rest - call me before you take off if you get a chance." Lou punches off the phone and scrolls back through his text messages until he finds the phone number Jack had sent him earlier. He keys it into his system and starts the search routines. Strictly speaking this wasn't legal, but NSA had been using kleptographic backdoors for years and it only seemed right to have placed some in the systems he was deploying for them — call it a check and balance — more than ten years ago Snowden had shown the world NSA couldn't be trusted.

232

The system processed for only a few seconds before returning the listing for the phone number Lou had keyed in. He had expected a masked or untraceable number and was surprised to see an inside line for the US embassy in London; now it was clear the CIA Station Chief in London had been compromised. He texts Jessie the information with a warning not to trust anyone in London.

He sits in his leather chair looking out windows, the sun is setting over the Flat Irons, spinning back to his monitor he drafts an encrypted email to Harrington and Simpson giving them the phone number and a brief update on Jack. He doesn't include whose number it is, let them do their own legwork – no reason to divulge all his secrets. He hits send, picks his phone up and heads down to the parking garage – it was going to be a long few days better get some sleep while he can – there were some heads that needed to roll in DC and he planned on making sure it happened.

Best Laid Plans

Young Salazar had driven through the darkened streets continuing out of town to the northwest for what seemed like an hour, it was probably only twenty minutes. She had called her dad briefly giving him an update and insisting he send the jet for Jack. Salazar had pulled into the short drive shortly after and come to a stop, he just nodded and pointed – Jessie knocks on the door hand on her pistol, she hears the car leaving even before the door opens. With her hand still inside the light jacket feeling for the butt of the heavy pistol she steps back as the light spills out; she doesn't expect the elderly woman, house coat wrapped around her, who opens the door and beckons Jessie in.

"You must be Jessie..." the woman says leading her down the short hall and into the kitchen. It's a brightly lit cheery room with a small table and two chairs, there is a tea kettle starting to whistle on the stove – everything seems so very quintessentially British.

Jessie enters hesitantly – she has already noticed the slight pull on the house coat's left side – *probably a thirty-eight* she surmises, "Yes, I'm sorry I didn't catch your name?"

"No, you didn't dear because I didn't give it to you." The woman retrieves two cups from the cupboard to the left of the stove, "come sit down, I just spoke with Jack?"

"I'm sorry, how do you know Jack?" Jessie asks, standing behind the chair, hands at the ready.

The woman gives her a smile and placing the small pistol on the table, "relax sweetie, Jack and I are old friends. Now sit a bit... I can't help you if you don't talk to me."

"You're going to help me?" Jessie asks, while sitting down keeping her eye on the pistol.

"Well of course dear, why else would he have sent you here?" she says patting Jessie's hand, "now have some tea and tell me everything that's happened."

Harriet's phone buzzes just as Jessie is getting ready to weave a story around why she is in London... "important?"

"Jack... he says some US soldiers just picked him up, he's headed to Mildenhall – that's an Air Force base about an hour east of here."

"That's great news, I hated leaving him there..." Jessie says.

Harriet smiles at her, "you really care for him, don't you?"

Jessie looks at her for a moment, "probably seems strange in our business, but he is my dad's best friend and my mentor – so yes I care a great deal about him."

"Not strange at all dear, I have known Jack for more than thirty years – there was a time..." she trails off the look in her eyes is clear. "Well anyway... we've known each other a long time."

Jessie reaches across the table and takes the older woman's hand, "you care too don't you?"

Harriet's smile is a bit melancholy, "we need to figure out how to get you out of here young lady," she says dodging the question.

Jessie nods, not willing to push and already knowing as much as she needs to, "yes, I've got some ideas on that..." She briefly explains who Mikhail is.

"You think this man will help you?"

Jessie smiles, "I do." She doesn't explain, but Harriet smiles.

Jessie frowns, "you don't approve?"

Harriet laughs, "oh no... I count on the predictable behavior of people all the time, just be careful... they can be just as unpredictable," Jessie nods thinking about her ex Tom, she hadn't seen his involvement with Sokolov coming – talk about unpredictable.

"Tell me about the young Jack," Jessie asks.

Harriet gets a faraway look in her eyes, "he was so handsome, and he had that special energy only you Yanks have..." She takes a sip of her tea, "those were good days, he would drop into town for a few days... we loved to dance! We would stay out all night," she pauses, "of course, I would have to drag myself into work the next day, but it was worth it."

"Did you know what he did? ...with the Agency and all?"

Harriet gives her a kindly smile, "honey I've been with MI6 as long as Jack's been with the Agency, we both knew, it didn't matter, we had something special."

"Oh..." Jessie doesn't really know what to say, "I'm sorry."

"Nothing to be sorry about dear, we had a good time, I think we both knew a normal life wasn't in the cards... we were married to our jobs."

"You loved him though..."

"Hmmph still do... I shouldn't though!" She laughs. "Now back to business young lady, we have a lot to do and not much time if what Jack tells me is true..."

Jessie should have asked what Jack had told her but things were moving quickly, "I should be okay as long as Mikhail is on-board, Langley set me up with most everything, hard part was surviving London and getting out of here..." Jessie pulls out her phone, "I guess it would help to know what's going on and if anyone is looking for me, really need to know how much time I have and if I should bother checking in with the Station Chief."

"Let me make a couple of calls, you go ahead and call Mikhail and I'll see what I can find out," Harriet says getting up from the table. Jessie eyes the pistol wondering if it's a test or just a sign of trust – she dials Mikhail's number.

He picks up on the first ring, "Jessie?"

"Mikhail, I need your help."

"Anything you need Jessie, I will help," he answers without hesitation.

"But I haven't even told you what I need..."

He pauses for a second, "doesn't matter, tell me what it is."

"I need to get to Tel Aviv as soon as possible... discreetly."

"Where are you now?" he asks.

"Just outside London, but I can be anywhere you need within reason."

"Can you get to Farnborough? It's a private jetport South of the city, very discreet and I can be there first thing in the morning."

"Hold on," she places her hand over the phone, "can I be at Farnborough in the morning?" she asks Harriet, who has just come back into the kitchen.

"Definitely," Harriet mouths to her.

"Mikhail? No problem I can be there, what time?"

"Be there at eight and come in through the main gate, they'll shuttle you right up to the ramp to board, if you're not there I'll wait an hour."

"I'll be there no worries," she answers hanging up and turning to Harriet who is standing in the middle of the kitchen, "shouldn't be a problem right?"

"No, shouldn't be a problem," the woman answers.

Jessie has her pistol out in one fluid motion, "what's the deal Harriet?" She looks around slinging on her backpack, "tell me now!"

"I'm sorry, really I am, but they are coming..."

"Who, who is coming..." Jessie demands moving toward the door. Harriet leaps toward the table and her pistol, faster than Jessie would have thought possible for a woman her age; Jessie doesn't hesitate though and places two rounds in the woman's chest. Harriet crashes to the floor behind the table eyes already glassy and sightless.

"Goddammit, why would you do that?!" Jessie screams at the dead woman. She takes the 38 off the table and slips it into her backpack wondering how much time she has and who exactly is coming, the Brits, her own people or ALPHA? None of this made sense, had it been a setup since the beginning? She wasn't going to find any answers here, it was time to get out while she still could.

She quickly reloads the 45 and chambers a round in each pistol; the Springfield XD held thirteen rounds in the clip and with one in each chamber she had twenty-eight rounds plus the seven in the thirty-eight if it came to that, she hoped it wouldn't.

The cottage was small which was an advantage, she flips the light switch in the kitchen, the soft glow from the stove and refrigerator night lights the only illumination, she moves cautiously to the front hall and douses those lights as well – no point giving someone an easy target – now to find a backdoor if there was one. She proceeds down the hallway the kitchen is on her left, bedroom on the right and the living room is straight ahead. The large windows overlook a small garden and back yard, it is inky black beyond that with only a few lights in the distance. Jessie opens the back door leading out to the yard and leaves it open before moving back toward the kitchen. It's harder to disappear in the country than it is in a city or town, especially when you don't know the area – so it's a debate on whether to just leave or hunker down and see what happens.

The debate is settled for her as two laser sights crisscross through the kitchen windows, so they were using night vision and lasers she thinks as she dives for the floor, rolling toward the living room. If they were coming from the side odds were that there was at least one at the front door and another at the back – which she had left open.

They would have the advantage in the dark, but she could even the odds if her timing was just perfect. She moves quickly plastering herself against the hallway wall reaching for the light switch, not yet she tells herself, just a little longer as the lasers crisscross the kitchen windows again. The sudden light would throw off anyone wearing the night vision goggles, but it wasn't like the movies, they wouldn't be blinded or incapacitated - at best it would buy her a couple of seconds to act, but a couple of seconds was a lifetime in a firefight.

The wall over her head erupts in splinters in the same instant she ducks hitting the switch, the shots had come from the back door, she unloads three rounds into the shadowy figure entering there. The first two pitch the man back, but the double thump makes it clear he is wearing body armor, her third shot catches him in the neck and he goes down. Jessie is already rolling into a crouch semi concealed by the couch as two more men enter through the kitchen door. She doesn't waste any rounds on center mass instead taking the harder head shot – both men are down within seconds of each other.

She can hear the man behind her gurgling - three, five, seven rounds, she counts them off in her head as she pivots into the kitchen, *probably at least one more at the front door and maybe another driving* she thinks. Time to change the game again, she hits the light switch plunging the house back into darkness and moves into the hallway. She pauses for a second halfway to the front door letting her eyes adjust to the darkness, she has seven rounds left in one pistol and fourteen in the other.

It's a common misperception that a wooden door will stop a bullet, most won't, and Jessie knows this. She switches to the full pistol empties the clip chest high through the door splintering the center of it to pieces. She doesn't wait to see what happens but pulls the door open while pressing herself against the wall second pistol drawn and ready to fire. Looking out she surveys the man lying on the ground, the wooden splinters and at least two rounds have penetrated his face and neck killing him. She picks up the night vision goggles lying next to him, two full clips and an individual med kit – in the Rangers they had called them IFAKs – she crams all of it in her backpack. Donning the goggles, she sees his SA80 in the grass to the left, the HK assault rifle is standard issue for the Brits, she checks the magazine and slings it over her shoulder – so did that make this a British unit – not necessarily.

This was a mess she thinks, pausing for a moment, five dead including four commando types, it was late on a Friday night unlikely anyone would be coming through here, but still didn't make sense to leave a body in plain sight. She grabs the man and trundles him into the front hallway shutting what's left of the door behind her propping him against it to hold it shut, she maneuvers the others just inside the doors to the house and locks the side door. Surveying the house one last time, she takes Harriet's phone and collects three more clips from the two dead men in the kitchen. She leaves out the back door, locking it behind her and starts across the dark field on the side of the house in a cautious jog. She tries to remember the small town they had driven through on the way – it couldn't be more than a mile or two.

The adrenaline is bleeding off now as she slows to a walk and finally comes to a halt looking around. She drops down into the grass, backtracking through the chain of events. Harriet had unknowingly tipped her off, something about the way she had been looking out the kitchen windows, it was dark outside but the woman had been deliberately looking for something. Jessie's instincts had kicked in at that point, the move for the pistol had just been confirmation. From that point forward everything else had been training. Jessie was lethal in close quarters combat and her daily range work had saved her again.

She was missing something obvious though, what was it? Of course, they hadn't walked here – there had to be a vehicle, she hadn't seen one in the drive but that made sense, they would have parked somewhere close by and worked their way in. She is back up and jogging toward the house again, she cycles the slide on the SA80 opting for the higher capacity weapon, it felt like being in the Rangers again weapon at the ready jogging through the dark.

The black Range Rover was parked half a mile down from the house, pulled off onto the grass berm on the side of the road; obviously they hadn't been concerned about anyone seeing it. She doesn't see anyone and wonders if her luck is going to hold, she tries the door, it's open. "Please God, let the keys be in here," she whispers – the prospect of going back to the house and searching four dead bodies didn't appeal to her at all. She pushes the start button and the engine purrs to life; Range Rovers didn't roar anymore – well the evening had started as a serious cluster-fuck but maybe things were looking up.

Final Preparations

David didn't look back, he wasn't worried about Daniel taking any action, if the man had been here to eliminate him it would have happened already. *It didn't make sense though, why come at all, why shadow him, why, why, why?*

Clearly Mossad had wanted him dead, they had been hunting him since the day he had dropped off the grid, but when he took out the younger man Daniel hadn't reached for a weapon, made a move, nothing at all. David had been ready for it, but nothing had happened, what was he missing? It was time to move though, they had been able to follow him this morning and that meant they knew where his apartment was. He increases his pace, finally realizing that Daniel and the younger man may have been decoys – what if there were multiple teams here for him? He should have thought of that. He castigates himself as he starts the car and heads back towards his apartment.

He parks six blocks away and makes his way through the alleys entering the building from the service entrance, no sign of anyone yet, but he had no illusions Mossad was the best in the world and he wouldn't necessarily see them until it was too late. He reaches the third floor via the stairs cracking the door to the landing and listening quietly – nothing. If there was another team, odds are they would be in his apartment waiting for him or would have already rigged a trap that would detonate when he opened the door or the refrigerator – Mossad was masterful at disguising their traps, but David was an expert too and short of a direct shot he could diffuse just about anything they might have left for him.

Nothing to do but find out, he approaches the door, there are no tell-tale signs, scratches on the lock, hair thin trigger wires, he inspects it thoroughly before inserting the key and wincing slightly as he turns it – nothing. He takes a deep breath and pushes the door open, he is alone, he locks the door behind him and begins inspecting the refrigerator. Not finding anything he opens it and takes out the hummus container – the VX17 is still there – which means no one has been here... yet. He packs the few belongings he keeps there in the small roller bag he travels with.

He won't be back and can't leave anything behind, he rinses the vial off and dries it carefully with a hand towel before carrying it to the small table. He had been experimenting on how to disguise the vial for weeks, the volume wasn't an issue, but he needed something that would be overlooked in any normal security inspection. He had gotten an idea after watching late night TV, in an American monster movie *Jurassic Park,* one of the characters had used a shaving cream cannister to sneak out genetic material.

That would never work in today's security restricted world it was simply too big to carry through an airport or into the restricted areas of the Zamzam well, so he had searched the local stores until finding SWISH mouthwash spray, it was almost the perfect size and cinnamon flavor was almost the same color. The spray came in a metal cylindrical atomizer – and the size was perfect. It had taken a dozen of them before he had successfully drained the mouthwash and cut the cannister lengthwise allowing him to flatten it out so it could be wrapped around the VX vial. He would have preferred to solder the metal back together, but that was just the type of item that could get you noticed. The hardest part was going to be gluing the atomizer spray top on tightly enough for it not to come off, he had decided to use a quick drying epoxy that would harden completely around the spray top holding it in place.

He surveys his work, not bad he thinks, you would have to actually test the sprayer to know it wasn't real. He dumps it into his laptop case mixing it in with the collection of pens, acetaminophen packs, and chewing gum, just one more thing in his collection. He slings the bag over his shoulder grabs the roller bag and with a quick look around exits the apartment. He had thought about setting a few traps of his own, but why create a reason for the authorities to begin asking questions about the quiet man who had lived in apartment 319.

The two young boys look up from their game of marbles at the end of the hall, David hesitates before giving them a small wave and heading down the back stairs. They were innocents in a war they knew nothing about, so be it his sweet Tania had been an innocent too. He starts the car and heads for the airport, four flights, three identities and he would be home, probably for the last time. Something still doesn't add up, but David can't see it – he knows the easiest way to solve it is to let it resolve itself – concentrating on a riddle only made it impossible to solve; the answer would present itself when he let the pieces fall into place on their own.

His flight lands in Rome mid-morning and grabbing his bag out of the overhead he walks through the concourse until he gets to the Alitalia gates in Terminal One. With a little more than an hour's wait he camps out in the food court with a double scoop of ginger cinnamon gelato and watches the foot traffic scurry from gate to gate. Humanity rushes by oblivious to the monster sitting among them, he takes another bite savoring the creamy concoction as he watches a young family struggle with their bags, stroller, and two young children. There was a time not so long ago when a sight like that would break his heart and he would have to turn away to hide the tears, but today he searches for a spark, something, some sign that he is still alive inside.

Hearing his flight called, he dumps the remaining sugary sludge into a nearby trash can and pulls his bag along. The ticket reads Gabe Levin, just another weary businessman heading home – in a little over three hours he will be back in Israel, back in the nation that betrayed him, a final farewell to his girls.

The plane touches down at Ben Gurion airport outside of Tel Aviv three minutes ahead of schedule, its Shabbat in Israel – the Sabbath – public transportation doesn't operate and most businesses are closed. David catches a cab outside the terminal giving the driver directions to the Kalamata a small Greek restaurant a few blocks from his apartment, it was one of the few places open. The Greek family was respectful of course, but business was business and there were enough tourists looking for a hot meal on a Saturday for them to stay open.

He doesn't bother going inside, but walks up the street toward his apartment, he pretends not to see the young woman watching him from the window as she dips her pita in tzatziki. She was surprised to see him, they hadn't expected Azrael to return to Tel Aviv until after he had released the VX17, there hadn't been any messages out of Daniel or Mitch though.

Rina sits perfectly still watching him trudge up the street, *he looks old and tired.* She thinks, *of course, that's exactly what he wants everyone to think*, she realizes. Now what to do, Daniel had been clear they were to take Azrael down if he made it back to Tel Aviv... *but what if he hadn't completed the objective then what?* There was no way to reach Daniel and Mitch, she could reach out to Neil and see what he thought, but that would be breaking protocol, she was on her own.

She signals for the check and leaving the cash on the table she hurries out into the street. Azrael has turned the corner by George's and is almost to his apartment. She slows, blending into the tourist traffic on the sidewalk, still not sure what she should do once she catches up to him. The pistol tucked in her back seems heavy and unwieldly and the last thing she wants is a firefight with all these people around. Deciding to wait she angles towards the whale fountain across the street from the apartment and sits on one of the benches.

She feels the sharp prick in her right arm as the man sits down next to her, "good afternoon Rina," Azrael says politely.

She rubs her arm, "what did you do to me?"

"Androctonus Scorpious – native to Saudi Arabia – ironic, don't you think?" he says with a smile. "The venom is lethal without the serum," he looks at his watch, "in just a few hours."

"But why..."

"Rina, Rina, did you think I would let Mossad stop me, did you think you could just sneak up on me and I wouldn't notice?" He sighs reaching behind her for the pistol he lays it on his lap. "You really should go, the neuro-toxin will stop your breathing in about an hour or so..." He stands up, "no more warnings, are we clear?"

Rina nods as she wobbles to her feet, imagining she can feel the venom flowing through her.

"Go now, save yourself child..." he waves her away and turns back toward the apartment. Well, Mossad would either be showing up with a commando unit or he would have a few hours peace, either way he was ready. Returning to the apartment he packs a change of clothes, his BFP shirt and ID, three passports, two stacks of cash – one Israeli one Saudi – a faded photo of his girls and the Jericho 941 pistol he had been issued in the Army. He sets the backpack and his bag with his laptop by the door. Sitting at the desk he pulls up the displays for the wireless cameras he has in both staircases and scanning all three streets approaching the building. Nothing, he figured it would take hours before the girl would break if she lived at all. He activates the pressure sensors wired to the apartment door and all the window, if someone tried to come in they were all going to go up in one tremendous fireball. He takes a look around, why had he come here – like the jilted lover that ignores the pain of betrayal and returns for that final kiss, he lays on the bed closing his eyes trying to find some peace his mind hurtling forward.

Chicken Nuggets

Jessie keys Farnborough Airport into the SUV's NAV system and waits as the directions load; it's a series of smaller roads until she is able to merge onto the eight-lane highway M25 towards London, the NAV unit predicts an hour's drive. Traffic is light at just past one in the morning and she is making good time, unfortunately she is going to arrive significantly earlier than Mikhail, she reaches for the phone and dials his number.

"Any chance you can get here a bit sooner?" she asks without waiting for him to say anything.

"I can wake my pilot… it's about a three-hour flight, is everything okay?" he answers sleepily.

"No everything is not okay," she tells him about the shootout at Harriet's, "I'm just worried about being here any longer than necessary, somebody is going to expect to hear from those guys pretty soon is my guess."

"Okay, we can be there by five or six local time, where are you now?" he asks coming awake.

"I'm driving their SUV to the airport, bout an hour away… why?"

"You need to get out of that car now, find a parking lot or somewhere immediately, do you know how to – how do you say - hotwire a car?" he asks anxiously.

"Why would I do that?" she asks.

"What kind of vehicle is it?"

"Range Rover SUV, very nice by the way, like yours," she says a bit teasingly.

"Jessie, they have GPS trackers in all new cars, they will find you... you have to get rid of it now... look for an old car, one that doesn't have a navigation system in it... do it now okay?"

"Got it, dammit, I didn't think about that," she says hanging up and pulling off the next exit looking for somewhere to park. Spotting a Ramada Inn, she pulls into the almost full parking lot and heads toward a dark corner in the back. She kills the engine wishing she knew how to disable the GPS system. She had never stolen a car before and although they had taught her how to hotwire vehicles at the Farm it wasn't a guaranteed success and even old cars could be retrofitted with alarms.

No, it would be much better if she could find a motorcycle or even a scooter, they all used a three-prong connector for the ignition switch and a quick wire bridge was all you needed to get one started. Only down-side was she was going to have to lose the rifle, she couldn't very well ride a motorcycle around London with that strapped to her back.

It takes her twenty minutes of exploring the Ramada parking lot and the low budget hotel next door before she finds an older Honda Shadow parked by the rear service doors. She hates that it probably belongs to a night clerk or janitor, but *she really has no choice* she thinks quietly rolling it away from the doors. Pulling the ignition wires out she uncouples the connectors and cuts off a three-inch piece of wire from the side she isn't using. After stripping both sides she folds it into a "U" shape and inserts both ends into the connector leading to the ignition switch, she hears the telltale click of the bike turning on and gives herself a small smile, *still got it!* She secures her backpack, zips her jacket up concealing the pistols and pushes the ignition button. The deep throated purr of the engine is just about the best feeling she has had in days and jumping on she kicks it into gear and heads back toward the highway.

She takes the left exit off M25 the street lamps casting pools of light as she flashes by, leaning into the turn then shifting her weight to take the right-hand exit onto M3, the lane reversals took some getting used to, especially the exits. The inside was outside and the outside was inside and if you weren't careful you would miss the left exits. She slows down as she approaches the ramp to A331, she had decided to get off a couple of exits before the airport and work her way over, it would be easier to see if anyone was waiting for her.

She almost misses the exit for Finley and A325 but quickly corrects and loops the circle twice before picking the right spin-off and heading into a residential section of small shops and homes. With no traffic on the roads and everything seemingly shut up tight for the night the golden arches gleam beckoning her in as she rounds the curve to merge onto A325. Unable to ignore the sudden hunger pangs she glides into the drive through. Ten-piece nuggets, large fries and a chocolate shake, it had been her go-to meal as a six-year-old – back then she had gone weeks eating only nuggets, fries and cream cheese bagels. She had eventually grown out of it, but there were still days she would sneak a drive through run just to have the hot salty fries, too thick shake and the crunchy nuggets.

She sits on the curb squeezing the ketchup packet onto the last nugget, mashes a couple of fries on top and pops it into her mouth, another long draw finishes off the shake – brushing the salty residue off on her jeans she dumps the bag in the nearby trash and gets back on the bike. She had left it running, not wanting to chance it not starting back up, she heads out of the parking lot toward the airport hoping McDonald's wasn't going to be her last meal.

Mikhail had said he could be there by six or seven at the very latest, it was a three-hour flight and he was going to have to track his pilot down earlier than expected, that gave her a few hours to burn and plenty of time for whoever was looking for her to regroup.

Worst case scenario she was a fugitive from justice and the British government was looking for her, that would make getting out of the country difficult – best case the commando team was put together by ALPHA and covert. Neither option pleased her but definitely better if it wasn't official – they had the power to shutdown borders, plaster you on the news, pretty much put you on the run from everything and everyone. Jessie's problem is there really wasn't any way to know and no one to call that could tell her.

The whole strategy of routing through London to create a smokescreen was starting to seem like a really bad idea. ALPHA or somebody had been a step ahead of them or at the very least they had been betrayed. Jessie needed time to think through that, if Harriet had betrayed Jack, well that debt was paid, but if it was Salazar or his son – there was a reckoning coming when this was finished.

She circles the airport twice surveying the parking lots looking for any vehicles or activity that would seem out of the ordinary; not exactly sure what that might be at two in the morning. Other than a couple of maintenance crewman, a janitor working in the main concourse the only other person she can see is the gate guards controlling access to the tarmac. Because this was a private jetport for corporate clients it did not have the normal security presence a public airport would, which didn't mean it was going to be easy to sneak onto – it was still fenced and access was controlled.

She still had two alternate identities she could use, but even a simple artist's sketch or stock photo would be more than enough to identify her if the authorities were actually looking, never mind who shows up to a private airport at two in the morning? So, sneak on and find a place to hole up or camp out till Mikhail's plane landed and saunter in, brass balls swinging - no choice, hide in plain sight and act like you own the place. She would have to stash some things like the night vision goggles, her pistols and ammunition – you couldn't very well enter an airport, even this one, armed to the teeth.

She heads back out to A325, she had passed a twenty-four Shell station and convenience store on the way in, she was going to need a few supplies to pull this off.

Decisions

Rina lays back in the hospital bed, she had stumbled into the emergency room three hours earlier, her entire body on fire. She had been unable to speak clearly and finally had to scribble "scorpion bite" on a pad. To their credit the nurses and doctors had rushed into action immediately – only problem is they had shown her three pictures of different scorpions and asked her which one it was. She had been pretty sure at that point she was going to die, with a one in three chances of saving herself she had picked the one on the right figuring it was the most common. She must have gotten lucky because the pain was starting to subside in most of her body, but she still had a splitting headache and her right arm was noticeably swollen.

The curtain pushes aside, "Rina?"

She looks up, Daniel is standing there, "What are you doing here?" she asks with a slight slur.

"Long story," he looks around coming to the bedside and pulling up the chair next to her. He takes her hand, "what happened?"

She tells him how she had been eating lunch, getting a feel for the neighborhood when Azrael had suddenly gotten out of a taxi across the street. "I made a mistake," she says, starting to cry. "When he stuck me on that bench I thought I was going to die," she sniffles.

"He killed Mitch in Jeddah," Daniel says matter-of-factly. "My fault, he saw me, knew we were following him..." he trails off.

"Can't we just kill him?" Rina asks plaintively.

He has a pained look in his eyes, "you know we can't, it's almost done, then we'll do it, right now you rest, I'm going to try to reach Neil."

She leans back on the bed, "okay, but are you sure we are doing the right thing?" Her brush with mortality had made her reconsider the value of life, not just hers, but all life. The thought of killing a million people seemed like much more than some mission parameters all of a sudden.

Daniel understands, he had faced the same struggle just a few nights ago as he had kissed his boys goodnight, "I don't know Rina, but this is our mission..." he hesitates, "I'm not sure we could stop him even if we wanted to."

She just nods turning her head away so he won't see the tears starting again, "Daniel... be careful... he really is Azrael..."

"I know," he whispers as he pulls the curtain closed. Part of him wanted to believe that Azrael hadn't killed her out of some still-remaining kernel of compassion, but he knew better. It was simply a quiet and expedient method of getting her out of the way, if she died so be it. He hadn't expected David to be here, but the man seemed to be two steps ahead of him at every turn. It didn't make sense, well at least not to him, why even come back here? The Hajj was happening in the next week and at least a million pilgrims had already started to strain the resources there, why come home now. He wasn't going to figure it out, he had never fully understood the depths of the man's hatred, he had rationalized the political motivations behind ALPHA, but David's willingness to kill a million people was something he just couldn't get his head around.

He walks out the main entrance of the hospital and checks his watch, another forty minutes or so until the Sabbath ended, he hails a cab and heads to his hotel, he isn't worried about running into David or even bothering to watch his back – if Azrael wanted him dead it would probably have happened already. He climbs the four floors to his room. He wasn't as observant of the Sabbath customs as he probably should have been, but he tried and the elevator was off for the next half hour or so and the pre-programmed elevators stopped at every floor – he would take the stairs.

Daniel lies on the bed staring at the ceiling, he needed to reach Neil, but he wasn't sure what to tell him. Azrael was back in Israel and as far as they knew he hadn't deployed the VX17 yet, it was too early – unless he was using some kind of time delay or remote trigger. Damn was that even possible, he wonders. Mossad used them all the time, cell phone triggers, time delay explosives there were a thousand variations, but would Azrael have taken the chance? Would Azrael have left the VX17 in the system where it might be found, he didn't think so this was too personal to leave to chance – and that meant they were going to have to wait and watch.

He checks the time again and punches up the speed dial on his phone, he breathes a sigh of relief when the ringing stops, "Neil, glad you picked up." They were on a first name basis, having joined Mossad together fifteen years ago, they had become friends over the years.

"Is there a reason I wouldn't?" the man asks.

"I'm in Tel Aviv, Azrael is back here..." he hesitates, not sure what to say next.

"What is it Daniel, tell me," Neil knows him well enough to sense something is wrong.

"He killed Mitch in Jeddah and we almost lost Rina today, I don't know why he is back here my friend, but I am worried."

"Did he do it?" he doesn't need to elaborate.

"I don't think so, we would have heard something by now, it's too early though you know he is going to wait till it will have the biggest impact and that's later this week."

"Shit... I guess that makes sense, why is he here then... you don't think he's planning something here do you?"

Daniel doesn't respond, he hadn't actually considered that, what if the Hajj had been a red herring all along just to draw their attention away from the real target? "I don't know, I hadn't really considered that, we've been so focused on the other." The possibility that Israel was the real target was almost too surreal for Daniel to contemplate.

"Well, I think we need to consider it..." Neil says emphatically.

"Fine, but what are we going to do about it?"

"I don't know Daniel, I just don't know... but don't we have to do something?" Neil asks softly.

"Yes, my friend, keep your eyes open and don't approach him if shows up there, just call me okay?"

"I will, but Daniel... if I have a shot at him I'm taking it, I won't take a chance this lunatic lets that germ loose here..." he waits for a response, "you understand, don't you?"

"I do, but please, please, wait for me, I don't want to lose you old friend."

"I can handle it Daniel... I'll call you if he shows."

Daniel doesn't argue the point, "Shavua tov, my friend..." He hadn't intended to revert to Hebrew, but it felt right somehow. He closes his eyes trying to remember everything Azrael had said to him over the past few days, was there a clue there, how was he supposed to make the right decision?

Intersections

Jack comes awake as the hand gently shakes his shoulder, he reaches for the HK before realizing where he is.

"It's okay sir, just time to go," Captain Williard says.

"Oh, uh sorry... Captain thanks for everything," Jacks says coming fully awake, "where are they taking me?"

"Private ambulance, going to run you down to Farnborough about two hours south of here."

"Private ambulance?" Jack asks.

"Yeah, just came in through the main gate, says they were cleared by someone out of DC, there a problem?" the Captain asks.

"What time is it local sir?"

The Captain looks at his watch, "bout 0330, is there something I need to know?"

Jack does a quick calculation in his head its ten thirty in DC, "Let me make a quick call, can we stall them for a couple minutes, it's just after this mess tonight I'd feel better with some confirmation that they are who they say they are."

"Alright Jack, I'll review your condition with them, see if I can drag it out for a few minutes, make your calls," he says leaving the room.

Jack dials Vance Simpson's number, it rings half dozen times before the man picks up. "It's late old man, you doing okay?"

"Been better, but your son-in-law took good care of me, thanks for that - bit of a surprise when those Air Force boys showed up," Jack laughs. "Quick question though, you arrange for private ambulance transport?"

"I did, Lou didn't give me much choice, said to have you at Farnborough no later than six your time," he laughs, "you know how he is, thinks we all work for him."

"Sounds like him, just wanted to make sure these guys were on the level before I went like a lamb to slaughter."

"I understand Jack. Listen, Lou was worried about the same thing, they're supposed to give you his code name from when you guys were in Manila – that mean anything to you?"

Jack smiles, "Yeah, that's a story I should tell you one day..."

"Alright, we all good?"

"Yeah, thanks again Vance, see you soon I hope..." Jack hangs up as Captain Williard and two men in scrubs come into the room pushing a stretcher. They look innocent enough, which is exactly what your assassin of the day should look like Jack thinks. "Okay, someone needs to convince me you guys are on the level," Jack says looking from one to the other.

The younger man on the right smiles, "they told us you might be skeptical."

"I think what they said was he's a cheeky bastard," the other says with a matching smile, "oh, and that you are very, very dangerous..." He looks at his partner then back at Jack, "that true sir?"

Jack smiles, "Sure is, I am a seriously cheeky bastard," he says in his very best British accent. "Oh, I am also very dangerous," he continues dropping the accent and lowering his voice, "but I'm sure there is no reason to worry, now which one of you is going to convince me I should let you take me out of here?"

The younger one steps forward, "sir, I was told to tell you that Evergreen says get in the ambulance and don't be a pain in the ass..." he grins, "that's verbatim sir."

Jack shakes his head, "well, that's exactly what I would expect out of him, you going to vouch for this guy?" he says pointing to the other man.

"Yes sir, he's my brother."

"Ok, let's go then..." He turns to the Captain, "any chance your fellas brought my jacket along and my bag?"

"Sure, I'll get them and meet you out front."

They load Jack on the stretcher and roll him out to the ambulance, Captain Williard hands him his bag and jacket, "here you go Jack, take care of yourself..."

Jack nods and holds onto the bag and jacket as they load him into the ambulance, the older brother starts to attach the safety restraints. "Son, no way you're tying me down for the next two hours, I'll just sit in the jump seat here you guys sit up front, I'll let you know if I have a problem, clear?"

"That's not regulations sir," the man replies.

"Well regulations or not after the night I've had nobody is tying me down, so let's just get on the road, what do you say?"

The two men look at each, "ok sir, whatever you say," the younger brother answers shutting the doors and getting into the driver's seat.

They dim the lights in the back, which is fine with Jack, and head out of the base. It's just past four in the morning, the older brother leans between the seats, "it's about two and half hours down there, buckle up and try to get some rest."

Jack doesn't answer, time to catalogue what he has left to protect himself, just cause these two had the right answer didn't mean Jack believed them, his paranoia was running high and it was better to be prepared for every eventuality. He checks the coat pocket first feeling for the garotte. It's there, but not really going to be much use in the ambulance against two of them. Checking the bag, he is surprised to feel the outline of a pistol, old school six shooter – has to be the Captain's personal piece he thinks to himself. Not much use in a gunfight but more than enough to take care of these two if something should happen. He tightens the seatbelt low around his hips, careful to avoid the wound in his side feeling much better about things.

Jessie enters the convenience store, it doesn't take much to change your appearance a few accessories and a whole lot of attitude is really all she needs. A pair of garish knockoff sun glasses, a pack of hair ties, and some glitter lip gloss and she has what she needs. She pays cash and leaves giving the clerk a wink and a smile. Stowing the bag in her backpack she wishes they had Waffle House here. She would pay dearly for a coffee and a bathroom where they don't ask any questions and aren't surprised by anyone that walks through the door. Checking her phone, it's a quarter to four, time is passing slowly – she should have checked in with Jack and probably her dad earlier, but she is hesitant to make any calls this late.

Sitting on the bike off to the side of the gas pumps, time to go, she thinks. Too many lights and at this time of night she didn't need to be bringing any attention to herself. She was going to have to improvise, heading back to the airport she pulls into one of the industrial complex parking lots surrounding the airport. Digging into the bag she pulls out the hair ties and quickly braids her hair into two matching pony tails, taking the glitter gloss she runs her finger over the ball and applies it above each eye, before applying a thick layer to her lips – yuck strawberry kiwi! She looks around spotting a garbage dumpster. She drops the pistols, boxes of ammunition and the night vision goggles, she hesitates to drop the knife in, but finally lets it go as well. She studies the two remaining passports and opts for the Stella Woods one, it sounds like it would fit an American celebrity. Time to go, she dons the ridiculous sun glasses, even more so in the middle of the night – time to hide in plain sight.

The motorcycle actually wakes the gate guard as she pulls up to the barricade, she holds out her passport as if showing up at four in the morning, riding a motorcycle and wearing shades is as normal as bangers and mash.

"American?"

"All day, every day," she says, flashing a smile and adding a bit of sass to her answer.

The man looks her passport over again, "you know this is a private airport right miss?"

Jessie tips her glasses up, "of course, my jet will be here at six, I can camp out in the lounge, right?" she says, sounding mystified that he would even mention it.

"Your jet?"

"Uh yeah, you don't recognize me? Uhh... *boys don't matter to me...*" she sings. "I just played two shows in London, you need to get out more..."

"Sorry miss, you have anything to declare?"

"Nope, just me and my backpack... wanna see?" she says holding it out to him.

He takes a perfunctory look inside before handing her passport back to her, "Ok miss, straight through to the left, security screening won't be open till five, but there are drinks and snacks in the lounge area."

"Thanks," she says blowing him a kiss and revving the bike up before taking off through the gate. Piece of cake, she had spent time with enough celebrity princesses working for Thompson Security that this performance hadn't been much of a stretch, but a gate guard wasn't the same as waltzing through UK Border Security, the real test was coming. She parks the bike in the far corner of the lot hoping she will be long gone before anyone takes notice of it.

The lounge is definitely VIP and obviously caters to the luxury high end traveler, she grabs a Diet Coke out of the glass cooler and a protein bar from the basket on the counter. The coffee smells good, but she knows it will just increase the acid already churning in her gut, leaning back in the leather lounger she takes a bite of the strawberry filled bar and lets out a sigh. This had been one hell of a day, or couple of days actually. She hoped Jack was alright, at least he was on a US base and should be safe there, she hadn't felt good about leaving him, but he had insisted. She didn't want to think about how to tell him what had happened with Harriet.

She wakes with a start, she must have drifted off – *Christ, that's a good way to wake up dead*, she thinks...

"Jessie, Jessie..."

The voice is familiar, but she can't really place it, she opens her eyes squinting, the morning sun streaming through the floor to ceiling glass makes it hard to see.

"Jessie, what are you doing here," Mark asks his hand on her shoulder.

She is awake now, "Mark, what the hell? Why are you here," she asks shaking herself fully awake. She looks around, they are the only ones in the lounge, "the name's Stella Woods, you can't act like you know me, understand, now why are you here?" she whispers.

"Hey fine, be whoever you want," he says the hurt showing in his voice, "your dad sent me to collect Jack and bring him back to the states... uh what are you doing here?"

Jessie pauses, "two things Mark, you know I work for the government and can't talk about it, it's not personal. Seriously you just have to understand, and two did you say you were picking up Jack?"

He holds his hands up defensively, "Ok, sorry about that. I get it, really I do, and yes he is supposed to be here any time now in a private ambulance, I had a nice tail wind so I'm about forty minutes early, I was just surprised to see you here... even with the glitter," he says with a smile.

Ignoring the glitter comment, "It's okay, no harm done, but I need to get it together, thanks for waking me up..." Jessie stands up and stretches, "I'll see ya when I get back." She heads to the security checkpoint adding a bit of a prance to her walk and donning the sunglasses, time to be Stella Woods pop icon. Her phone starts buzzing before she gets there, "Hello?"

"Jessie we just landed, are you here?" Mikhail asks.

"Yeah, just got to make it through security, be there in a few minutes," she says hanging up. She sashays up to the check point, "Okay boys, my ride is here, who gets to check me out?" she says in an overtly sexual tone holding out her passport.

The security process is surprisingly benign and she is through in just a few minutes, the concierge staff shuttles her out to Mikhail's Gulfstream. She pauses at the top of the stairs watching the ambulance enter the tarmac, must be Jack she thinks, wishing there was a way to talk to him, but what she had to say wasn't meant for a phone call. She turns back into the jet as the stairs are pulled up, "Thanks for coming Mikhail..."

The Unraveling

Rina had finally been released from the hospital late Saturday night well after the conclusion of the Sabbath, she had called her parents to pick her up, their apartment in Tel Aviv was relatively close to the hospital. Her parents doted on her, an only child - like most fathers, hers took great pride in the work his daughter did in the defense of Israel. They weren't aware of all the details, like her transfer from the Army to Mossad five years earlier, but that didn't diminish their pride or willingness to talk to anyone who would listen.

It had started innocently enough, she had tried to keep the story simple as her mother had pushed her to eat something, they had been on a training mission when she had been accidentally stung by a scorpion. How it had penetrated her uniform and why she was in a hospital in Tel Aviv weren't going to hold up to the rigid inspection of her dad's incessant questions. He had forced her hand and the web of lies had snowballed from there. She had been busy trying to calm her mother down when he excused himself and called his Rabbi whose son was a Captain in the IDF, he didn't want to make any trouble but there was clearly more to the story and his only goal was to protect his daughter.

It had been half past one in the morning on Sunday when Colonel Yitzak Adler of the IDF Criminal Investigations Division had knocked on the door. When Rina's records had shown a discharge five-years earlier it had started to raise serious questions about who she was and why she was claiming to be involved in an IDF training accident no one knew anything about. The Colonel didn't have any of his questions answered though, two senior Mossad agents showed up a few minutes later and shut the whole thing down.

They had zip tied her hands behind her back and led her out of her parent's apartment; her father's protestations falling on deaf ears, leaving him staring dumbfounded at the door as they had driven off. Rina was broken, the humiliation in front of her parents combined with the sheer terror of Azrael had destroyed any remaining allegiance she had to ALPHA. Daniel and Neil were on their own, though they didn't know it yet. She leaned against the window watching the street lights pass by during the short ride cross-town to Mossad headquarters.

The pale green room was empty except for the metal table bolted to the floor, the plastic chair she was sitting on and the two-way mirror covering the wall in front of her. There was probably at least two cameras and a microphone as well, but she didn't bother looking for them, what was the point she wasn't keeping any secrets. The two agents had taken an initial statement from her, before leaving her alone for more than an hour. It was almost three in the morning before the interrogation started, she didn't know why they had waited but she was too exhausted to care.

It felt like she was babbling, "there were seven of us, including Control..." she wipes her eyes, "four Israelis, a Brit, Russian, and American."

"But Control was Israeli?" the man in the grey suit asked.

"Yes, yes, I told you that," in her head she has named him Mr. Grey – he was actually Nathan Lieber one of the most senior Mossad agents and a personal advisor to the Director, "who are you?" she asks.

He ignores her question looking down at his notes, "you said earlier that this ALPHA team was working with Azrael... explain that to me..."

"That's not what I said, we weren't working with him. We were just, I don't know, I guess we were pushing him in the direction you all wanted..." she starts crying again, "we were just doing what they told us to."

"Who told you... who wanted?" He pauses, "Rina, I need to know who *they* are..."

"I don't know, Control always gave us the information we needed, I don't know who they are... I mean it must be from higher up right?"

He doesn't answer instead asking, "who is Control? At least you must know that, you said he was Israeli..."

"I can't tell you, please don't make me tell you," she cries.

"Rina, don't make this harder than it has to be, tell us what we need to know…" the man leans in and in a soft voice, "why are you protecting these people? They're going to kill millions of people, you want their blood on your hands… Rina?" He had purposely allowed her an emotional loophole – the ability to separate herself from ALPHA and by extension the killing of a million people. It was a ploy of course, but in her weakened psychological state it was just the straw she needed.

"Daniel Gilman…"

The man leans back in his chair, "Daniel Gilman, the head of Mossad Intelligence?"

"Yes sir," she answers hanging her head.

"Where is he Rina?"

"I don't know… I really don't."

The man picks up his phone and dials, "it's Gilman, yes that Gilman, find him now…" He hangs up and turns back to Rina, "you did the right thing young lady… now sit tight, we've got work to do."

The man leaves her sitting in the chair, she lays her head on her arms and cries softly. She remembers the day Daniel recruited her, it had seemed like important work protecting her country. Now the lie was exposed though, how could killing all those people really protect her people or country? There weren't any answers forthcoming.

The two men watch her through the two-way mirror, "so what is going to happen to her?" the young man asks.

"She is never going to see the light of day..." Lieber answers. He looks through the mirror again, "this is a story that can never be told..." He shakes his head, "it's an unmitigated disaster. Can you imagine what will happen if an Israeli - an ex-Mossad agent at that - unleashes this weapon during the Hajj?" He looks at the other man, "no, I can't either, we will be the pariahs of the modern world..."

"But the Americans and the British are involved as well..." the younger man interjects.

"Don't be naïve my young friend, they will turn their backs on us quicker than you can imagine, and then the war will start – the last war." He puts his hand on the man's shoulder, "We have to neutralize this now, and that means rolling ALPHA up and finding Azrael."

"How are we supposed to do that?"

"Gilman will give us ALPHA and we will involve the American and British intelligence agencies – they can clean their mess up and we will take care of our house."

The younger man hesitates, "okay, but what about Azrael, nobody's even been close to bringing him down..."

"I don't know, it may mean involving the Saudis – I don't like it, but that decision isn't going to be ours to make." He doesn't say so, but there is no way they can come clean to the

Saudis – this isn't something the Kingdom would be understanding about.

There is a knock on the door and an agent sticks his head in, "Gilman is in room four sir…"

"Thanks," Lieber turns to the younger man, "let's go Ben, time to see what he can tell us." The walk down the hall and into a grey room identical to the one holding Rina.

"Daniel…" he says in greeting as he sits down, "Ben take those ties off of him."

"Yes sir," the young man says as he cuts the ties off Daniel's wrists.

"Thanks Nathan," Daniel says, rubbing his wrists together.

"Daniel what have you done?" Nathan asks.

Daniel hangs his head, "I love our country Nathan," he looks up tears in his eyes, "I did what I had to."

Nathan tries to control his anger, but it bleeds through in his voice, "you have put us all in jeopardy, if the Muslim nations…"

"If they what Nathan? We have created a completely new identity for Azrael, David Eisen doesn't exist anymore." Daniel starts to stand up.

"Sit down sir!" Ben orders drawing his weapon.

Daniel sits, his hands raised in supplication, "Nathan, this will work, the Arab nations will tear each other apart and we will finally have assured the safety of our people…"

"You are a fool Daniel, Azrael himself will make sure they know it was a Jew that did this to them, don't you understand?"

Daniel smiles thinly, "that's why my team is going to eliminate him, he won't leave Jeddah alive, even if it means sacrificing ourselves."

"Daniel do you hear yourself?" Nathan shakes his head, "you already lost one of your team in Jeddah and young Rina is down the hall... this is over, how can you not see?" He leans forward, "our only hope now is to stop Azrael before he can unleash this holocaust."

The choice of words is intentional and hits Daniel with the force of a physical blow. "How can you equate this to that?" he asks angrily.

"Daniel how can we not – the world will..." he leans back in the chair and with a sigh, "now tell me where to find Azrael and I will send a team to end this."

"It wasn't supposed to be like this Nathan... I don't know where he is... we didn't even expect him to come back here..." He turns to Ben, "Can we get a few minutes alone?"

Nathan nods to the young man, "it's okay Ben, why don't you get us all some coffee..."

As the young man leaves Daniel turns back to Nathan, "are you sure you want to do this? My group was put together at the highest levels – this isn't going to go away quietly Nathan..."

"How high, give me names Daniel… otherwise it's just talk…"

"You know I can't do that…" he says exasperatedly.

"Then I can't help you… you have to give me something, tell me who on the US side and the Brits – let's start there."

Why not expose the Americans and the Brits, it won't change anything, maybe he can delay long enough for Azrael… "okay, okay, Anthony Moyer on the American side and Lord Arleigh Fields on the British… satisfied?"

"National Security Director Moyer?" Nathan asks surprised.

"Yes, that Moyer, I told you this was at the highest levels, we have to do this Nathan, it's not too late… Fields is one of the top men in the British Foreign Office. These are our country's biggest supporters, was I supposed to say? No?"

"They approached you directly?" Lieber asks incredulously.

"No, of course not, came down from Liebowitz, told me to put a team together to help track down Azrael, this was over three years ago…" Daniel stops, realizing he has given away more than intended. "Look Nathan, this all started as a joint effort to track down and eliminate David, it didn't change direction until we were already deep into it…"

"Why would we need an international team for that, we knew Azrael was Eisen from the start?"

278

Daniel leans back in his chair and spreads his hands, "I don't know... Liebowitz says do it, so I do it, what would you have done, seriously?"

"You should have said something Daniel, I would have helped you... who is left from your team?"

"Neil Weinberg, he is up in Nahariya in case Eisen decides to go home."

"You think that's a possibility?"

"I don't know I didn't think he would come back here at all... Neil is worried he is actually targeting us and the whole Hajj thing has been a red herring from the start..."

"What do you think? Is that possible?"

"Possible, yes, probable, no... he went through a lot of trouble to penetrate Mecca and their holy water supply, why take the risk just to come home? No, I think he will do what he intended..."

Ben comes back in with three coffees, setting two between the men and sipping his own.

"Ben, keep Daniel here," he turns to the other man, "do I need to put the ties back on you?"

"No, no I'm not going anywhere..."

"Okay, I've got to advise the Prime Minister... this is his call..." Nathan stands up and heads for the door, he looks back, "I'm sorry Daniel... really I am."

Accountable

Presidents and Prime Ministers don't like bad news, they like it even less when someone wakes them up with it. The Israeli Prime Minister had made the calls himself, such was the importance of communicating the proper message, that it also allowed executive privilege to be invoked, was a bonus. The American President believed in the prescription *early to bed, early to rise...* he had turned in an hour earlier and upon being wakened had exhibited the customarily coarse language he had become known for. Considered a bit of a cowboy on the world stage, he was quite the opposite of the British Prime Minister, she was calm and serene under even the most stressful circumstances and this call at four in the morning certainly qualified.

After a brief explanation and the promise to forward a complete security brief with all the details, they had both agreed to clean up their piece. In almost identical language, both Western leaders had made it clear; Azrael was his problem and don't expect any support if somehow, Azrael managed to pull off this horror – it wasn't anything he hadn't expected. He had made the calls from his personal home office, Nathan had been sitting on the couch listening. He set the phone down, "I want you in charge of this, whatever it takes – no mistakes, understand?"

"Yes sir…" had been the simple reply.

Six thousand miles away and nearing midnight, an irritated President Campbell dons his Navy sweats and shambles down to his office calling for coffee, cinnamon rolls, the Attorney General – and his Chief of Staff – Mindi Holbrook. The rumor was that Mindi was either clairvoyant or kept a cot in her office, she was the first female Chief of Staff and always seemed to magically be there when the President called. AG Jack Mulcahey was able to make it in before the President had started on his second cup of coffee.

Halfway through his second or maybe third cinnamon roll the President had fully briefed his two most trusted advisors. "I know we don't have a lot of details, but we have to get out ahead of this… Jack who is our best guy at Justice to lead an investigation on this?"

"Jim, you sure you want to go in that direction, there won't be any keeping it out of the press?"

Mindi watches the exchange, "we can't sit on this, God forbid something does happen and it looks like we were dragging on our feet. Everything we've worked for over there will go up in flames, literally… no this has to be done by the book," the President answers.

He looks over at Mindi – she nods her assent – "going to be a political firestorm but we'll hit all the morning shows and get our story out before anyone knows what's happening – going to have to burn Moyer at the stake though." She takes another sip of her black coffee, "I'll call Simpson at the Agency, he is career – let me drop this on him and see how he reacts..."

"Ok, if you're comfortable with him, see what resources we have over there we can use." The President turns to the AG, "who are you thinking?"

"I've got just the guy," the AG smiles, "Alberto Jimenez, sharp, tough, fearless just the type we need for something like this..."

"Moyer is going to try to intimidate him, can he handle it?" Mindi asks.

"No problem, Alberto grew up on the mean streets of Albuquerque, trust me, this is our guy."

"Ok, make sure he understands, I want everyone involved in this, no one is protected, doesn't matter who it is, clear?"

"Yes sir," the AG takes his leave.

"What do you think Mindi?" the President asks.

"I think we better hope the Israeli's can stop this guy, but either way we are in for a new Jihad against the Great Satan, and this lunatic Aza is going to latch on to this like a rabid pit-bull."

"Alright, nothing we can do about that now, let's get Simpson up tonight, if we aren't sleeping, nobody else is either..."

"Yes sir, you want me to call Director Jacoby first?"

"No, if you trust Simpson just call him. If Moyer was part of this then let's find out who else knew about it before we let the cat out of the bag, make sense?"

"How much can I tell him?"

"Up to you, I trust your judgement, enough to gauge whether you think he's involved... you can leave me out of it for now, just say we have some information coming out of the Israeli government – can't divulge any more than that... you know the drill."

"Yes sir, I'll have an update at the morning brief, anything else?"

"No, no, that's fine and Mindi..."

"Yes sir?"

"Thanks, you know I couldn't do this without you..."

She gives him a smile, he has always been a great boss, "thank you sir, get some rest, I've got this..."

She watches him for a moment as he heads back to the residence side of the White House, before turning and walking to her office. She would do whatever she could to protect him, but a scandal of this magnitude would unfairly overshadow two terms of progress. The peace in the Middle-East, something they had worked tirelessly on would be destroyed, not to mention the specter of a resurgent Caliphate – *it just pissed her off and fucking Moyer... what the hell was he thinking...?*

She picks up the phone linking to the White House Switchboard, the operators were legendary for being able to find literally anyone, anywhere at any time... she had tested it once or twice and had yet to stump them. "Yes, can you find Deputy CIA Director Vance Simpson for me please, connect him to my office if you will..." she says before hanging up. It was going to be another long night, and contrary to popular belief, she did not have a cot in her office, but she had spent more than a few nights on the very comfortable couch, her diminutive frame fit nicely on.

She had just started jotting down some talking points when the phone starts ringing. She smiles, they truly could find anyone, "Mindi Holbrook..."

"Good evening Miss Holbrook, Vance Simpson, what can I do for you?"

"Vance, thanks for taking the call so late. Listen, I'll get right to it, we've had some disturbing information come in tonight from the Israelis and I wanted to get your take on it before we go any further..." she pauses waiting for him to respond.

"Ok," he says noncommittally, "what do you have?"

"Well, according to the Israelis they have taken down an unsanctioned top-secret group called ALPHA that's connected to Azrael..."

The silence stretches out for a few seconds, "you're kidding, right?" he tries to keep the shock out of his voice, "when did this happen Miss Holbrook?"

"Call me Mindi, last few hours. Vance, if you know something about this I have to know, the President has to know..."

"That information isn't completely accurate, but I don't know that we should be discussing this over the phone..."

"All White House lines are secure..." she answers.

"Yes, I know, but I am at home and my line is not..."

"I'll send a car for you then..."

"No need, I'll drive myself. Just tell the gate to be expecting me, I can be there in forty minutes... can I ask a question?"

"Sure what?"

"Do we know where Azrael is right now?" he asks.

She doesn't answer right away, if he is part of the conspiracy any tactical advantage will be lost by telling him, "why?"

"I have an operative on the way to Israel as we speak, she will be on the ground in a few hours; if he is there I need to warn her..."

Mindi wonders if that's true, it's a pretty elaborate story to concoct on the spur of the moment, making her decision quickly she says, "yes, he is for now, the Israelis are putting together a team to go after him… now get here as quickly as you can."

"Yes ma'am, I'm on my way." He hangs up, shakes his wife awake, "duty calls honey, sorry." He kisses her forehead and heads to the closet, grabbing the SAT phone off the night stand. It rings half a dozen times before going to voicemail: "Jessie, Azrael is in Israel, things are starting to break loose, I can't go into it now, but the Israelis are on to ALPHA – please be careful." He hangs up hoping she checks the message before she lands.

The White House

Vance turns the key to start the BMW Five series, the car was twenty years old, but ran like a top, he loved it too much to trade for a newer one. His wife refused to ride in it, preferring her Porsche SUV, he didn't care though, he loved the old styling and had refinished the interior two years earlier, with over three hundred thousand miles together it was more of an old friend than a car. He dials Albert's number on the SAT phone and waits while the encryption syncs.

A groggy Jimenez picks up a few rings later, "what the fuck Simpson it's like one thirty or something... you lonely?"

"Pay attention Albert, this is starting to go down and I need some advice, just got a call from Mindi Holbrook – you know Mindi?"

"Uh yeah, what do you mean you got a call?"

"From the White House, she said the Israelis are taking ALPHA down as we speak, and they believe there has been collusion with Azrael..."

"She actually said 'collusion'" Albert asks sounding much more awake all of a sudden.

"Uh no, why?"

"Cause it's one of those legal words you never want associated with your name... what does she want with you?"

"Well, if I had to guess they're going to try to get out in front of this, I'm headed into the White House now to meet with her."

"You're going there? Fuck me... okay, okay, let me think a second." Albert gets out of bed and heads for the kitchen, this was going to require some thinking and that required sustenance. "Alright, here's the deal, we probably know more than they do, at least for now – which means she is going to want to know why you didn't send this up the chain or reach out to the White House directly. That's easy though, you didn't know how high up the conspiracy went and wanted to gather as much information as possible yada, yada... maybe not completely Kosher, but plausible." He looks in the fridge, pulling out a container of left-over chicken lo-mein, gives it a sniff and pops it in the microwave.

"Are you eating? Come on Albert..."

"What, you fucking woke me in the middle of the night, it's just a snack... listen though best advice on this – tell the truth, if she is reaching out to you they probably didn't see this coming, you don't want to be sitting in front of a Senate Committee explaining why you lied to the White House six months from now... and think about this Vance, why call you and not Moyer?"

"Thanks Albert I appreciate it, what do I tell her about Lou and Jessie, you know our group?"

"Little as possible, Jessie is fine, she works for you, but I would leave the rest out if you can, but you know what, if you feel it's the right thing to tell her I think everyone would understand..."

"Okay, thanks again, go back to bed..."

"Way ahead of you..." Albert answers.

Twenty minutes later he stops at the gate and shows his credentials, after a bit of scrutiny they wave him in and direct him to the parking area. He knows the drill having been here a time or two over the years, but in the middle of the night it has a clandestine feel to it. He signs in and passes through the security screening before finally being given a badge and led to Mindi Holbrook's office by a serious looking Secret Service agent.

"Vance thanks for coming," she says offering her hand and greeting him as if it was the most normal thing in the world to be holding a meeting in the White House at two in the morning.

"Miss Holbrook, I hope I can help," he answers a bit noncommittally.

"Coffee?" She offers, pouring herself a cup.

"Sure," he says, sitting down across the desk from her. The pleasantries done with, an awkward silence develops. "Miss Holbrook, how are we going to decide to trust each other," Vance finally asks with a small smile.

"We don't have much of a choice, do we?" she says with a sigh. "Here's the problem Vance, it's my job to protect the President, and clearly you know something about all of this already, so now I am in the unenviable position of trying to decipher whether I can trust you or if you were part of this mess to begin with," she spreads her hands, "so help me out here."

"Well, I am asking myself the same thing," he answers setting the coffee cup down. "You see Mindi, I am a little surprised you would call me and not DNI Moyer, he is after all the President's senior intelligence official and a Cabinet member."

Mindi Holbrook may have been one of the smartest folks in this administration, but in the midst of a crisis in the middle of the night crossing swords with a very well trained senior intelligence officer like Vance Simpson, she was at a clear disadvantage and he knew it.

She hesitates long enough for Simpson to nod his head, "Miss Holbrook," he says, reverting to a more formal tone, "why don't you tell me the whole story, I'll fill in whatever gaps I can and then let's see how we protect our country and the rest of the world, shall we?"

She makes a quick calculation and seeing there really is no choice gives him a brief and concise overview of what they know, which admittedly isn't much. "We don't have much more than that, call came in from the highest levels of the Israeli government – this is pretty much happening real time so there isn't a lot of detail right now."

"Mindi, you didn't mention DNI Moyer? Are you aware of his role in this?"

She hesitates again, she wasn't fond of playing poker when the other guy could see her hand... "Okay, from what we were told Moyer is the senior official on our side that... I guess initiated this catastrophe... satisfied?"

"I'm sorry Mindi, I just needed to make sure the information you were getting was real."

"Satisfied?"

"Yes, but there is a lot more to this than you've been told..." It takes forty minutes to walk her through the details, including the VX17 and the working hypothesis on the Zamzam Well as the primary target.

"Okay Vance, but how did you develop this... what did you call it – a working hypothesis?" she asks.

It's his turn to feel the pressure, "combination really; intel developed from agents, a lot of predictive analytics based on data we've gathered and sometimes you get lucky with tips honestly. Anyway, we've put it all together and think we have a pretty good picture of what's going on."

She gives him a long searching look, "and there's still plenty you have elected not to tell me... still not sure if you trust me? Give me a second Vance okay?" She doesn't wait for his answer picking up the phone and keying in a three-digit extension. "Sir I hate to bother you again, any chance of you coming back down for a few minutes? I think you need to hear this... Ok, thanks." She turns to Vance, "follow me..." she says getting up from her desk.

They have been standing quietly outside the Oval Office for just a few minutes when the President comes down the hall still in his sweats trailed by two Secret Service agents. He holds out his hand in greeting, "Vance, thanks for coming over tonight, I understand we have a bit of a mess on our hands."

Vance is a bit overwhelmed, the whole thing is surreal, "Yes sir, I think that may be a bit of an understatement."

They follow him into the office and sit in the two opposing wingback chairs as the President takes his place in the large leather chair behind the Resolute Desk. Leaning forward his elbows on the leather-bound blotter he looks from one to the other, "Ok, who is going to start?"

"Sir, I think you need to hear what Mister Simpson has to say, he has significantly more detail and context than we do on this ALPHA group." She turns to Vance, "I know you're skeptical, but the President needs to have as clear a picture as possible..."

Vance nods in assent, "Sir, I need to start at the beginning if that's okay?" He gives them brief but thorough background on Azrael including a top ten list of assassinations. "We've been searching for this guy for almost four years, he disappeared shortly after the Syrian incident and rumor was he had managed to smuggle a vial of the VX17 – you familiar with this sir?" The President nods and motions for him to continue. "Well anyway there isn't a worse scenario than this lunatic with a WMD. We think this is when Moyer and his group developed this warped idea to set the Middle East on fire."

The President interjects, "do you know who is in the rest of this group?"

"No sir. I only know DNI Moyer because he is in my chain of command and he started asking some questions that didn't make sense. That, combined with an attempt to take one of my top agents out because she was getting too close to this..."

"Wait a second Vance," Mindi interjects, "you didn't mention this earlier."

"I know and I'm sorry, there is a group of us that have been working on this for the past couple of weeks under the radar if you will." He looks at Mindi before turning back to the President. "Sir, we developed most of our information outside the confines of the CIA and DC in general. I've got a young agent, Jessie McIntyre on the way to Israel as we speak, I have authorized her to take whatever action necessary to neutralize this threat, she may be the best chance we have sir."

"What about this group you mentioned, people from Langley?" the President asks leaning forward elbows on the desk.

"No sir, FBI, Justice, and all the analytics came out of Paradigm Tech in Boulder – they are a government contractor design and deploy basically all our encryption and system security programs… They've got this data analytics engine called NEO it's like science fiction sir…" Vance stops realizing he has been babbling a bit. "Sorry sir, things have been moving pretty fast…"

"Okay, two questions – who at the FBI and Justice?"

"Well Harrington at the FBI, he's based here in DC…"

"Isn't he the one that broke the human trafficking ring last year?"

"Actually, him and Jessie McIntyre but we stepped aside and let the Bureau handle everything stateside…"

"Who at Justice?"

"Alberto Jimenez…"

The President looks to Mindi, "okay, I hear he is excellent, now tell me about this attempt on your agent."

Vance gives them the short version, "this guy was a retired SEAL working at NSA, Miss McIntyre and her father Lou called in some favors at the FBI and that's how Tim and Alberto got involved, we all met out in Colorado where Paradigm is located, one thing led to another and when we pooled all our data using Paradigm's data analytics tool, all arrows pointed to Azrael, ALPHA and DNI Moyer… I'm sorry sir." He had left Kirilov out of it for now, not even the President needed to worry about navigating that mess right now.

"Alright, as of right now I'm appointing a Presidential Commission to uncover this mess and figure out how we can keep this from happening again, I think you should lead it." He turns to Mindi, "I can do that, right?"

"Yes sir, but I think we should focus on preventing the imminent disaster first, there will be plenty of time to do a post mortem on this..."

"Sir, I am not the right guy to head up your commission, I'm CIA, an old spy. You need someone like Alberto – he knows the law and would be much better at putting something together like this, besides this is a domestic issue you need to let Justice and the FBI take the lead on this..."

The President nods, "you're right, but I still want you involved, I'm sure there is a foreign component to this and I may want you to weigh in on that." Mindi nods her agreement, "ok now what about your operative, this McIntyre, I want her to have whatever she needs. If it's in this country's power I want it to happen, and put her father on the commission, sounds like we need his smarts."

"Mister President, she is probably landing in Tel Aviv in the next hour or so, any chance we can ask the Israelis to incorporate her into their team? I think it's better if she isn't operating over there without some official coverage..."

"Consider it done, now I'm going to get a few hours..."

"Yes sir," they say in unison as he stands.

"Mindi, I want an initial brief on this at the ten AM."

"Yes sir," she responds.

"Vance thanks for coming out at this time of night, good to have you on the team," he says with a pat on the shoulder before heading back to the residence.

Mindi turns to Vance, "I'll get it all written up and official for his signature, it's not as simple as he likes to make it unfortunately... Do you want to talk to your team before it's announced?"

"Yeah, that would be great," Vance answers still trying to catch up with what's just happened.

"I'm sure the AG is going to be the one to announce this and formally tap Mister Jimenez, but I think we're okay if you tell him it's coming but it probably won't be until Monday. We need to get out ahead of this first, and Vance thanks again..." she says with a small smile leading him to the security desk.

He takes his leave, retrieving his car and heads home, there won't be any sleep the horizon to the East is already starting to brighten.

Confrontations

The Gulf Stream landed after finally receiving clearance from Tel Aviv tower, not a guarantee these days, the airport was busy and it wasn't unusual for the Israeli Military to delay or reroute private air traffic without warning. It was extremely difficult to even obtain permission to fly into Israeli airspace, the approval process was a myriad of forms, background checks and documentation — they took their security seriously here. Fortunately, Kirilov was a known identity and since he was doing business with Mossad some accommodations had been made.

The door to the cockpit opens, "sir, I am being directed to the tarmac by Terminal Four, what should I do?"

Kirilov looks at Jessie before answering, "go ahead, nothing we can do on the ground, what is Terminal Four?"

"It's ceremonial only sir, not even on the airport maps..." the pilot replies nervously.

Kirilov turns to Jessie, "what do you think?"

"I think someone must have known we were coming, I'm not going down without a fight though, what do we have on board?"

Kirilov smiles, "well, I happen to be in the business..." he leads her toward the back, "but Jessie, there is no winning a firefight with the Israelis, especially not here, let's see if we can talk first okay?"

She gives him a skeptical look, "okay, I'll follow your lead on this, but if they make a threatening move I'm not going to die asking questions." Her phone starts ringing as they pull to a stop, she checks the number. *Shit, what does Simpson want, this is not a good time...*

She clicks the answer button while taking the HK machine pistol and three thirty round clips from Kirilov, "got a bit of a situation here sir, what's up?" she asks in a clipped tone.

"Please tell me you haven't shot anyone..."

"Not yet sir, we just landed at Ben Gurion, but it looks like the Israelis knew we were coming, they've shuttled us off to an empty part of the airport..."

"Jessie listen to me closely, they knew you were coming because the President told them... I can't explain all of it now, but Mossad broke ALPHA last night and they are putting a task force together to eliminate Azrael... Our President insisted they put you on the team..."

"Are you serious sir? What about Mikhail?"

"Yes, I'm serious, and don't let Mikhail shoot anyone either..." Simpson sighs, "I don't know about Mikhail, he has good contacts over there so he should be able to take care of himself."

"Okay sir, who's my contact on this side?" she asks.

"Nathan Lieber, he's heading it up – very senior in Mossad, and a serious operator so pay attention."

"Okay, got to go sir... I'll update you later." She looks over at Mikhail, "going to be interesting, you hear enough of that?"

Mikhail nods slapping in a clip, "I did, and it makes sense... let's be careful anyway..."

They pop the door and drop the steps, three blacked out SUVs and half a dozen uniformed Israeli soldiers, weapons at the ready, greet them. A young man in a navy-blue suit calls out, "Miss McIntyre, I'm Ben Shapiro – Nathan Lieber asked me to escort you to his office." He says politely. Noticing their weapons, the soldiers elevate theirs, Ben puts his hands up, "you won't be needing those, please put them down."

"I'd rather hold onto it if it's all the same to you..." Jessie responds only slightly lowering hers.

"I'm sorry Miss McIntyre, I can't let you do that, leave them in the plane, I promise nothing will happen to you."

Jessie lets out a laugh, "I appreciate your confidence Mister Shapiro, she hands the gun to Kirilov and whispers "cover me," as she descends the steps. Walking directly up to Ben, "what about my friend?"

"Mister Kirilov is free to stay here or we can arrange for hotel accommodations," he answers.

She ignores the obvious attempt to surprise her and turns back to the plane, "Mikhail," she calls waving him down.

He sets the guns on the seat and calmly joins her on the tarmac, "good to see you Ben," he says holding out his hand.

"Mikhail," the man answers with a nod.

"So, you two are old friends?" she asks.

"Not exactly," Mikhail answers, but we know each other. Turning back to Ben, "I'll be staying at The Norman, I've got a suite over there," he says matter-of-factly.

"That's fine, my people will take you over," Ben answers in a tone that discourages any further discussion. "Okay, let's go then, any bags or anything?"

"Nope, just my backpack," Jessie answers holding it out, "I suppose you'll want to take a look..." Ben takes a quick look but doesn't say anything.

Turning to Mikhail, "look I'll call you as soon as I have some details, no worries okay?" Jessie says, touching him on the arm.

He doesn't say anything as he watches her get into the back seat of the lead SUV, before turning to the remaining two soldiers, "you my escort?" Neither one says anything as they open the rear door for him and get in the front. It's a silent thirty-minute drive to The Norman before they pull up and the valet opens the door for him.

"Ahh, Mister Kirilov, so good to see you again."

"Thanks George, just the duffle... is the room ready?" Kirilov asks, ignoring the two in the front of the vehicle.

"Of course, sir right this way."

On the other side of Tel Aviv Ben and Jessie pull into the Israeli Defense Forces headquarters — there simply is no precedent for allowing a foreign agent into Mossad's headquarters — even an American one. It's been an awkwardly quiet ride with Jessie ignoring Ben's attempts at small talk. They pass through a thorough security screening before being escorted to a small office where Jessie is given a visitor ID badge with her picture on it. The security officer explains that she must wear it at all times and is not to be unescorted while in the building.

With the formalities completed Ben leads her to a bank of elevators. They get off on the sixth floor and enter a large conference room, just above the table a three-dimensional map is being projected. The four men studying it stop talking when she and Ben approach them.

"Nathan Lieber, you must be Miss McIntyre," a well-dressed older man says extending his hand.

"Yes, pleased to meet you sir," she answers, giving him a firm grip in return. He introduces her to the other three, all officers in the Israeli military: Captain Hamlin, Lieutenant Golson, and Lieutenant Kashman nod their greeting.

They turn back to the map projection, which from what Jessie can see looks like an older neighborhood, she guesses this is where they believe Azrael is. The men are speaking Hebrew ostensibly dismissing her, she has been studying Hebrew for a bit more than a year and the Agency's intensive language program is able to accelerate the time it would normally take to master a language. That, combined with her natural linguistic strength means she can follow most of the conversation. The men are discussing a SWAT style breach and elimination of Azrael at his apartment, having listened long enough she breaks in speaking in Hebrew, "with all due respect sir that's a terrible idea..." The men all look up trying to hide their surprise.

Nathan with a thin smile, "why would that be Miss McIntyre?"

She switches to English, "well, two things actually, first you trained him... think he doesn't have the whole area under some type of electronic surveillance, he will know you're coming a mile away and my guess is that whole place is wired to go up should someone get close enough to have a shot at him..."

"And the second thing?" he asks.

"I need to talk to him..." she says simply.

Golson breaks into a laugh, "that's insane..."

"Maybe, but if you kill him and he's already placed the VX17 there won't be any way to stop it in time... I've been studying this guy for a year now and I think I can get him to talk to me."

"Why you? What makes you think you know him better than we do? We trained him, he was one of us," the Captain says

302

forcefully. He turns to Nathan, "why are we even including the Americans in this?"

Nathan ignores him, "go on, tell me what you're thinking," turning back to the Captain, "she is here because their President and your Prime Minister want her here, clear?" He turns back to Jessie and nods for her to continue.

She sits down and leans in, "sir, this is going to seem overly simple, but I learned everything I could about him in the first couple of months of trying to track down his identity, his training, skills, style, choice of targets, perceived ideology, everything our intelligence community had on this guy. None of it seemed to make sense, his targets were all over the place, wasn't motivated by politics, religion, anything I could put my finger on and say — this is what drives this guy. Clearly, he was trained beyond the capabilities of most people, a total anomaly if you will," she looks at the men.

"Go on..." Nathan encourages her.

"So, when we finally cracked who he was a couple of weeks ago, I started to think we were approaching this all wrong, Azrael isn't an assassin, not in the true sense of the word, he really is the Angel of Death, that's how he sees himself. This isn't about anything more than the bringing the Lord's vengeance upon those responsible for killing his wife and daughter." She pushes forward, "he's intent on not only killing as many Muslims as possible, but doing it in a particularly horrible way during their holiest of holy days... and the topping on this death sundae... as an Israeli he will make all of you, all of Israel an international pariah... cause nobody is going to believe you didn't know about it... so I need to talk to him..."

Before Nathan or the others can respond Ben sticks his head in the door, "he's on the move..."

Task Force - Justice

"I'll have a number two with an extra hash-brown and small black coffee please," Vance pulls up to the first window and hands the young woman a ten-dollar bill before pulling up to the next window. McDonalds wasn't his first choice for a gourmet breakfast, but he had been inexplicably hungry after driving out of the White House grounds and the twenty-four-hour McDonald's was about the only thing open at five in the morning. Besides a sausage and egg McMuffin was a bit of a guilty pleasure, and if a 2AM unexpected meeting with the president didn't earn you a free pass from the cardiologist well what did?

He had called Jessie to give her a quick heads up, of course she had seemed skeptical, he just hoped she could keep herself in check, the Israelis didn't take well to outside interference and they weren't going to be very happy about having to include her in their operation. He hadn't bothered to argue the point with the President, he was just glad to have him intervene on her behalf.

He needed to call Tim and Albert, but they could wait a few more minutes, he parks in the empty lot and blows on the hot coffee before taking a sip. DC had plenty of swanky restaurants and an equal number of greasy spoons, but there was something delightful about that first bite of the preformed salty, crunchy, potato cake fresh out of the deep fryer. He takes the last bite of the sausage sandwich, wishing for the millionth time that they toasted the muffins better, he smiles to himself – *critiquing McDonalds...... too funny*! He dials Albert's number and waits for the sync and he is sure going to be the miffed answer.

"I can't believe you are calling me again, Jesus man have you no humanity..."

"Good morning Albert, just left the White House, you mind if I dial Tim in for a three way?"

"Go ahead, best offer I've had all week..."

Vance smiles to himself the man was incorrigible he thinks, as he dials Harrington's number.

"Tim Harrington," the man sounds as if he has been up for hours and was just waiting for the call.

"Morning Tim, sorry to call so early, I've got Albert dialed in as well, need to brief both of you on a meeting I just left."

"Little early for a meeting isn't?" Tim asks.

"It's a little early for anything," Albert growls.

"Listen fellas, last night Mossad took down ALPHA or at least their piece of it, their Prime Minister called the President directly and fingered Moyer..."

"No fuckin' way..." Albert blurts out.

"Yes, anyway Mindi Holbrook called and asked me to come over... long story short, the President is announcing a Special Commission to investigate the whole thing and provide a recommendation. My guess is they are going to try to insulate themselves from this and we'll probably end up with a Special Prosecutor and a number of indictments... anyway Albert, the good news is you're going to be tapped to head it up..."

"Congrats Albert you'll be famous," Tim laughs.

"Just what I want to be... fuckin' famous," Albert says quietly. "Any idea when this is coming Vance?" he asks.

"My guess is you'll get a call from the AG this morning, Holbrook said he would be the one announcing it."

"Looks like I dodged the bullet this time," Tim says laughing again.

"Bullshit dude, you are going to be my lead investigator!" Albert exclaims.

"You would do that to a friend?" Tim says.

"Count on it amigo!" Albert says, dropping back into his street accent.

"Listen fellas, I've got to run, heading home for a quick shower and I owe Lou a call also, the President wants his brain on this one too," Vance says.

"This is going to be crazy," Albert says, "alright take care guys, looks like I better find a clean shirt."

They exchange goodbyes and hang up, life was crazy sometimes – he never would have figured to be working with the likes of Albert and Tim, never mind Lou. He looks at this watch, six o'clock already, that would make it four in Boulder, he decides to catch a shower at home and change no reason to roust Lou out of bed, he was pretty sure the man wasn't going to be excited about serving on a Presidential Commission.

Two hours later; shower and clean shirt and back in the car, Vance dials Lou's number. The man picks up quickly, "everything okay Vance?"

"Yeah Lou, everything's fine, you got a couple of minutes."

"Sure, but have you talked to Jessie?" he asks, "last I heard she was heading for a safe house, someone Jack knows over there, but she hasn't called since then."

"She's fine, just talked to her a couple of hours ago, landed in Tel Aviv with Mikhail and was meeting up with the Israelis..."

"Wait, did you say meeting up with the Israelis? What Israelis?" Lou asks his voice started to rise.

"Slow down Lou, let me fill you in."

"Okay, sorry about that go, ahead..." Lou says calming down.

Simpson recounts the events of the last twenty-four hours, concluding with Albert being tapped to head up the investigation, "and Lou, the President wants you to be part of it also..."

"Oh, for the love of God, why?" Lou exclaims.

Vance smiles to himself, he had expected something like this, "probably my fault I'm afraid, he wanted to know how we had cracked the whole thing open on our end... and well, you were the brains behind it all – I had to give you the credit," he says with a laugh.

"Very funny Vance, I owe you one, Jesus you know how I feel about this stuff..."

"I do actually Lou, it's one of the reasons I think it's important we include folks like yourself for a change."

"I don't know Vance, I'll have to think about it, don't we need to worry about ending this mess first though?"

"Yes, we do, but either way we need to clean this up and make sure it's not swept under the rug. Lou, they sent someone to your house my friend, we can't let that stand... the people running this country can't think that's okay..." He pauses, not having really thought about it this way before. "You know, we had some dark times after 9/11, did some things we all thought were necessary, but Lou, we can't slip back to those times and this mess reeks of that attitude... so you have to make sure we shine a big bright light on it..."

"Okay Vance, you're right – I guess I needed to hear that."

"It's okay my friend," Vance answers.

"But what about right now, what can we do to help Jessie, do we have any details on what the Israeli plan is?"

"I don't have anything Lou, they aren't sharing, but my guess is an all-out manhunt to terminate this guy before he can release the VX17."

"Christ, I hope she's careful, leave it to my girl to be in the middle of the biggest mess possible."

"I wouldn't worry Lou, I'm sure they will have her in more of an observational role than anything else, no way Mossad is letting an American agent take the lead on anything, besides Jessie is one of the most capable people I have ever known..."

"Thanks again Vance, sometimes I forget she isn't six years old... a father's curse I guess."

"I understand..." he didn't but he figured it's what Lou needed to hear, "stay close to the phone I'll call you as soon as I hear anything."

"Will do!" Lou hangs up and punches a few keys on his system, bringing up a list of servers. He was sure Vance would call him, but he also had real-time access to many of the SIGINT systems NSA and other agencies used to monitor communications around the world. It shouldn't be too hard to isolate Israeli military communications and listen in on some chatter... what could it hurt?

Memories

Jack extracts his passport, phone, and remaining cash before stowing the backpack under the stretcher hoping the gate security wouldn't search the whole ambulance. Sticking his head between the front seats he can see the tarmac and a couple of corporate jets reflecting the rising sun. "Well boys, looks like we made it and I didn't have to kill either one of you... good show!" once again using his best British accent.

They drive directly up to the Paradigm jet and a waiting security officer. "They are going to check you here and then you can board the jet sir," the driver tells him. It only takes a few minutes to review his passport before Mark helps him up the steps and pulls the door closed.

"Jack this is Jerry Franklin, Lou asked him to come along to make sure you were okay..." Mark says introducing them. "And this is Tom Farmington, another one of our pilots, we're switching on and off since this is a quick turn-around, you guys get settled in while we pre-flight."

"Please to meet you Jerry," Jack says, holding out his hand, "combat medic?"

"Yes sir, three tours in Afghanistan, saw some action in Somalia and places I can't talk about," he says with a smile. "Why don't you give me a quick run-down on what happened. I've got Captain Williard's notes but give me the one-two anyway."

"Fellas strap in, so I can get us out of here," Mark calls from the front.

The men buckle in as Jack explains the events of the previous evening to Jerry. He leaves out a lot of detail but it's obvious the man knows enough not to ask too many questions.

"Jack, I think we're probably fine with this, but if you feel any dizziness or nausea or that thing starts bleeding I need to know right away, okay... no hero stuff."

"You got it, I'm too old for the hero stuff..." Jack answers with a laugh.

"Right, of course you are, which is why I had to fly over here to babysit you home... just tell me if you don't feel right, now let me get a quick blood pressure and temp, got to earn my pay," he says reaching for his med bag. He is quick and efficient as the jet levels off and turns West heading out over the Atlantic as he finishes up.

Mark comes back to where they are sitting, "He doing okay" he asks, motioning to Jack, "not going to have anywhere to divert to for at least a few hours."

"Yeah, no problem, I think we are good to go," the medic answers, pulling out his ear buds, "Jack, shake me loose if you need something," he says putting the buds in and reclining his seat.

"Jack, you got a minute," Mark asks taking the seat next to him.

"Sure son, what's up…"

"Didn't have a chance to tell you earlier, but figured you would want to know, I ran into Jessie in the airport lounge about half an hour before you guys showed up."

Jack sits up, "seriously, was she okay? What did she say?"

Mark lets out a sigh, "well not much as usual, was using a fake name or at least not her own - left on another jet right as you pulled in." He sits back in the leather chair, "I know you probably can't tell me, but what do you guys really do?"

Jack can see the young man is taken with Jessie and why not, who wouldn't be, "sorry Mark, I can't tell you…" he says with a smile, "but listen, it's important work, and I think you probably already have a pretty good guess, am I right?"

"I guess so sir, you're either international drug dealers or spies, I'm not sure which one is worse actually…" he says almost forlornly.

"You like her, don't you?" Jack says softly.

"That obvious?"

Jack nods, "pretty much, but listen to me son, folks like Jessie and I, we're no good at relationships – too many secrets, too many things that we can't talk about and normal folks wouldn't understand anyway…"

"I could try?"

"...And you would, I don't doubt it, but people like us just can't let our guard down, we don't or probably won't trust anyone enough to let them get close, I mean really close..." Jack hesitates, "Mark, I'm sorry, I wish I could tell you different, but it doesn't mean she doesn't care about you and she probably even likes you just fine, but Jessie doesn't let anyone in, just the way it is... she can't afford to." He knows it's a weak explanation and probably more than she would have liked for him to say, but the young man seemed so melancholy, better to give him some bitter medicine and save the heartache.

"I kinda figured..." he says, "thanks for talking to me though..." he seems ready to say more but changes his mind. "I'm going to catch some z's in the back, thanks again sir..."

"No problem son," Jacks says as he watches him head towards the back. He seemed like a nice enough young man, but Jack knew Jessie well enough by now to know she was too focused and moving too fast to be tied down by a normal relationship, the mess with Tom last year had probably cauterized any feelings she had in that direction. He wished he didn't understand so well, it wasn't something most people could understand, and it didn't do any good to talk about it anyway.

He looks out the window at the sun glinting off the miniature waves below thinking about the past few weeks and beyond – where had the time gone? He had finally come face to face with his mortality, not that he hadn't been in dangerous situations before, but this had been the first time he had seriously considered that he might die, and it had put him in a reflective mood. This moment had seemed so far off back in the early days when he and Lou had been in the field but looking back the brevity of it all struck him, history was like that though it seemed so far away viewed through the lens of youth, not so much though the closer you got to the end.

Jack shifts uncomfortably in the seat. He has been lost in thought watching the clouds speed by as he catalogues the memories and experiences of forty years in the field, had it really been that long, didn't seem like it. His side is throbbing as he unbuckles deciding to head to the galley in the rear for a bottle of water.

Gunshot wounds create direct damage as the projectile passes through the body, tearing the flesh as it goes. Secondary damage however can be even greater from the shockwave caused by the release of energy, but not necessarily as obvious. Jack had been fortunate that the round had not torn or ruptured organs or major blood vessels, however the shockwave had weakened his spleen and the arterial structures feeding it. The damage was undetectable without some advanced imaging and had been progressing over the past twenty-four hours until the slow leaking had started to progress rapidly now turning into a major internal bleed. He passes out before he can take two steps going down between the seats.

Jerry sits up and stretches looking across the row to check on Jack, he comes fully awake immediately noticing Jack is not in his seat, unbuckling he turns to the back seeing Jack prone in the aisle he grabs his kit and starts yelling.

"Mark, Mark I need you now."

Mark sits up in the back row, "shit, what happened?"

"I don't know, come help me get him in a seat so I can take a look," Jerry is already checking for a pulse and respirations. "He's breathing but his pulse is a mess. Let's go, now lift him over here."

They place Jack in one of seats and recline it all the way so he is almost laying down... as Jerry begins to examine him, "Fuck me," he whispers mostly to himself.

"What, what is it?" Mark asks.

"See this," Jerry says, pointing to a darkening bruise on Jack's side above the bandages, "that's internal bleeding, we need to get him on the ground now, he needs a surgeon."

"Can't you help him?"

"Not with this, we probably have an hour maybe a little longer at this point, get moving kid, find us somewhere to land..." Jerry shoves him toward the cockpit, "go, we don't have time..." He turns back to Jack fastening the seatbelt around him and completing his exam. *Goddammit, an ultrasound or CT on the ground might have caught this, now he was probably going to lose the patient at thirty thousand feet, fuck!*

The plane banks sharply to the right and accelerates, "I can put us down in Iceland in a little under two hours," Mark calls from the cockpit.

"You gotta do better than that," Jerry yells back, "Make sure they have an ambulance and surgical team on standby when we get there," he adds. "Dammit Jack, hold on..."

Sunday Morning News

Mindi Holbrook managed to hit all three networks and the two largest cable newsgroups as well, in spite of having stolen only a couple hours sleep, she looked fresh and vibrant. She had distilled the talking points down to three – The President was creating a special commission to investigate abuse of power rumors within the intelligence community, the Justice Department would take lead with full cooperation of the White House and no restrictions; nothing was to be off limits, and finally, the commission would be fully transparent with the American People in so much as it did not impact national security. The talking heads had been fully prepped and with the exception of the conservative cable host, had pitched her softball questions.

She had just finished up her last interview when her cell had started ringing, "Mindi... Anthony Moyer here, what the hell is going on? A special commission seriously? For what, and why wasn't I told about this?" he yells into the phone. Regaining his composure, "I'm sorry, but this is just not how things are done here..."

"Anthony, I'm going to give you a little advice, probably shouldn't but here it is... look out your front window... I'll wait, go ahead," she can hear him walking to the door, "see those fellas at the end of your drive?"

"Uh, yeah…"

"That's the FBI, they aren't leaving… so my advice - get yourself a good lawyer you son-of-a-bitch." She hangs up before he can respond.

Moyer will spend the next hour trying to reach the President to no avail. That same set of operators able to find anyone anywhere also won't put a call through that the president doesn't want. Failing to reach the President he will call the number he has for ALPHA Control seven times before finally giving up.

The phone records would have been a prominent fixture in Alberto Jimenez's case much to the chagrin of Moyer's attorneys, had things turned out differently. They didn't though, Anthony Moyer poured himself a double of Johnnie Walker Blue Label downed it standing in the study — poured a second and carried it out to the back porch downed it as well before sitting in his favorite rocker and eating a bullet from his father's forty-five service revolver. The agents stationed at the end of his driveway responded to the shot, but Anthony Moyer had efficiently and effectively delivered the justice he so richly deserved.

His death would be carried on all the news shows and although no-one came right out and said anything, it was pretty clear there was a correlation between the morning blitz by Mindi Holbrook and the events transpiring soon thereafter.

Half a world away Nathan Lieber has a decision to make, "Ben, where is he headed?"

"Don't know sir, left the apartment with a backpack and laptop bag, we are tracking him using the city-wide video system. But sir, I think he knows we are watching or just doesn't care, he isn't trying to hide."

Nathan turns to Captain Hamlin, "Captain, I want the airports on lock down – every one of them, even the private ones, anything leaves the ground that doesn't have clearance I want brought down immediately – understand."

"Yes sir, got it..." he says leaving quickly.

"Golson, you take your team over to the apartment, be careful, remember who we're dealing with here," he says looking at Jessie, "I want to know what's there, especially the vial you've been briefed on... nobody touches anything I just want to know if it's there, are we clear? You understand what happens if it's released right?"

"Yes sir, we'll be careful."

"Kashman, have your team ready when I call, I want at least four snipers ready to go, only your best, okay..."

The man just nods and starts talking into his radio.

"Alright McIntyre you're with me, let's go..." he says heading for the door.

Jessie slings her backpack over her shoulder and hurries to catch up.

There is only a skeleton crew in the Paradigm offices on Sunday afternoon, mostly system maintenance and a few programmers that simply don't have another life. Upstairs Lou is watching the news shows replay the morning interviews with Mindi Holbrook, a half-eaten tuna sub and a warming root beer sit next to his keyboard – on his screen is a monitoring program listening for SIGINT out of Israel – it's been quiet all morning.

The screen blossoms as the news tickers announce the death of Moyer, Lou punches a few keys and the TV's go quiet, he plugs in a set of earphones and listens to the hurried commands of an Israeli Captain and two Lieutenants seven thousand miles away. *Here we go* he thinks; *please, please be safe Jessie...*

Just outside Keflavik Iceland, Mark's radio starts to squawk, "Gulf Stream N112PI cleared to land on runway 01, correct to heading zero, zero, five - emergency vehicles will meet you at the tarmac.

"Roger Tower, correcting now."

Mark lowers the landing gear, bringing the nose up and slowing the jet's speed, "here we go, hold on we're coming in pretty hot..."

There is a significant bounce as the jet lands and settles onto the runway, Jerry is already unbuckling Jack as they roll to a stop. Mark pushes open the door and drops the steps, almost immediately two paramedics enter the cabin. "Status?"

Jerry looks up, "internal bleed, probably spleen, pulse is thready and respirations are fifty, unresponsive for the past ninety minutes..." They lift Jack up and trundle him down the steps to the waiting stretcher, Jerry following close behind. He looks back at Mark standing at the top of the steps, "I'll call you as soon as we know something..." he yells as he hops into the back of the ambulance pulling the door closed behind him, the ambulance speeds away, siren wailing as Mark watches.

Conversations

The thing about conversations is there are some we want to have, some we should have, and some we need to have - balancing these has always been an exercise in futility, human beings simply aren't circumspect enough to choose properly in the moment. Jessie was hurtling toward a need-to-have-moment and struggling with what she wants to say or at least how to say it...

Lieber had stopped in front of a non-descript door and was pressing his palm against a bioscan lock as Jessie catches up to him. The door clicks open revealing an extensive armory behind another locked door, to the right is a multi-inch plexiglass window with a built-in intercom system. They are buzzed through and Jessie looks around the hardware is impressive. Row after row of automatic rifles, pistols and various other hand-held weapons, she whistles – "sweet!"

He lets a small smile show, "here, this should fit," he says handing her a tactical Kevlar vest. Looking through the shelves he picks up an HK machine pistol but sets it back down, choosing instead a pair of Kimber Custom II .45s with the rosewood Crimson Trace laser grips, he hands them to Jessie, "I think these will be right up your alley... no?" He smiles, seeing her eyes light up, "there's a rack of holster rigs over there take whatever you need, I'll grab a couple boxes of rounds for you, any preference?"

"I use the Hornady Critical Defense Cartridge, when I can get it," she replies running her hands over the pistols.

"I'll see what we have," he replies.

She picks a double shoulder rig, it's become her favorite way to carry, the newer Kevlar tactical vests are so thin they don't get in the way any longer. She tightens the rig and shrugs her shoulders to get it just right. Everything in place she joins Lieber at the counter where he hands her two boxes of rounds. "How did you know I preferred the Kimbers?" she asks.

He just smiles at her, "it's my business to know, you like them?"

"Best pistol I've ever owned, I usually carry the 9MM but I've started using the .45 at the range a lot lately."

"I prefer them too, that's my personal set, I hope it serves you well," he says.

"Seriously? You sure sir, I'm happy to use whatever you have..."

He shakes his head, "carry them well Miss McIntyre, hopefully you won't need them – time to go."

"Sir, where are we going?" she asks trailing him back into the hallway.

"You said you wanted to have a conversation with Azrael, well you may get your chance, he's headed to Nahariya..." They take the elevator to the roof where a chopper is waiting, things are moving fast and Jessie is trying to marshal her thoughts. The sun has just set in the Western sky and although it's still light out, a few stars are starting to prick through the deepening twilight to the East. Lieber hands her a set of head phones, "Azrael just boarded the train North, takes about ninety minutes to get to the Nahariya we'll be there in forty-five…"

She nods keying the mic, "sir, where do you think he is going?"

"General consensus is back to the neighborhood where he and his family lived, they never rebuilt most of that area, it's on the far North side of town…"

"Sir, where are his wife and daughter buried?"

"I don't know, why?"

"He's not going home sir, he's going to say goodbye… we need to know where they are sir…"

Lieber nods pulling his phone from its holster and keying in a message to Lieutenant Kashman requesting the information. "Alright, we should know before we get there, what's your plan McIntyre?"

She hesitates, she hadn't developed a clear plan, things have been moving too fast. She had thought to appeal to his humanity but that was a fool's errand and she knows it. There wasn't going to be any forcing him to tell her where the VX17 was either, why would he, especially if it was already in place.

No, she needed a way to get him talking, if she could get him to reveal enough then they might have a chance, the key word being might. They needed to end this before it started. "Sir, you're not going to like this but... I need to get to the graves, I'll have my SAT phone dialed into you, so you can hear me, but I need to get him talking... we need to know where the VX17 is and if possible, how he plans on triggering it..."

"McIntyre, that's a suicide mission and assuming he doesn't kill you on sight, what makes you think he is going to tell you anything?"

She had been thinking about that part, Azrael was marching inexorably toward a spectacular conclusion to this journey, but he was leaving some interesting clues along the way. Clearly, he was willing to kill anyone that got in the way or might try to stop him... however, he had left Daniel and Rina both alive, no reason to have done that. For that matter, why come back here at all, it was an unnecessary risk, but one he seemed bent on taking... Azrael was the Angel of Death, no question, and probably the most capable operative she had seen short of Jack, but glimpses of his pain and humanity were escaping the façade he had tried so hard to create. She was counting on it, counting on being able to tap into that pain, maybe get him to release some of it and in doing so give them the clue they would need to avert this disaster. It wasn't much, but she had reconciled herself to the risk and the potential sacrifice it might require.

She turns to Lieber, "short answer sir, I think he wants to... wants to share his pain, a confession if you will before going off to war..."

"McIntyre... Jews don't do confession..." he responds, "but I don't have a better idea so if you're game I am..."

She nods, "let's do it sir, we have to try..."

They set the chopper down on the beach, Raisa and Tania Eisen had been buried together in the old city cemetery bordering the beach on the South side of Nahariya.

"I'll get snipers set up as best I can, but these stones are stacked almost on top of each other, it's unlikely we'll have a shot... you're going to be pretty much on your own..." Lieber cautions.

"Yes sir, I understand..." she studies the diagram of the cemetery on his phone, orienting herself to the water before taking a leg up and scrambling over the cemetery wall. She dials Lieber's number making sure he can hear her before setting the screen brightness to zero and clipping it to her belt. "Here we go sir..."

Jessie makes her way through the maze of gravestones, the older markers occasionally interspersed with a new one, the cemetery is old though and clearly overcrowded. She looks back toward the entryway and the lights of the street running parallel to the wall, it's a long way off and the sky is growing dark.

The graves are almost at the back wall, the shadows are long and it's grown fairly dark. To her right she can hear the soft crash of waves on the beach, she was surprised how close to the water they were. She turns back studying the names; Raisa and Tania and wonders what that horrible night must have been like for the little girl, no father there to comfort her, the rockets raining down and exploding all around them.

She doesn't see anyone but out of the dark to her left a low voice asks, "Have you come to mourn with me Miss McIntyre?"

Jessie doesn't answer immediately, "is that what we are doing David?" she finally replies.

She can't see him moving in the darkness but somehow senses it as suddenly he is standing next to her, "my girls, my sweet, sweet girls," he says with a melancholy sadness.

"I'm sorry..." is all she can come up with.

He lets out a short laugh, "really? How very comforting..."

Jessie knows she is going to lose him if she doesn't re-engage the conversation, "was that you in St. Eustatius?" she asks without looking at him.

"Yes, it was, you're my only miss and now here you are..."

"Why didn't you take another shot? I holed up in that dive shed wondering if you were coming for me..."

David stands quietly, not answering, "that first shot was meant for you, I couldn't have Ismael talking to the CIA..." he pauses, "I guess you weren't meant to die that day..." he continues without emotion.

"Are all these pilgrims meant to die?" she asks softly, finally turning to look at him. She can see the pain in his face as he returns her gaze.

"You wouldn't understand, what do you know of loss, the blood of innocents spilled for nothing, nothing I tell you..." He turns back to the dark marble stones, "the blood of my girls soaked this land, and our countries... yours and mine betrayed them," he says angrily.

"So now more innocents must die to balance those scales," she asks...

He laughs again, "there are no innocents Miss McIntyre don't you see... death is all we deserve... it's our legacy."

"I don't believe that David and I don't think you really do either, a week ago people in my government tried to have me killed... you know why?" She doesn't wait for him to answer, "they were protecting you..."

He turns to her, "protecting me... what are you saying..." it's just an underlying tone, but she can hear the questions in his voice.

"I think you know what I am saying, why do you think this man Daniel didn't try to stop you?" She looks around, "I'll tell you why... because he was part of a team trying to manipulate you... they want you to do this... this isn't a religious war, it's not vindication for the death of your wife and daughter," she says nodding to the graves, "David, this is what all wars are about... power, politics, money..."

"I don't believe you... this was my idea!" he says his voice rising, "this is my vengeance..."

Jessie doesn't get a chance to respond as a shot rings out from among the stones striking her square in the back, knocking her to the ground, David ducks down next to her pulling his pistol. He rolls her over and she groans, "Mother-fucker that hurts," she gasps looking up at him, "you believe me now, you still think this is about you?"

He doesn't have a chance to respond before a voice calls out, "David we need to go now, they are surrounding us..."

"No, no, no it can't be..." he whispers looking at her, "stay here..." he says shuffling to the left a half dozen feet. David stands rapidly letting off four rounds, Jessie ignores the pain and struggles to her feet. She can see David moving quickly forward between the markers to where a man is slumped against one of the stones.

She manages to make her way over, "who is it?"

"I know this man, he is Mossad..." David exclaims, the disbelief evident in his voice... "but, why would he shoot at you?" he asks turning toward Jessie.

"I told you why... they want this to happen, they want to set the world on fire, who do you think benefits in the end? You?

Me?" she unclips her phone and turns it off... "David, we have about two or three minutes before this place is full of troops, what do you want to do?"

He gives her a strange look, reaches into his bag and slips a small cylinder into her hand, "keep this safe, my country can't have this..." He turns his back to her, "it's time for you to go Miss McIntyre..."

She can hear the rapid-fire shouts in the distance as Lieber and his troops enter the gates and overhead the syncopated whir of a chopper approaches, "I can't let you leave David, you know that..." she says to his back.

"I know... it's okay..." he says, turning, his pistol pointed at her... She reaches for her holster, "don't," he says shaking his head.

The first round catches him in the shoulder, knocking him back against the stone behind him, Jessie has her pistol out and unloads half a dozen rounds into his chest. She walks over to him, "dammit David why..."

He smiles up at her weakly, "thank you..." he whispers before sliding over a crimson stain hi-lighting the names of his wife and daughter.

Kirilov touches her on the shoulder, "sorry Jessie, thought he was going to shoot you..."

"I don't know Mikhail, maybe he was, I just don't know..." She kneels down in front of the grave as Lieber and his men come running up, disaster may have been averted but there wasn't anything good about this – had anything really been resolved – was the world truly a safer place, she didn't think so...

Epilogue

The sharp crack of the rifles firing ripples across the long rows of white stones, once – twice – three times, finally echoing into silence as a solo bugle mournfully renders Taps. The plain wooden casket has been lowered and the folded flag is warm in her hands, "be at peace Jack, I miss you already…" Jessie whispers as she leans against her dad and lets the tears flow. He kisses the top of her head, they don't need words, they both feel the same way.

The "team" had met last night at Rasika's for dinner. It seemed like an appropriate setting for a farewell dinner, Jack hadn't made it out of the Keflavik Hospital, passing before the surgeons had really even started. The beers and tears had flowed last night interspersed with plenty of stories and laughter – Tim, Albert, Vance, even Mark and Jerry had joined Jessie and Lou. Jessie had taken it hard, feeling responsible for him even being in the field again and particularly in London. She had kept it to herself though, it was still a bit of a boy's club and she wasn't going to play the weepy woman role… but she also knew it was going to be a long time before this one healed.

It had taken three days for Jessie to get out of Israel and head back to the States, that was almost two weeks ago, and the two governments were still arguing over the vial of VX17. She hadn't been able to keep it out of Lieber's hands, but at least it wasn't going to disappear accidentally this time. Neither country was making too much noise though, if it actually got out that a rogue Mossad agent had been hours away from releasing it during the annual Hajj, the Middle East might have gone up in flames anyway.

Albert and Tim were off and running under the auspices of the new Presidential Commission and were now working with their counterparts in Britain and Israel. Stonewalling the press had become Albert's favorite past-time, well, that and breakfast. It was unlikely they would ever completely unravel the ALPHA group's activities, but at least the attention might dissuade others from walking down that path in the future, at least that's what they kept telling themselves.

As she walks the concrete path back to the parking area with her dad she looks back towards the grave site – a lone figure stands head bowed hands clasped – Mikhail. She tugs on her dad's arm, "Jessie, you got a second?" Vance Simpson asks.

She stops and looks up, "uh, sure," she looks back again, but the figure is gone, maybe she had only hoped it had been him. The Israelis had whisked him out of the cemetery that night before she could really talk to him. She hadn't heard from him since and Lou had remotely wiped and disabled his phone as soon as she had told him. Turning back to Simpson she says, "I'm sorry sir, what did you say?"

Simpson pauses as if deciding what to say, finally giving her a smile, "take a few weeks off then come see me okay?"

She looks at her dad as Simpson walks back up the hill, "what do you think that was about..."

"I don't know kiddo, but let's go home..."

Acknowledgements

This book is dedicated to my wife and kids for their unfailing support. Many thanks to the family and friends that have provided encouragement, feedback, suggestions, and have been steadfast supporters through this process. A special thanks to James Coyle for his editing. Continued thanks to retired Colonel Randy Williams – US Army Rangers for his insight on the military, the Army Rangers, and his specific knowledge of the Middle East and the rich and varied cultures in that part of the world. Missy Heckler for proof-reading and support. Once again Krysteena Runas has captured my vision and created a cover beyond perfect for this story. Any errors or exaggerations are solely a reflection of my inability to listen and in no way reflect on the expertise of these fine people.

If you enjoyed this story please consider posting a positive review on Amazon. My other books can be found at the following link: www.amazon.com/author/jjcastagno

Once again thank you for giving me the opportunity to pursue this love of mine and use up a little of your time with my tales...

JC